The Purple Quest

The Purple Quest

A NOVEL OF
SEAFARING ADVENTURE
IN THE ANCIENT WORLD

by Frank G. Slaughter

Doubleday & Company, Inc., Garden City, New York

With the exception of actual historical personages, the characters are entirely the product of the author's imagination and have no relation to any person in real life.

*This book is affectionately dedicated
to my niece,*

PATSY SLAUGHTER

The rising city, which from far you see,
Is Carthage and a Tyrian colony.
Phoenician Dido rules the growing state,
Who fled from Tyre, to shun her brother's hate.
Great were her wrongs, her story full of fate;
*Which I will sum in short.**

* The above and all quotations at chapter headings are from Virgil's *Aeneid*, translated by John Dryden, copyright 1909 by P. F. Collier & Son.

The Purple Quest

One:

*Not far from hence, if I observed
aright,
The southing of the stars and polar
light.*

THE TALL MAN balancing himself upon the swaying afterdeck of the Phoenician *gaoul* was as sunbronzed as any of the crew handling the great vessel. His garb—a loincloth of durable Tyrian weave—was no different from that of the slaves resting upon the long oars to keep them out of the water while the black ship, driven by sail alone, ploughed steadily eastward through the azure waters of the Mediterranean, known since the beginning of time to those who dwelt upon its shores or sailed its waters as the "Great Sea." Yet even the most casual observer would have recognized him instantly as the master of the vessel and a natural leader of men.

Straton, Son of Gerlach, was no ordinary shipmaster. A member of the wealthiest and most influential of Tyre's merchant families and a descendant of Phales, last king in the line of Hiram the Great—under whose rule the immensely profitable treaty with King David of Israel and his son Solomon had been consummated—his heritage was fully as regal as that of Tyre's present ruling house. A skilled navigator, he was also deeply learned in the age-old lore of his people concerning the sea and the far places of the earth bordering upon its shores.

His face was lean with the characteristic bold profile of his people, who for five hundred years—since the decline of the Minoans of Crete—had ranged in their galleys and gaouls over the vast reaches of the Great Sea, from Egypt in the south to Cilicia in the north, and from the Phoenician coast in the east beyond the Pillars of Melkarth, the twin headlands marking the entrance to the boundless reaches of the Western Sea. In his deep-blue eyes burned a light that marked an eager and questing mind, ever seeking new answers to old riddles and—like all Phoenicians—new ways to gain profit in seaborne commerce.

As he steadied himself against the sway of the ship, Straton's eyes were fastened upon a disc of wood floating in an open cask filled with sea water—a device whereby the disc could always be kept level, no matter to what angle the deck was canted by the thrust of the wind against the great black sail. At the center of the wooden disc stood a perpendicular stick, known generally by its Greek name of *gnomon* —the "guiding line." The history of the device went back to the Babylonian astrologers, who had charted the heavens and its bodies before the time of Hammurabi, the Lawgiver. But its use in navigation had been discovered only a few centuries before by Phoenician seafarers and kept a closely guarded secret, as was most of their treasured lore.

On the surface of the floating board a set of circles had been drawn, with the upright stick at their center so arranged that, when the sun shone upon the device, the gnomon cast a shadow across the circles, a shadow whose length—always shortest at exact noon—could be measured and recorded accurately for any place upon any day of the year. For centuries, Phoenician shipmasters had been observing the length of the sun's shadow at noon by means of devices similar to the one Straton was using. Carefully recorded upon rigorously guarded papyrus rolls in the alphabet they had introduced to commerce, this information allowed a shipmaster—as long as the sun was shining—to determine whether his vessel was pointing toward the port of his choice. If the shadow of the gnomon were too long at noon, his position was to the north of the course he desired to follow; if too short, it was to the south. Joined with their knowledge of the heavens, particularly the north-pointing stars in both the Great and the Small Bear, this pathfinding skill had long since made Straton's people the foremost mariners of the world.

The steersmen handling the great sweeps at the stern that guided the gaoul; the overseers at the center of the deck, always within whip-reach of the slaves at the oars; the topmen who handled the great sail straining against the mast; the pilot at his perch above the cutwater at the prow; even the mercenaries whose task it was to defend the vessel in case of attack—all were watching the scene upon the after-deck. And in all the great ship at the moment there was no sound of human voice, only the creak of the yards against the mast and the low hum of the wind against the drumhead-taut sail.

Slowly the shadow of the gnomon shortened as the sun approached the zenith, until finally it seemed to pause, before lengthening again as the sun started its daily descent. For a moment the shipmaster waited, making certain beyond doubt that midday had been reached, then his voice broke the silence that had gripped the ship.

"The shadow is at the shortest!"

Turning quickly, Straton scanned a section of papyrus held by his servant Ares, a wizened little Greek who had been in his master's service since the younger man's birth. His eyes ran down the papyrus strip, scanning the letters and figures written there in a neat Phoenician script. Then he glanced once again at the slender shadow of the gnomon measured by the circles drawn upon the floating wooden disc. And when his face broke into a smile, even the soldiers, who knew little of navigation, sensed the answer before he shouted jubilantly:

"On course! We will dock at Tyre before nightfall!"

While a cheer rose from all parts of the ship, Ares busied himself rolling up the papyrus containing the precious sailing directions. Wrapping it in cloth, he tied a string around the twin wooden cylinders to protect the writing surface made from the pith of reeds that grew best in the lowlands of Egypt along the banks of the Nile. Finally, he placed the roll carefully in a small chest of polished cedar and, drying the gnomon with a soft towel, added it to the contents before lifting the cedar box so it could be locked with the small key Straton wore around his neck upon a silver chain.

Every Tyrian shipmaster swore by the wrath of Melkarth, patron deity of Tyre, to guard with his life both key and chest. He was further required to jettison the latter over the side, if capture by an enemy appeared imminent, and as an added precaution, the bottom of the chest was weighted with lead so it would sink instantly. The lid, however, was so closely fitted as to be waterproof, allowing recovery by diving—if the outcome of a fight should change for the better.

Only the pilot, besides Straton, knew how to take the daily readings of both the sun's shadow and the so-called "Phoenician Star," judging the ship's position from previous observations recorded upon the papyrus roll. The pilot, a weather-beaten veteran named Amathus, who had sailed the gaoul the length of the Great Sea to bring Straton back to Tyre had taught the younger man all the lore accumulated in a lifetime at sea, most of it in the service of the House of Gerlach. But now that Straton commanded the great vessel, only if he were ill or wounded in battle would Amathus move from his perch at the bow above the bronze-sheathed prow to take charge of the precious cedar box and the task of guiding the ship.

Straton had been driving both vessel and crew hard since they had left Gadir, the thriving Phoenician port city at the mouth of the river Baetis in the district of Tartessus, beyond the Pillars of Melkarth on the shores of the seemingly boundless Western Sea. Not even the slaves at the oars resented their master's eagerness to reach port, however, for all were familiar with the story of his decision five years before not to return to Tyre, after his betrothed, Princess Elissa—popularly known by her nickname of Dido—had been married under the terms of her father's will to Sicharbas, the High Priest of Melkarth and Astarte. And all knew that only a few weeks earlier Straton had been recalled by his father—though for exactly what reason not even he yet understood.

"The stars spoke truly when you observed them last night, Master," Ares said. "If you will lock the chest, I will put it away."

Before turning the key in the lock, Straton removed a small papyrus roll. And while Ares was busy in the small cabin that formed the captain's quarters, placing the navigating instruments and sailing directions upon a shelf beneath the stacks of papyrus rolls containing the manifests of the cargo, he unrolled the small strip of papyrus and read it through for perhaps the hundredth time, since his father's summons had been brought to him from Tyre by this very vessel.

ii

The letter was cryptic, as if his father had hesitated to commit to writing information which might fall into other hands:

My beloved son,

The time has come, in both my opinion and that of others whom you respect, for your return to Tyre. You have served our house nobly and well in the Western Land, but you are needed now at home. Six months ago I ordered a start upon the new gaoul for which you sent me the drawings. It will be larger and faster than any ship of its kind that has ever sailed the seas, but I would not entrust it to anyone save its creator. Arrange a cargo of whatever can be easily and quickly obtained in Gadir and depart for home as soon after you receive this letter as you can. I, and many others, await your coming eagerly.

May the favor of Melkarth and Astarte be with you on the voyage. I have made a special sacrifice to each in your name.

Your loving father,
Gerlach

"Five years is too long for a man to moon over a woman—even the fair Dido." Ares spoke with the familiarity of affection and long devotion. Among those on the gaoul, only he had remained with Straton during the entire five years of his voluntary absence from Tyre. "Perhaps your father had decided it is time you married and gave him grandchildren to comfort him in his old age."

"I was anxious to do that once."

"And you will be again. Your line made Tyre great in the days of King Hiram, and who is to say it will not rule there once again?"

14

It was an enticing prospect and Straton allowed himself to dwell briefly upon it, as he bit into a hunk of bread, tearing it off with strong white teeth. He reached out with the point of a slender dagger, its handle inset with exquisitely fashioned plates of papyrus-thin Egyptian tile in many colors, to pick up a slice of meat roasted over coals in the huge sand-filled cooking pot upon the afterdeck. The dagger had been a gift from Dido and, even though she was married to another, he wore it constantly at his belt.

The wind had freshened almost to a gale, and the fifty-oared gaoul —black in color, like all Phoenician ships even to the sail, so an attacker, or one being attacked, could not easily see it at night—moved swiftly over the long swells. The slaves chattered among themselves as they leaned upon the long sweeps, while those selected to bring food moved along the catwalk between the rowers' benches, giving each man his allowance in a wooden bowl and pouring him a cup of thin Tartessus wine.

It was a scene to bring joy to a shipmaster's soul, for the wind had held steadily from the northwest almost since they had entered the Great Sea, cutting days off the sometimes laborious voyage under oars. But Straton's thoughts were elsewhere for, though five years had dulled somewhat the memory of the lovely young Princess Dido, who was to have been his bride, with Tyre lying just beyond the curve of the horizon, he found the memory returning. And no peace came with it, for, married to the High Priest Sicharbas, whom he had respected since childhood, Elissa, the Queen, was as unattainable even in Tyre as she had been during the five years he'd spent in Tartessus at the western end of the known world.

Though his thoughts were far away, Straton's ears were attuned to the symphony of the ship, the hum of the wind through the rigging, the creak of mast and yard, the rush of the waves beneath the cutwater. It was a familiar and beloved fusion of sounds in which any false note would have brought him immediately out of his reverie. He hardly noticed when Ares took away the meat and the bread, substituting a dish of pomegranates purchased in the shops of Itanos on the island of Crete, where they had paused overnight to take on water and food. Only when the servant spoke again did the spell break and Straton look up, grateful to the gnomelike little Greek for lifting him out of the bottomless morass of his own thoughts.

"Food, women, a place to sleep—what more does a man need?" Ares posed a philosophical question, a favorite trick of his when he wished to hold forth at some length on a subject of his own choosing.

"The favor of the gods, perhaps."

15

"You have that, too. Look how the wind has held at our backs all the way. I would wager a debenweight of silver—if I had it—that no gaoul has ever made the journey eastward in so short a time."

"You would win the bet, I am sure."

"I have prayed to the Greek gods for you, too, Master," Ares confided. "Everyone knows they participate in the affairs of humans more often than your Melkarth or Astarte."

"You mean meddle, don't you?"

"Who could blame fair Juno or divine Aphrodite for falling in love with such a one as you?" Ares demanded indignantly. "Particularly when they look down from Mount Olympus and see you sailing the greatest ship in the merchant fleet of Tyre faster than any man has sailed a gaoul before?"

"How can I be sure I am so favored?"

"Someday you will meet a woman so lovely that you will know at once she is a goddess," Ares assured him. "She will drive all others from your mind and your heart—even her for whom you went away."

"And then?"

"You will indeed be the most fortunate of men, for such a prize is even greater than what you will exhibit to the merchants tomorrow."

Straton glanced toward the small cedar chest, visible on the shelf through the open door of the cabin. It had rarely been out of his sight during the entire voyage, for hidden in its bottom was a cake of purple gum, resembling a dark piece of amber. And though the fragment of congealed color was small enough to carried easily in the palm of a man's hand, he was sure it was more valuable than the entire cargo of the gaoul.

iii

During the afternoon, while the ship plunged eastward before the wind, Straton finished the log of the voyage and gave a final check to the papyrus-roll manifests listing the cargo he had taken on hurriedly at Gadir. Much of it was made up of tin and tin ore, which, mixed with the copper of Cyprus, formed bronze. An almost universal metal, bronze was fashioned by the artisans of Tyre into armor, weapons, tools, ornaments and large plates used as reinforcement for the hulls of the gaouls. In fact, much of the success of Phoenician mariners could be attributed to the brazen prows and reinforced hulls of their vessels, which were able to withstand the impact of mountainous waves in a storm, the crash of ship against ship in battle, and the grinding of the sand when put directly upon the shore for trade where no suitable harbors existed.

In exchange for tin, silver and emeralds, largely unobtainable in their homeland, canny Phoenician traders in the Tartessian markets exchanged glassware, exquisite vases, jewelry and olive oil, purchased on the way westward at Utica and other colony ports of the northern Libyan—or African—coast, as well as spices, perfumes and particularly the richly dyed fabrics loved by women the world over. For centuries, in fact, much of the wealth of the Phoenician city-states—Arvad, Byblus, Berytus, Sidon and Tyre, the greatest of them all—had come from a virtual monopoly over the production of the rich purple dye for which, more than anything else, the region had been famous for more than a thousand years.

While Straton worked, Ares bustled about, putting up the engraved silver plate and cup from which his master had eaten, selecting the robe he would wear when he went ashore, and polishing his finely tooled leather sandals. As he worked, the servant chattered steadily.

"What reward will you ask tomorrow when you face the Council of Merchants?" he asked.

Straton had asked himself the same question more than once, since he had realized the importance of the fragment of purple gum safely stored in the small chest with the gnomon and the haven-finding scroll. "What would you suggest?" he asked.

"To be king. What else?"

"Tyre already has a king."

"Pygmalion is only a boy. What does he know of ruling a great city?"

"The reports say Queen Elissa and her husband have guided him well as regents."

"Tyre's king should be a merchant from a noble house—like yours. Amathus tells me King Pygmalion has been courting the favor of the artisans of Tyre over the merchants, hoping to remove Queen Elissa and Sicharbas from the regency and rule alone."

"That could be only sailor's gossip."

"I think not." Ares' monkeylike features were screwed up in thought. "Artisans always envy merchants their profits. But men like you and your father have made Tyre great, not workers in silver and bronze, who risk nothing worse than a mashed finger. What do they know of kingship?"

The government of Tyre, like all Phoenician city-states, was not an hereditary monarchy. If the son of a reigning monarch proved himself worthy, he usually won his father's scepter, but a king could also be elected by the Royal Council. This powerful body was composed of the heads of the great trading companies, with a few of the leading members of the artisans' guilds representing those engaged in dyeing, glassmaking, the working of silver and gold, weaving and other arts. But as long as Straton could remember, the artisans had been seeking a greater degree of control over the state's affairs, so what Ares said might well include a kernel of truth.

"As a hero, you will certainly be entertained by the King and will have access to his cup." Ares' voice intruded upon Straton's thoughts. "A poisoner in Memphis once sold me—"

Straton gave the servant a clout, but the wiry Greek only rolled with the blow and came up grinning. "It's a good thing you have me to think for you where trickery is concerned, Master," he said impudently. "In Greece, Phoenicians are called thieves. Why have a reputation and not trade upon it?"

"As a poisoner?"

"King Pygmalion's great-grandfather Ithobel murdered King Phales, your ancestor. You would only be paying him off in kind."

"Did vengeance bring happiness to the Greek King Edipus your poets sing about?"

"Perhaps not. But when you want to kill somebody, it always helps to have blood guilt as an excuse."

"I will kill in a fair fight, or not at all. Now be quiet while I finish what I am doing."

"L-A-N-D!"

The cry of the lookout perched at the top of the mast echoed throughout the ship, and a great cheer rose from the crew. Straton climbed quickly to the masthead and perched beside the sailor stationed there. Cupping his fingers together to form a tube, he squinted through it, having learned long ago that, by shutting out the surrounding sky from his field of vision, he could see distant objects far more clearly.

Now he was able to distinguish what appeared to be the Ladder of Tyre, a jutting, upthrust peak among the cedar-clad Lebanon hills not far from the city, cut at one side by a chasm through which the surging waters of a mountain stream met the sea. A few moments later, a flash of white halfway up the elevation marked the location of the chalk cliffs forming part of the gorge, giving him the clue he needed to be certain of his identification. Viewed from the sea at this distance, the queen of all Phoenician cities appeared to nestle at the foot of Mount Hermon, a massive peak far to the east in the Anti-Lebanon range, whose snow-clad summit shone in the afternoon sunlight with the color of old rose above the drifting clouds that partially obscured it.

18

"It is Tyre!" Straton called down to the deck. "An extra measure of wine to all, if we make port by nightfall."

The slaves at the oars needed no urging, for reaching port meant rest and shelter from the wind, cold and rain, as well as more food and some leisure. Rowing while the ship surged onward under the impetus of the great sail was a tricky job, but they were a highly trained crew. With an overseer pounding out the rhythm of the strokes upon a great drum, the two rows of oars dipped into the water and swung smoothly toward the stern, as the men fell back upon the benches in the jarring stroke that imparted the greatest possible force to blades.

Straton remained at the masthead for another half hour, calling down to the steersmen to change the course slightly from time to time, as he guided the gaoul toward the harbor. Finally, when the mass of the city upon its foundation of solid rock was easily visible, he slid down the mast and strode back between the lines of rowers to his cabin.

Ares was already standing at the bulwark between the long steering sweeps, holding a jar to which a rope was attached for hauling up water. It took only a few moments to douse Straton's muscular body, while the Phoenician captain rubbed himself vigorously with a flat piece of pumice stone. Drying himself with a soft towel then, he donned a fresh loincloth while Ares was removing scissors, comb, tweezers and a razor from a small leather case.

Clipping deftly and keeping up a constant chatter while his master worked at a flat-topped table, completing the final examination of the records, Ares trimmed Straton's beard. The upper lip he shaved after the fashion of the Greeks and, this finished, carefully combed his master's hair with a silver comb which, like the jeweled dagger, had been a gift from Princess Dido. Next he rubbed a fragrant ointment into Straton's beard and, moistening his hands with a rich oil purchased in Tartessus, began to massage the skin of his master's torso.

All the while the ship had been plunging eastward toward the heights of Tyre, which were easily visible now. But the wind, which had been driving them steadily homeward for several days, chose this moment to become perverse, so the great sail had to be lowered and the vessel moved by oars alone. Had there been a harbor on the western side of the island, it would have been simpler to set a course directly toward it. But only the rocky base upon which the city stood rose there, surmounted by the forbidding mass of the great Temple of Melkarth and Astarte upon a jutting outcrop.

As a boy, Straton had prowled this reef-guarded and largely avoided side of the island, where rocky teeth waited to tear a boat apart, seeking an underwater cave by which, it was said, the god came and went in secret. He had found the so-called Cave of Melkarth, but it had turned out to be little more than a pocket in the rocky face of the outcrop at the water's edge containing a moldering bronze image of the god to scare off curious boys, but no sign of the awesome presence of the Baal of Tyre.

The rocky base of the city—actually, it was built on two islands, with a canal between—acted as a breakwater, creating a deepwater anchorage on its eastern side. So great was the shipping entering and leaving the port, however, that the docking space had been extended to the north and south by means of stone breakwaters.

The section facing the older city of Palaetyrus, on the mainland a short boat journey away, was so well protected that ships moored directly to the stone quay at the foot of the towering wall protecting Tyre from attack across the narrow channel. Here was a district called the *okel*, made up of warehouses, docks and ways for ship construction and repair, where the great gaouls were tied up for loading and unloading, as well as smaller ships engaged in the coastal traffic. But those awaiting their turn at the protected mooring were forced to anchor in either the Northern or Southern—often called the Egyptian— Harbor. And, since the Northern Harbor was the largest, it was toward this that Straton ordered the gaoul steered.

Now that he was almost beneath the ramparts guarding the city of his birth, Straton felt a strange reluctance to go on. The city, rising abruptly from its rocky base, had never seemed more beautiful, with the rays of the setting sun softening the sharp corners of the buildings that rose, story on story, to tower above the surrounding ocean. There was none of the glare of midday that made its whitewashed walls visible far at sea, but even from the water level he could see people moving about on the rooftops, which, in the warm weather that prevailed much of the year, served as gathering places in the evening and for sleeping at night.

As a boy, he had raced with his fellows across what was sometimes called the "road of the roofs," for the houses were jammed against each other so as not to waste any of the precious land space. And as the ship swung into a more northerly course to negotiate the entrance into the protected anchorage, he could see people gathering in little knots on the rooftops, looking down at the gaoul.

Even though the Son of Gerlach was, by birth, a member of the nobility of Tyre and had been, prior to his five-year stay in the West, the favored suitor of Princess Dido, not even his own family would greet him, when the great ship was moored to the quay making up one side of the Northern Harbor. For rigid custom demanded that the approach of a ship from a distant port be ignored by those on shore, since, being a beautiful and willful woman, the patron goddess Astarte, spouse of Melkarth, was also capricious.

Only after the shipmaster had visited the shrine of the goddess and made a gift of gold or precious objects, was the city free to welcome the newcomers. Until then, not even a slave upon the stone quay would take a line to secure the vessel to the shore. What was more, an agreement between the shipowners of Tyre forbade Straton from reporting to his father before he gave the Council of Merchants an account of the voyage, so none could gain a lead over the others by withholding some new discovery for himself.

Skillfully conned by the pilot at the bow and Straton at the stern, giving quiet orders to the steersmen, the vessel approached the harbor. Only the oars drove it as they rounded the northern point and Straton kept the course a little south of due east until the end of the protecting mole appeared. Then, at his command, the rowers on the seaward side strained at the great sweeps, while the slaves on the landward side lifted their oars from the water. Like a bit of flotsam caught by a current, the ship swung around and, when all fifty oars dipped into the water on the next beat pounded out upon the huge drum, it shot through the narrow harbor entrance and into the protected anchorage.

The topmen, who kept watch at the masthead and handled the sail when at sea, were already perched on the side nearest the quay at the end of the spar that supported the sail. From long practice everyone concerned knew his task, and the only sounds were Straton's low-voiced commands, the splash of the oars as they bit into the water, the creak of the yard as the topmen crawled out upon it, and the faint groan of wood upon wood when the ship finally came gently to rest against the timbers guarding the hull from grinding against the stone. Even before the ship touched the quay, the topmen had dropped to it from the yard, seizing the mooring lines cast to them by their fellows upon the deck and securing them on shore. Meanwhile, aboard the ship others were busy swinging a short ladder across the distance from deck to the quay below.

Ares came from his master's quarters as the ladder dropped into place, carrying in his outstretched hands an exquisitely fashioned small jewel box. Darkness had fallen while they completed the mooring, and when Straton lifted the top of the jewel case, the light of a torch burning upon the afterdeck revealed the ritual gift to Astarte, a necklace of exquisite emeralds lying upon the cushioned bottom. Much of the price of the necklace had been borne by the House of Gerlach, which owned the ship, but every man there had shared a little in its cost, thus earning his portion of favor from the goddess.

"Surely the High Priestess herself will welcome you when you make such a great gift," Ares said with a smirk.

"The High Priestess is old enough to be my mother." Straton closed the box and put it beneath his arm. "I shall seek my welcome elsewhere."

"Our arrival has already been noted in many of the great palaces up there." Ares nodded toward the upper levels of the rocky island, where the most magnificent of its buildings were located—including Straton's own home. "Once the gift is made, you can remain at the shrine, and I'll wager many a young woman would be pleased to meet you there."

Straton, however, was still oppressed by the sense of melancholy that had come upon him with the first glimpse of Tyre once again. He knew its source, the anticipation of the pain he would feel tomorrow at the meeting of the Council of Merchants when he saw Elissa again for the first time in five years. But even that gave him no armor against the knowledge that she now belonged to another or the memory of a night when, for a few hours in the very grove toward which he turned his steps as he left the waterfront, she had belonged to him. Painful though the brief journey was, however, he could not turn back from the shrine where he must make the ritual gift of thanksgiving to Astarte, freeing the crew to seek their own pleasures in the waterfront brothels and the pleasure houses of the mainland town of Palaetyrus across the narrow channel.

iv

The sacred grove devoted to the worship of the goddess Astarte, divine spouse of Melkarth, the Baal of Tyre, occupied the very topmost level of the city, its loveliest section. Traditional in the worship of the Earth Mother was the requirement that, before becoming eligible for marriage, every maiden must visit the sacred grove and there give herself to the first man who offered her a gift. Only when the sacrifice of her virginity to the goddess had been accomplished and the gift she received added to the temple coffers, was she free to marry the husband of her choice—or the one her dowry would secure for her.

According to a long-established custom, the more desirable maidens of Tyre arranged to meet their lovers in the grove on the night they elected to perform the ritual sacrifice of virtue to Astarte. But the less attractive and impecunious were forced to come there night after night, hoping some man—if no more than a drunken seaman—would drop the required gift in her hand and free her.

Straton was fully cognizant of the eager glances from the young women sitting in the entrances to the wooded bowers lining his path through the grove to the shrine. Several even got to their feet hopefully as he approached but, when he looked to neither side, they turned back disconsolately to their places. Some men, he knew from the stories of Ares—who improved his own fortunes considerably that way when the ship was in port—earned money by accepting gifts for relieving grateful maidens from their long wait, especially in winter when the nights were chilly here on the highest point of the island.

The small shrine of Astarte was the most beautiful structure in Tyre. Approached by a long colonnade roofed over with timbers hewn from the great cedars that grew upon the mountainsides of the barrier range called the Lebanon, it stood at the very center of the grove. Here temple priestesses waited to reward those making a gift, their bodies gleaming through the sheer byssus of their ceremonial robes. But they drew back when Straton held up the jewel case he carried as a sign that he was on his way to make a sacrifice to the goddess.

"Noble Straton," one of the priestesses called out to him softly as he approached. "It is I, Thamus, the servant of the goddess. Come to me when you have made your gift to the Divine Mother."

It had been more than a month since he'd held a fiery, dark-skinned beauty of Tartessus in his arms. Straton remembered the lovely temple courtesan well, too, for the priestesses of Astarte were highly skilled in pleasing men. But he was concerned tonight with the enigma at which his father's letter of summons had so clearly hinted, and with the purpose for which he had been called home after five years of absence.

Now he was in the forecourt of the shrine, a pillared hall constructed from blocks of stone fitted together with the well-known skill of Phoenician builders that left the joints barely distinguishable, even to close scrutiny. The topmost part of the wall was given over to an exquisitely carved frieze depicting events in the worship of Astarte, her marriage to the great Baal, and her subsequent fecundation of the earth. Here Straton put down the carved box long enough to wash his hands ceremoniously in a great silver basin, accepting a towel of soft white cloth handed to him by a lovely slave girl, who was naked except for a garland of flowers about her hips.

Though inside the shrine, he was still not within the inner sanctum, for only the Chief Priestess, the High Priest and the goddess herself could go there. The central court before it, where gifts to Astarte were received, was square and paved with stones worn smooth by many thousands of feet. Hidden lamps illuminated the room with a soft glow, and upon the ceiling were painted scenes depicting the life of divine Astarte.

At one side of the room was an altar made of marble covered with a thin layer of gold. According to tradition, the marble had been brought from the sacred grotto of Adonis on the mainland, where the goddess went each year in the spring to perform the annual union with her lord that gave new life to the land. There, in a cave from which poured a softly rushing stream, the sacred marble had been quarried and brought to Tyre, where it had been placed in the temple as its focal point. Advancing to the golden altar now, Straton placed the box in the center, opened it and lifted the emerald necklace so the light shone upon the green stones, making them seem to come alive upon his fingers.

"Straton, Son of Gerlach, brings an offering for himself, his ship, and his house," he intoned in the ritual of worship. "A necklace made from green stones discovered in the mountains of Tartessus."

"Your offering is accepted, O Straton," a musical voice said. "The goddess rejoices that you have returned home safely. You and your men may go and find pleasure for yourselves."

His gift made, Straton left the shrine and started back through the grove toward the broad street marking its boundary. But though she called softly to him once again, he did not pause to acknowledge the invitation of Thamus, for his memory had been seized by a far more alluring picture, one he'd hoped had been erased from his mind but which, he realized now, was as vivid as ever.

Two:

*For Tyrian maidens bows and quivers
bear,
And purple buskins o'er their ankles
wear.*

IT HAD HAPPENED on a night long ago, following his return from his first voyage to Tartessus. That voyage had almost ended in disaster, when the gaoul which was his first command had been tossed about like a cockleshell during a great storm that turned even the protected harbor of Gadir into a fury of wind-lashed waters. Driven upon the shore, the ship had seemed a total loss, for the city lacked the elaborate ways and facilities for repair available at Tyre, until he'd noticed something in the Western Sea which did not exist in the waters washing the shore of his homeland, the tides that twice daily caused the level of the sea to rise and fall sharply.

Choosing a protected cove near Gadir, Straton and his crew had put the stricken gaoul upon the shore at the flooding of the tide. After draining the water from the vessel and patching the damaged hull, they had taken the ship up the river Baetis toward the inland city of Tartessus, for which the district was named. There the crew had worked hard under his direction during the mild Tartessian winter, cutting trees in the hills, hewing them into new timbers and completing the overhauling made necessary by the shipwreck.

There had also been time to mine a new find of silver they discovered not far from the river. And when the gaoul finally sailed for home with the coming of spring and the end of the season of storms, they had carried such a heavy load of silver that even the anchor blocks were made of the precious metal, so highly prized by the smiths and jewelers of Tyre.

The city could deny nothing to those who brought news of so important a find, but Straton had desired only one reward, the hand of lovely Princess Dido, with whom he had been in love since they both were children. The Princess had desire to be courted, however, as was her right, and he'd devoted the whole summer to that effort, spending much of the time hunting in the hills back of the mainland shore, for she was very fond of the chase.

Never quite sure just how his suit was being received—for one day

25

Dido would be charming, her eyes promising delights he could only dream of, and the next as cool as the snow that covered the peaks of the Lebanon range in winter—he'd almost despaired of winning her. Then, suddenly—the night before he was to sail again to Tartessus, seeking another fortune in silver and emeralds—his prospects had brightened.

He'd been on deck, supervising the placing of the last of the cargo for sale in the West, when a slave girl he'd recognized as the Princess' personal maid sought him out.

"I have a message for the noble Straton," she said. "One known sometimes as Dido will visit the Grove of Astarte tonight."

The words could have only one meaning, and Straton had felt his heartbeat quicken at the thought. By giving herself to him in the sacred grove, Elissa would fulfill the vow made to the goddess by every Phoenician maiden and name him her betrothed at last.

"Will your mistress sacrifice to Astarte?"

"If perchance she is offered a worthy gift."

Straton had taken a purse from his belt, opened it and extracted a piece of silver with its weight stamped upon it. "This is for you," he told the girl, "if you will tell me where she is to wait."

"Just inside the south entrance to the grove, within the second bower. She will come when the glass is turned the second time after the sun sets."

Straton knew the spot well; it was a favorite trysting place where young women from the noble families of Tyre's aristocracy could meet their lovers for the ritual yielding. The temple authorities had even built a latticed enclosure, whose wooden framework had long since been hidden by flowering vines, where highborn lovers might have privacy.

"Your mistress will be met there," he assured the girl. "And my servant will give you another piece of silver before my ship sails tomorrow."

In his eagerness to claim a prize beyond price, Straton had gone to the grove a full hour before the time of assignation. There he had waited in the secluded bower while murmuring, soft laughter, and occasional sharp cries of suddenly experienced pleasure filled the night around him. As impatient as a bridegroom waiting for the end of the wedding feast, he had almost decided that Elissa had chosen not to come, when he'd heard her voice on the path outside the bower.

She had come directly from the hunt, with quiver and bow still slung over her shoulders and the boots of soft leather dyed with Tyrian purple—known to the populace who adored her as "Dido's buskins"—upon her feet. Caught up by the eagerness of their bodies, when she came into his waiting arms in the darkness, they had quite forgotten the ritual gift until she was preparing to leave the bower a little before dawn. He'd given her the customary piece of silver then and had watched her disappear into the shrine to make her gift to the goddess.

Straton had sailed the following morning without seeing his beloved again, confident that they would be wed when he returned from Tartessus in the spring. But word had come with the last ship from Tyre in the autumn that King Mattan was dead and, according to the provisions of his will, Elissa had been wed to the High Priest Sicharbas—who was actually her uncle—to serve with her husband as regents for her brother Pygmalion, then about fourteen years of age.

With only his memories as comfort, Straton had chosen to stay in Tartessus and supervise the operations of the House of Gerlach in the West. He'd even been fairly content—for there was much work to be done and no lack of feminine diversion—until the strange, cryptic note had come from his father, summoning him home.

ii

The harsh laughter of drunken men shattered Straton's reverie. Caught up by a memory, he had not noticed where he was going, but his thoughts had guided his steps toward the secluded bower just inside the southern entrance to the grove, where he had waited for Elissa on that night five years ago. And to his startled eyes, the girl he saw poised in the midst of the bower might have been the Princess herself—until a closer look told him she was taller and slenderer. She moved her head just then, too, and in the light of one of the torches burning at every entrance to the grove, he saw that her hair seemed to have been spun of purest gold, while Elissa was raven-tressed.

Even in the first, quick glance, Straton realized that the girl in the bower was far more beautiful than Elissa had ever been. The carriage of her head and neck, the proud loveliness of her face, with its high cheekbones and dark eyes, her rounded though slender body—in fact almost everything about her reminded him of a fawn he had come upon hardly a month before while hunting in the hills back of Gadir. For it, too, had possessed the same loveliness, the same look of wariness but not of fear, the same tense grace, as if poised for flight.

The harsh laughter that had startled him sounded again and he saw now the reason for the girl's wariness. A hulking lout of a man, a caravan driver, judging by his clothing and the stink that came to Straton's nostrils, had stepped into the open space where she was poised for flight. He reached out to seize her and, when she eluded him with a swift movement, Straton knew at once what must have happened. The girl had no doubt come to the grove to meet her lover, since this spot was reserved by common consent for such arranged encounters. But the lover had somehow failed to meet her, and the caravan driver, having strayed into a part of the grove where such as he was not supposed to go, had found her there. Now he sought to press upon her the gift that would obligate her to yield to him.

Without pausing to plan a course of action, Straton stepped off the path into the underbrush and moved toward where the girl was standing. Whoever she was and whoever her lover, he had seen at first glance that she was not such as gave herself to the man seeking to claim her, so he would have come to her aid under any circumstances. But in some strange way that he could not understand, she also seemed familiar, as if she were someone he knew yet whose name he did not remember.

It could not be, he decided, because of her white robe of soft and expensive byssus, caught simply at her shoulders with golden scarab pins to leave her arms bare, and girded at the waist with a jeweled belt. Originally a Grecian garment, the *kiton*, as it was called, had long since become popular with both daughters and wives of the rich everywhere, because its soft clinging folds flattered almost any feminine figure. This girl, however, needed no such flattery, for the tense grace of her body as she waited for the next move of her attacker was like a painting or a lovely statue. And with that thought, Straton suddenly knew why she seemed familiar to him. Except that she wore the long kiton, while they had been garbed only in the briefest of loin girdles, the girl was a counterpart of the feminine bull dancers he'd seen depicted at Knossus on the island of Crete in a frieze on the walls of an ancient temple of the Minotaur—the half-man, half-bull deity for whose worship that island had once been the major center.

The worship of the Minotaur had characterized an earlier seafaring race called the Minoans, who had inhabited Crete until driven off by the Dorians and Ionians, Greek tribes who had overrun the island under the leadership of their legendary hero, Theseus. But though the Minoans and their cruel sport had long since disappeared, the artist had caught the sheer beauty of the bull dance, preserving it forever in stone and pigment by painting the handsome boys and girls, selected from among the pick of the youth in all the islands for the bull dance, in the act of vaulting nimbly over the horns of the sacred animals to land lightly upon their backs and thence leaping to the ground. And this girl, with no change except dropping her kiton, could have stepped into the frieze and become a part of it.

The girl in the bower had not yet seen Straton; she was far too busy dodging the hands of what, he saw now, was not one but three men, each seeking to thrust his gift upon her. Moving quickly, he came up behind her, just as her attackers forced her back against the underbrush forming the wall of the bower and into his arms. He had already removed the gold ring he wore, and now he reached across her shoulder to drop it into the cleft between her breasts, partially revealed by the loose folds of her robe.

"She has accepted my gift," he announced to the startled attackers, as he stepped into the bower, thrusting the girl behind him with the same motion. "By the law of Astarte, she is mine for tonight."

His sudden appearance startled the men who were badgering the girl. Two of them drew back, realizing he was a nobleman by the authority in his manner and his rich garment. But not the third, an evil-looking brute of a fellow who was heavier and broader of shoulder than Straton.

"Now I shall have the girl and your gold, too," he growled. "But first I will break you apart with my two hands."

As the man moved confidently to seize him, Straton stepped back—but only to gain room for a trick he'd seen a Tartessian miner use in a drinking brawl. He had hired the miner to teach it to him afterward, and, watching the other warily now, he balanced himself lightly upon the balls of his feet, hoping to end the whole affair with one forthright move. His only regret was that he had not worn a heavier sandal, but it was too late to remedy that now.

The ruffian's arms were already beginning to close when Straton raised himself upon the toes of his left foot and kicked upward with his right in a flashing blow. He could hardly miss at that close range, and the edge of his sandal struck his opponent just behind the point of the chin. There was a sharp crack of breaking bone, and an exquisite stab of pain in Straton's own foot, as it jammed forward in the light sandal and struck the chin of his opponent.

Half-stunned by the blow that had broken his jaw, the man sagged forward, but this was no time for mercy—with two more still able to fight. Completing the trick the Tartessian miner had taught him, Straton chopped down with clenched fists upon the back of the man's neck, driving the hulking body to the ground, where it lay inert.

Not certain whether the sudden ferocity of the attack had intimidated the others, he turned quickly to face them. But the big man had evidently been their leader and, with him half-conscious on the ground, they showed no desire to continue.

"Does either of you dispute me the possession of the girl?" Straton demanded sharply.

Both shook their heads. Then, unaccountably, one of them started to snicker and the other joined in, guffawing and slapping his partner on the back at some joke that Straton did not immediately perceive.

"Your quarry has escaped you, sir." Overcome with laughter, the man could not go on, and Straton turned to see that the bower was empty, save for him and the other men.

The girl had fled!

At another time he might have shrugged and gone on his way, or laughed with the other two at the way she had tricked him into fighting her battle, then fled before he could demand the customary reward. But as he turned, the sudden lancing pain in his bruised foot almost nauseated him, and the knowledge that he had probably broken it in vain sent a wave of frustrated rage surging through him.

Alternately cursing the girl and himself, he thrashed through the brush in pursuit, but she was fleet and the pain in his foot made him stumble often. By the time he burst through the hedge surrounding the grove, the girl was almost out of sight, running along the street marking its southern boundary like the fawn she had resembled. Without looking back, she crossed the street to enter a house fronting upon the grove.

Cursing impulsive girls who got themselves into situations from which they must be rescued, Straton limped across the street and hammered on the door of the house into which she had disappeared. It was opened after a few moments by a bent old man with a gray beard, whom he recognized as Pallas, one of the lesser merchants of Tyre engaged largely in the coastal trade and in serving as an agent for merchants in other cities. Pallas peered up at him in the light of the candle he carried, then his face broke into a welcoming smile.

"My house is honored by the Son of Gerlach," he said. "Will you enter?"

"The girl!" Straton said hoarsely. "Where is she?"

"What girl do you mean, sir?" a tall man standing behind the Phoenician merchant asked. "There is no girl here except my daughter, Hera."

"I gave a gift as ransom for a girl just now in the grove, but she ran away," Straton explained. "I may even have broken my foot fighting to save her from three ruffians."

"You think she came from here?"

"I saw her enter this house."

"My name is Diomedes and my daughter retired some time ago, sir," the Ionian said. "You are obviously under a strain and, no doubt mistook another house for the home of my friend, Pallas."

"I saw her come here with my own eyes," Straton insisted.

"Do we have guests, Father?" It was the girl of the grove. She stood just behind the Ionian, wearing a sleeping robe and with her hair tumbled about her shoulders, as if she had just risen from her couch. While Straton stood gaping in astonishment that she could be even more beautiful than when he had come upon her in the grove, she lifted her hand to rub her eyes, as if she had just awakened—but not before he saw a light of mirth in their depths.

"Is it customary for the men of Tyre to thrust themselves into the houses of those who have visitors and disturb their rest?" she asked coolly.

Straton had lost—and he knew it. But he was determined not to let this cool goddess escape unscathed. "Then you deny being in the grove just now?" he asked.

The girl drew herself up proudly. "Do I look like a courtesan, sir, who must needs go about seeking men?"

She had defeated him with the question, for against the girl's refusal to admit her identity he could marshal no evidence, save that of the three who had tried to attack her. And even if he could find them, they would have little reason to help him, after he had broken their leader's jaw.

"I apologize for disturbing the rest of a visitor to Tyre, sir," he said courteously to the Ionian. "My friend Pallas here will tell you that my word is accepted as truth in Tyre and wherever the House of Gerlach sends its ships. Tonight a beautiful young woman accepted my gift in the Grove of Astarte. According to our law, she belongs to me and cannot marry until she has ransomed her body by giving its price to the goddess."

Turning, he limped down the steps to the street and set his face toward the harbor where his gaoul was berthed. He was soaking his swollen foot in sea water, cursing all women, when Ares returned shortly before dawn, vastly satisfied with himself and the pieces of silver jingling in his purse.

iii

Ares took one look at the swollen foot and started blowing on the coals of the cooking fire, which were always kept alive in a huge sand-filled pot upon the afterdeck. Next he drew a pot of sea water and put it to heating over the flame. Highly skilled in the treatment of wounds, the little man claimed descent from Podalirius who, with Machaon, it was said in tales told by the Greeks, had served as physician to the invaders at the siege of fabled Troy, centuries earlier. While Ares was applying steaming compresses and massaging soothing ointments into the bruised tissues of Straton's foot, he easily wormed the story of last night's events out of his still indignant master.

"You say the girl was a Greek?" he asked.

"An Ionian, I would guess."

"They are the most beautiful women in all the isles."

"This girl was even more than that."

"Did you learn her name?"

"The father called her Hera."

"Her-r-ra!" Ares almost dropped the foot he was massaging; it was the first time Straton had ever seen him pale with fear. "A-are you sure?"

"I heard the name plainly. Do you know her?"

"What you call a girl was the goddess Juno—in human form! In Greece she is also known as Hera."

"This girl is no goddess! She and her father are staying at the house of Pallas, so he is probably master of a Greek trading galley and Pallas is his agent here in Tyre."

Ares, however, was not even listening. "You are indeed the most fortunate of men, Master, to be loved by the Queen of the Gods herself. But I told you it would happen, when the divine ones looked down from Mount Olympus and saw you sailing this ship."

"I shall be fortunate if I am even able to walk by the time the Council of Merchants meets this morning," Straton growled. "Get to work. We only have a few more hours."

Ares went on with his work—and with his conversation. "A goddess cannot give herself to the man she selects the first time she meets him in human form," he confided. "When she fled last night, it was only the first move in the game of love. You must play out the rest of it, as you would in *senit*."

An Egyptian invention, the game was played on a board marked into squares upon which pieces were moved according to patterns formed by a handful of polished sticks, when shaken up in a cup and cast out upon a flat surface. It was a favorite diversion on long ocean voyages.

"I have already made the first move, so the next is hers," Straton said with a shrug. "That is the end of it."

"Before another day passes, or at most two, you will see her again,"

Ares assured him. "This time you must seize her and make her yield. Such a prize is not for the faint of heart."

"I will seize her," Straton said grimly. "Goddess or not, she owes me a debt and I intend to make her pay."

"Now you are acting like a god, too," Ares said happily. "I would give much to witness your coupling. But alas, such things are not for the eyes of ordinary men."

"I would have thought you had your fill of that sort of thing last night. You were late enough getting back to the ship."

"Last night I was busy gathering information for you while gaining pleasure for myself," Ares confided. "Without me to look after your interests, you would have gone before the Council of Merchants with no knowledge of what has been happening since we left Tyre five years ago."

"What could I possibly learn from such as you were sporting with in the grove?" Straton demanded, but his grumpiness was already beginning to fade under the skilled ministrations of the servant.

"Last night I consoled the daughter of a merchant. She was very grateful—having waited overlong."

"No doubt because of a harelip? Or perhaps a large mole on the end of her nose?"

"She does have a mole," Ares chuckled. "And in a most interesting place. She is also a little fat, but in a woman that is not to be deplored. After all, nothing takes a man's mind off his troubles like admiring a well-rounded pair of buttocks." He wrung out another cloth from the small earthen pot he had set to boil over the flames and applied it to Straton's swollen foot. "Nevertheless, she is a most devout servant of the goddess Astarte. In fact, she would do no discredit to Venus or Aphrodite, except in appearance. We worshiped three times before the chill of dawn cooled our ardor."

"Spare me," Straton begged drowsily, already half asleep.

"Being a merchant's daughter, the girl knows much of what goes on in Tyre," the servant continued. "Did you know that King Pygmalion has fallen under the influence of a man named Mago?"

"Mago? The name is not familiar."

"For a good reason. He came to Tyre since we left."

"What does he do?"

"The King has allowed him to contract for the entire product of the silversmiths' guild."

"The Greeks have already taken much of that trade, so the contract would bring him little profit."

33

"Mago *claims* to deal in silver," Ares said. "But he spends most of his time with the King."

Straton made a quick calculation. "Pygmalion should be about eighteen years old."

"Nineteen—and a very lusty young man, addicted, they say, to strange pleasures. Mago caters to the King's tastes by supplying him with female slaves from other lands whose customs are different from ours."

"Such as?"

"Circassians—for one."

Straton whistled softly. "The young cub will not have much to look forward to when he grows older. But this Mago has a right to deal in slaves, if he wishes. Some of the most important trading houses in Tyre do—with much profit."

"It is also rumored that a plot is afoot to kill the High Priest Sicharbas and Queen Elissa, so Pygmalion can rule—with Mago as his chief minister."

Straton sat up, his painful foot forgotten. "Elissa and Pygmalion rule only on the sufferance of the Royal Council! The merchants have always been the kingmakers of Tyre!"

"Not much longer—from the things I hear Mago has been whispering into the young King's ear."

"Why would Pygmalion listen to such drivel? In a few more years the regency will be ended and he will rule alone."

"Why wait—if he can have it all now? Besides, it is rumored that the Assyrians will return this year and demand tribute once again. The merchants have been able to hold out before, because the Assyrians cannot take The Rock without ships. But the people of Palaetyrus are tired of being captured every twenty years or so and taken into slavery. Their voices have reached the King."

"Through this Mago?"

"Who else?"

"How much of this is idle gossip?"

"Some, no doubt," Ares admitted. "The girl says Queen Elissa and Sicharbas have been able to control King Pygmalion so far. But if Mago gains a greater hold on him, the balance could shift as quickly as a ship heels when the wind varies."

"I will discuss this with my father after the council meeting this morning," Straton said. "Get my sandals or it will be over, while I sit here listening to your chatter."

Ares brought the sandals from his master's quarters and Straton cautiously inserted his foot into the right one. But the servant had done his work well. The swelling was almost gone and, when both sandals were laced, Straton was able to stand upon the foot with little pain.

"Truly, you are as skilled as Eshmun himself," he told Ares, roughening the small man's dark hair affectionately with his hand. Eighth among the divine dwarfs called the Cabiri, who traditionally had invented and controlled the building of ships, navigation and—in the case of Eshmun—medicine, the Phoenician god of healing was much revered in Tyre, though on a lower level than Melkarth and Astarte.

"We Greeks have a god of healing, too," Ares confided. "We call him Asklepios, but I believe he is the same as Eshmun. One day you must visit his temples at Cos and Cnidus, Master. The priests there know the secrets of inducing the divine sleep in which all ills are cured."

"Or the throat cut." Straton took a few steps and was pleased to feel no pain. "I trust your countrymen about as far as a scorpion can cast a stone in battle. I have landed too many times on a foreign shore to trade, only to find a Greek there before me. Give me the purple gum and take the cargo lists to my father's warehouse. You can wait for me there."

With the precious fragment wrapped in a piece of cloth and stored in the breast of his robe, Straton descended the ladder to the quay and the street leading upward from the harbor to the summit of The Rock. In the morning sunlight, the white walls of the multistoried houses rising abruptly from the foundation of the island made a striking pattern. Each had its own cistern, hewn in part from the rocky base and completed aboveground with blocks of stone made waterproof with a thin limestone mortar. Thus every drop of rain that struck the roofs was channeled into the cisterns, for water was precious in Tyre. Only one other Phoenician city of importance—Arvad, about two days' sail to the north—was located offshore as it was. And Arvad had the advantage of a spring in the ocean nearby.

As he climbed toward the top of The Rock where the royal palace stood, Straton could look out upon the manifold activities of Phoenicia's major city. A new and almost finished gaoul stood on the ways before his father's warehouse beside the okel, and he noted, with a thrill of pride, that it was broader of beam and considerably longer than his own ship, as well as higher above the waterline.

The vessel had existed only in a set of sketches upon sheets of papyrus, when he'd sent the designs to his father from Tartessus. Now, he estimated, it could be made ready for sailing in perhaps two months. And, though he could not see them closely from where he stood, he was sure the timbers of its keel, the curving prow, the broad stern where the steering sweeps would be set into place upon their pivots before the ship was launched—plus the over-all sturdiness he had particularly insisted upon—were all there. For this was no ordinary vessel designed to sail the tideless waters between Tyre and the Pillars of Melkarth but a new type, built for long voyages beyond the twin headlands into the trackless expanse known as the Western Sea.

The royal palace lay toward the southwestern extremity of the city. Even by the time of King Hiram—Straton's famed ancestor and Tyre's greatest ruler—Tyre had grown to where there was not enough space on The Rock to contain its people, in spite of houses rising five and six stories above their foundation stones. Hiram had pulled down the old temple of Melkarth and used that space to expand the area devoted to housing the rapidly growing population, as Tyre quickly became the largest and wealthiest of the Phoenician states. By filling in on the western side, a considerable area had been added, and here had been built the new temple of Melkarth, Baal of Tyre, and Astarte, his divine spouse, adjoining the grove in which the shrine for worship of the Earth Mother alone was located.

Adjacent to the royal castle was the grand square called the *Eurychoros*, a public trading area with the establishments of the artisans, who had made Tyre's products famous throughout the world, ranged around it. The countinghouses of the leading merchants, on the other hand, were located for the most part in their warehouses near the water's edge, facing the mainland. In all, some twenty-four thousand people lived upon the island, with perhaps half that number in Palaetyrus across the narrow channel.

As he approached the royal palace, Straton felt a warm rush of pleasure when he saw his father waiting by the door, toward which men were now converging from all directions in preparation for the meeting of the Council of Merchants. Convened always following the arrival of the great ships engaged in the Tartessus trade, as well as on other occasions when some concerted action was necessary, the Council of Merchants was the real ruling body of Tyre and the older, but now far less important, city of Sidon a little way to the north. Its roster included the membership of the smaller Royal Council, a select group that served as an advisory body to the King as well as a restraining influence, since, acting together, they could depose him and elect another ruler.

"Welcome home, my son." Gerlach embraced Straton warmly. "I trust your voyage was pleasant."

"And profitable. Our coffers will be strained to hold the treasure we brought from the West."

"It is enough that you are safely home. Did you see the new gaoul on the ways?"

"Only a glance, but it is as beautiful as I knew it would be—"

"As you planned it to be," Gerlach corrected him. "Only the courage of youth could conceive of so large a ship and place the timbers and braces so it will not break apart in a storm."

"Even from the top of The Rock I could see that it is well built," Straton agreed, as they entered the meeting chamber. "You must have realized that I plan to sail it where our vessels have never been before."

Seats had been left vacant for Straton and Gerlach on the front row of the benches that filled most of the room, except for a small dais at the end. Upon the elevated platform stood four chairs, carved from ivory after the Egyptian fashion and inlaid with gold in a pattern featuring the Phoenician disc and crescent, representing the sun god—to whom even Melkarth paid homage. Surmounting this was the figure of Baal holding a lion cub in one hand and a battle-ax in the other, while his feet rested upon the figure of a full-grown lion, depicting the glory of conquest in the hunt or in battle.

As he looked about him, acknowledging the greetings of old friends among the merchants, Straton was struck by the changes that had taken place during his absence. Many familiar faces, most of them elderly, were gone, while others had taken their places. Some were friends with whom he had grown up, sons of merchants who headed the great trading houses from which came Tyre's wealth. But there were other and less patrician faces, more than he remembered seeing before among the members of this important council. And he was reminded of the gossip Ares had brought, that the make-up of those who wielded the power in Tyre had been subtly changing over the years.

Straton's eyes were fastened on the door at the back of the small dais, through which the royal party would enter the chamber. But though during the weeks of the voyage from Tartessus to Tyre he had been anticipating his first sight of Dido and the pain it would surely bring, he found her image dimmer in his mind now than he had ever remembered its being. And when she came into the room, just before her brother, Pygmalion, she seemed for an instant almost a stranger.

It was not that her beauty had been dimmed in any way by the passage of the years. In fact she was, he decided, more beautiful as the Queen of Tyre than she had been as its madcap princess of the purple buskins. Rather the years had given her a maturity since that night when she had met him in the Grove of Astarte, a maturity that became her well and had turned a beautiful girl into a lovely woman. And where he had expected to feel the sharp pain of heartbreak at seeing her the wife of another, he now felt only the admiration any man would feel for a beautiful woman who had once lain in his arms.

Elissa's eyes sought his as soon as she entered the chamber, and she smiled warmly as if, though married to another, she felt none of the change in attitude that had occurred in Straton during the past five years. He acknowledged her unspoken greeting with a bow but looked away quickly, as she went on to take her chair, lest she see in his eyes some hint of his own amazement at what had happened to him and realize how he had changed.

Pygmalion entered the room a few steps behind Elissa. Five years ago, the Crown Prince of Tyre had been a rather handsome boy with a weak mouth and a quick temper. Now he was a sulky-looking young man with a bored manner and dark circles of dissipation beneath his eyes. The High Priest Sicharbas, Elissa's husband, walked just behind the brother and sister, and Straton was shocked to see how much he had aged in five years.

A handsome, tall man then, in the prime of middle age, Sicharbas was bent now, as if by heavy burdens. His hair, which had been graying, was now pure white, and the normal finely chiseled outlines of his face had given way to what could hardly be called anything but emaciation. Straton had always admired and respected Sicharbas, even after receiving the news of the marriage of Elissa. But the man he was looking at now seemed already marked by the hand of death.

Behind Sicharbas walked a richly appareled man who appeared to be about Straton's own age. His skin was darker than that of the ordinary Phoenician and he carried himself with arrogance and assurance as he moved to a chair just behind the front three, placing himself at Pygmalion's elbow when the four took their seat. From his manner and his position at the side of the King, Straton was sure this must be Mago, the man of whom Ares had told him.

The merchants had risen at the entrance of the royal party and there was a brief pause while they resumed their seats. Mago leaned forward and whispered something into the ear of the young King, as if prompting him, and Pygmalion gave up gnawing upon a fingernail to speak.

"We are pleased to welcome home the Son of Gerlach," he said. "Our heart is warmed by the return of so skilled a shipmaster from the Western Land."

Straton bowed in the customary gesture of homage. "I place my life in the hands of King Pygmalion," he said in the formal words of a declaration of loyalty, then added rather pointedly, "—and Queen Elissa. The gift to Astarte has been made. I hope the goddess received it with favor."

Mago had given Straton a quick, appraising glance at his pointed reference to Elissa. Now he leaned forward again and whispered to the young King.

"The High Priestess informs me that the Earth Mother was pleased by your gift of a necklace of green stones." Pygmalion suppressed a yawn.

The first business of the meeting was the consideration of a petition from the Sidonians that Tyre defend her subject city to the north against an expected attack by advance elements of an Assyrian army which was reported to be advancing toward the upper Phoenician coast. Although Gerlach and others spoke in favor of the petition, the vote went against it on the ground that defending Sidon would weaken Tyre to a point where it might not be able to protect itself against the enemy, if the expected attack were launched against The Rock. When the discussion was ended, Pygmalion gave Straton the floor for a report of his voyage from Tartessus and his observations there.

"It is known to you all," Straton began, "that I have spent the past five years in the district of Tartessus and the city of Gadir, looking after the interest of our house and those of Tyre."

"In that order of importance?" Mago asked in a voice heavy with sarcasm.

"The welfare of Tyre and that of the House of Gerlach have been identical for centuries, sir," Straton answered curtly. "If you were a Tyrian, you would not need to ask such a question."

Mago shrugged and Straton continued. "On the voyage to Gadir, we made good progress to Utica, where we took on supplies and fresh water. Then standing well out to sea to clear the coast of Libya, we sailed a northwesterly course to the islands off the eastern coast of Tartessus and turned thence southwesterly to the Pillars of Melkarth, leading to the Western Sea. After sailing safely between the Pillars, we set a course northward again and so came to the great river at whose mouth Gadir stands."

"What of the city?" Pygmalion asked.

"It is thriving and the harbor is one of the best I have ever entered. The mines near the shore have largely been depleted of silver in recent years, but I had the good fortune to discover new ones in the hills that will furnish us with an ample supply for many years."

"You had no trouble in obtaining a cargo, then?" one of the merchants asked.

"I could have filled the ship three times over in Tartessus," Straton assured him. "But I believe we are on the verge of a new discovery, one that will make our nation the richest on earth—if we get there before the Greeks."

He had their attention now, for the rapidly spreading Greek mercantile empire had become a real challenge to the Phoenicians in recent years.

"What is this new area you propose to open for trade?" Mago inquired.

"A group of islands in the Western Sea."

"Farther away than Tartessus?"

"Considerably farther."

There was a murmur of objection among the merchants at the prospect of sending their ships any greater distance than was already traveled by vessels in the Tartessian trade. He had expected that objection, however, and was prepared to combat it.

"Have you seen these islands?" Mago asked.

"No," Straton admitted. "I was told of them by one blown there in a storm. He says they can easily be identified by a plume of smoke hanging over a mountain and a pillar of fire shining by night."

"Even such a spectacle could hardly be seen more than a day's sail away," Mago said contemptuously. "How do you propose to find these islands in a trackless sea?"

"The man who told me of them says the star Doube in the Small Bear is low in the sky there. And the Great Bear seems to reach his feet toward the ocean."

"What foolishness is this?" Mago snapped. "The Son of Gerlach should know better than to be taken in by a sailor's tale."

"I believed the story because it *was* told by a sailor."

Mago flushed at the contempt in his tone. "What does that mean?"

Before Straton could reply, one of the older merchants, a man highly respected by everyone in Tyre, intervened. "The sailor described how the sky would look from a ship driven south of the Pillars of Melkarth," he explained. "Had it sailed north, Doube would have risen in the sky and the Great Bear's paws would reach higher and higher above the water."

A murmur of agreement rose from the merchants, most of whom were themselves shipmasters and knew the truth of what the older man had said. Mago only shrugged, however, and continued his self-elected role of inquisitor.

"Do you have any further proof that such islands even exist?" he demanded.

"Only something that was found upon one of them. The people there call it The Dragon's Blood." Straton took a small cloth-wrapped packet from his robe and emptied the block of gum into his hand. He held it up to a shaft of sunlight pouring through a window as he moved closer to the dais, so those seated there could see how the block glowed with a hue so deeply red as to appear almost purple.

"Dragon's Blood!" Mago exclaimed scornfully. "Are you such a fool that you expect us to be impressed by a piece of red amber?"

It was on the tip of Straton's tongue to reveal just why The Dragon's Blood was so immensely valuable. But when he noticed a warning look in his father's eyes, he sensed that Gerlach did not want the knowledge revealed at the moment and, wrapping the fragment again in its cloth, placed it in the breast of his robe.

"As the ship of which I spoke was blown southward, its crew often saw fires glowing on the mainland shore at night," he said, deliberately diverting the attention of his audience from the purple gum. "They were able to distinguish groups of black men, but the water was shallow well out from the shore and they did not dare land in the rough sea."

"Did they take any slaves?" Pygmalion had leaned forward, showing interest for the first time.

"No."

"Then why do you think this voyage was so significant?" Mago demanded.

"It is well known that elephants thrive in the country of the black men south of our colony of Utica," Straton explained. "But by the time the ivory passes through the hands of the Libyans, who send caravans into the interior, the cost is greatly increased. If we could buy ivory directly from the black men, we could sell it to the Greeks at a considerable profit. All of you know how fond they are of furniture made from it."

He had improvised upon the first thought that came to him, seeking to turn the interest of the gathering away from the significance of The Dragon's Blood, until he could discuss it with his father. When he saw Mago nod agreement, he knew his thought about the ivory had been inspired, for trade in ivory was next in importance to that in the purple dye for which Phoenicia was most famous.

"How do you propose to reach the settlements of the black men on the Libyan shore?" one of the merchants asked.

"No doubt a river mouth or other harbor can be found along the coast south of the Pillars of Melkarth, just as we found the river upon which Gadir is located. By laying in supplies there, we should be able to trade along the coast as well as with the islands."

"If the Greeks don't get there before us."

"The Greeks have already taken much of the trade from us in the eastern half," Straton agreed. "At all cost, we must hold the western half of the Great Sea as our own."

Three:

*Who but a fool would wars with Juno choose,
And such alliance and such gifts refuse?*

NEITHER FATHER NOR SON mentioned the fragment of gum which had evoked such an outburst from Mago, until they were safely inside Gerlach's house and the servants, many of whom Straton had known since childhood, had greeted him.

"Is there something about this amber called The Dragon's Blood that you did not reveal just now?" Gerlach asked, when that pleasant chore was finished.

"It isn't amber, Father." Straton took the small block of gum from the pouch and held it up to the sunlight streaming through an open window. Once again it seemed to imprison the rays, turning them into a rich, purplish color. "Have you ever seen anything like this?"

"The color is beautiful!" Gerlach lifted the fragment and creased it with his fingernail, leaving a mark on the surface. "But it doesn't have the hardness of amber, which makes it less valuable."

Straton unfolded the cloth in which the gum had been wrapped. When he held it up to the light, the lustrous purple color was the equal of any tint produced by the dyers of Tyre.

"This fabric was the natural color of wool before I dyed it with water in which a small bit of the gum had been dissolved," he said. "Look at it now."

Gerlach caught his breath. "I have never seen anything like this before."

"Nor I."

"How costly is it?" The older man's voice was excited now.

"According to the man who sold it to me, the gum forms when the bark of a tree growing in the islands is wounded," Straton explained. "The natives use it to dye their garments but have no idea of its value."

"If the color holds, dyers everywhere would pay fabulous prices for this. A source of it not possessed by any other nation could make us all rich."

For many centuries, the secret of the purple dye obtained from the shellfish called *murex* growing on the bottom of the sea along the

43

Phoenician and adjoining coasts had been the greatest source of wealth to Tyre and its sister city-states. Each individual murex furnished only a few drops of the pure essence, however, and this was further condensed to no more than a sixteenth of its original volume by means of live steam.

Originally a milky-white color, the final shade was controlled by exposing the dyed fabric to sunlight for varying periods immediately after dyeing. In the hands of Tyre's skilled dyers a wide range of colors was obtained, ranging from a pale-green tint through pink, violet, and finally the deep purple, so rich that it was almost black. And since the wives and daughters of the rich and noble in all lands had come to feel they could not be fashionably dressed without the fabric dyed by the Phoenician art, a great industry had grown up around it.

Tyre itself stank with the drying piles of murex from which the dye had already been extracted. The leaders among the dyers were no less important in the kingdom than the merchant princes, and from the Nile to the Euphrates, men and women eagerly sought the fine fabrics woven in Canaan and dyed with the precious Phoenician purple. Recently, however, the always questing Greeks, having discovered for themselves the method of extracting the dye and located beds of the precious shellfish along their own coast, were beginning to take much of this important trade away from the Phoenicians.

"Have you told anyone of this discovery since you arrived in Tyre?" Gerlach asked.

"Only those aboard my ship have seen The Dragon's Blood. Ares and I dyed the piece of cloth in secret."

"You acted wisely. The ship you will need to discover the location of these islands is almost finished. And with a secret source of the dye, we may still save our nation from destruction at the hands of the Assyrians."

"How?"

"You will learn shortly," Gerlach said and called for the chief of his house slaves. "Go to the High Priest Sicharbas," he directed. "Ask him if my son and I, with Athach, the chief of the dyers, can wait upon him this evening."

"Why Sicharbas?" Straton asked when the slave had departed upon his mission. "Hasn't he been pushed into the background by this Mago?"

"It will take more than an upstart like Mago to destroy the confidence of Tyre in the High Priest of Melkarth," Gerlach said cryptically. "Do you have the records of this voyage?"

"I instructed Ares to take them to the warehouse and wait for us there."

"Good! We will set the scribes to counting up the profits while we wait for word from Sicharbas. But I suspect that your whole cargo is worth only a fraction of what The Dragon's Blood may come to mean for Tyre."

ii

It was early afternoon before Straton found time to undertake a pilgrimage he never failed to make upon his return to Tyre from a distant voyage. On the southwestern side of the main island, a small house was set in an isolated position at the very edge of a cliff whose sides descended directly into the water, forming a rock-walled cove hidden except from the sea. It was the home of Mochus, the philosopher and teacher who had molded Straton's youthful mind and given him his love for learning and for seeking out the mysteries both of the world and of the mind.

Nor had Mochus allowed his students, drawn from the most intelligent and promising young men of Tyre regardless of their station, to neglect the body in favor of the mind. Each day they had dived and swum for an hour before the noonday meal in the isolated cove just back of his home. And Straton had plunged deeper than any of the others dared to go, rising to the surface to display proudly the large whorled shells of the prized murex colony growing on the bottom.

The sun was shining brightly, the day warm, and the cove secluded from view, even from Mochus' house. It had been years since Straton had swum there as a youth, and he found himself wondering whether he still retained enough of the skill and wind of a diver to reach the bottom. From idle curiosity came the impulse to be certain and, stepping out of his clothing, he took several deep breaths, as he had learned to do while a schoolboy in preparation for a dive, and plunged deeply into the waters of the cove.

Surging downward, he scanned the face of the cliff beneath the water, seeking some scratches he had once made there to warn him when he was nearing the bottom. He was barely halfway down, however, when another swimmer came into his field of vision, heading upward from the depths. It was the girl he had rescued in the grove the night before, and she was so close that he could have reached out and touched her, had he not been so startled by her sudden appearance.

At first he thought she was naked like himself, then he saw that her sole garment was one of the woven loincloths he had observed Greek divers wear in the coves along the shoreline of Crete. Seen now almost unclothed, she was even more beautiful than she had been last night when he had first spied her, like a fawn held at bay by hunters, in the Grove of Astarte. And when he remembered Ares' assurance that, if the girl were indeed the goddess in human form the little man confidently believed her to be, he would surely see her again before another day had passed, Straton could not help wondering whether the prophecy had come true.

The girl's eyes were open and he saw that she was quite as startled by his presence as he was by hers. Instinctively, he reached out to seize her, but the act released her, too, from the shock of seeing him there. Kicking out sharply, she moved upward and his fingers only touched cool flesh, but her heel struck his shoulder and the force of the kick sent him tumbling end over end downward through the clear water.

Straton managed to right himself by thrashing about in the water but, conscious of his straining lungs, gave up any thought of reaching the bottom of the cove. Instead, he swam upward in pursuit of the girl, as angry once again as he had been last night when she'd run away from the grove. But when his head finally broke the surface of the pool, he had only a momentary glimpse of a slender thigh and foot, as she disappeared around the corner of the rocky ledge marking the boundary of the cove.

Thrashing across the cove in pursuit, he wasted precious minutes locating the steps, cut years ago by Mochus' students in the almost vertical wall of the cliff, and climbing out of the water. By the time he reached the level from which he had dived, the girl was nowhere in sight but, pressing along a path that led across the top edge of the cliff, he came out upon a vantage point and saw a slender, graceful figure moving ahead of him. She was fully clothed now and leaped from rocky outcrop to outcrop with all the grace of the fawn to which he had likened her in his mind last night. Still furious at being outwitted a second time, he started after her but, suddenly remembering that he was naked, hurriedly backed away and returned to the cove and his clothing.

Straton had almost finished dressing when he noticed a cord attached to a stake that had been securely wedged into a crevice in the rocks nearby. From the stake, the cord led down over the lip of the rocky cliff into the depths of the cove. Mochus, he knew, was no fisherman, so the line could hardly belong to him. And, unless one of the students had taken to fishing, its presence there could only mean that someone had been poaching in the cove. His curiosity aroused, Straton began to pull in the line hand over hand, his excitement rising when its weight told him a large fish must have been caught on the hook. But when finally the lower end broke the surface, he was so startled by what he saw that he almost dropped it back into the cove.

A wicker basket had been tied to the end of the line and weighted with stones, obviously to make it sink. In it were ten murex shells with —judging from the weight of one of them when he lifted it in his hand —the marine animals that furnished the precious purple dye alive inside. And with that knowledge came the answer to the girl's presence in the cove.

Obviously she had not come there for a casual swim, as he had first thought. Instead she had been engaged in a well-planned diving venture—as the basket and cord she'd not had time to recover proved—with the intention of examining the live murex growing upon the sea bottom. And for this there could be but one reason.

Through the years, the constantly increasing need of the dyers for more of the famous purple had put pressure on the fishermen, who used heavy nets and seines to drag the murex from the sea bottom. With so many of the marine animals being seined up before they were fully grown, however, the amount of the dye obtained from each had been growing steadily smaller—information that could be very important indeed to Greek dyers and merchants who competed with the Phoenicians for the trade in purple-dyed fabrics which, for centuries, had been a monopoly of Straton's people.

Briefly he considered taking the information he had gained to the Council of Merchants, but discarded the impulse. Neither Diomedes nor his daughter had broken any Phoenician law, since, having an agent in Tyre—the merchant Pallas—Diomedes was free to trade as he wished, and his daughter to swim wherever she desired. Straton did decide to keep a close watch on them, however, not so much because of what they might discover about the Phoenician dye trade as in the hope of seeing again the lovely girl who, in such a short time, seemed to have become closely involved in his own life.

Leaving the cove, Straton followed a path that wound between hedges of stunted cedars to the shadowed retreat beneath the spreading branches of a giant ailanthus tree that was Mochus' favorite place of discussion and meditation. He heard voices coming from the garden before he reached it but, knowing that Mochus was rarely alone, pushed on until he came around a corner of the hedge and realized the identity of the man with the old teacher.

It was Diomedes, the Greek merchant!

Mochus, however, had already seen him. "Straton!" he cried. "Come here!"

"I didn't realize you had a visitor," Straton apologized as he emerged from the path. "I can easily come again tomorrow."

"Diomedes is an old friend—and a shipmaster like yourself. You two will have much in common." Mochus turned to the Greek. "Straton is a former pupil, just returned from a voyage to Tartessus."

"The fame of the Son of Gerlach is known even in my native land," Diomedes said courteously. "I trust that your foot was not badly injured, sir."

"What is this?" Mochus demanded. "Have you met before?"

"Last night I mistook the daughter of Diomedes for someone else—perhaps a goddess," Straton explained. "My servant insists that among the Greeks divine beings often associate with ordinary people."

"It was a natural mistake," Diomedes said coolly. "Hera was named for the Queen of the Gods."

"And is as beautiful as Astarte herself! I am not so old that I cannot see that." Mochus looked at Straton closely. "Your hair is wet. I'll wager you stopped to swim in the cove."

Without waiting for an answer, the old teacher turned to Diomedes. "None of the young men I taught could dive deeper or remain under water longer than Straton."

"In Crete our young people learn to swim and dive almost before they can walk," Diomedes said. "Just before we left, my daughter helped to bring up some amphorae and other treasures from a Minoan vessel that sank in one of the coves of our coastline many centuries ago."

"When I saw her last night, I was struck by her resemblance to the bull dancers portrayed upon the walls of the temple at Knossus," Straton volunteered.

"The resemblance is not without reason. We are descended from the same Theseus who broke the power of the Minoans and destroyed the Minotaur." Diomedes got to his feet. "You and Mochus will have much to discuss, so I must not linger. I shall be in Tyre for a few days longer. Perhaps we can talk seafaring over a cup of spiced wine aboard my galley."

iii

"Tell me about your voyage," Mochus ordered Straton, when the guest had departed. "Did you use the method I taught you for locating true north by means of the sun's height at noonday?"

48

"Each day the sun shines, I record it at noon."

"And the north-south height from the angle of the south-gazing star within the Great Bear?"

"I sailed straight from the Pillars of Melkarth to Utica, then to Itanos on Crete and again to Tyre by means of it," Straton assured him. "But the star Doube in the Lesser Bear is a better guide."

"You are a worthy student." Mochus clapped his hands and one of the servants appeared with wine and sweet cakes. "After a plunge in the cold water of the cove, you need something to warm your blood. Even a strong man can take a chill."

Straton accepted the cup of wine and bit into one of the cakes. "Don't your students still swim in the pool?"

"Yes, but none can dive as deeply as you."

"The daughter of Diomedes can."

Mochus gave him a sharp look. "How do you know that?"

"I saw her just now in the cove. She had gathered a basket of murex from the bottom and was intending to pull them up with a cord, but my coming drove her away."

Mochus stroked his beard thoughtfully. "Diomedes is one of the shrewdest merchants among the Greeks. Word that our murex beds are failing must already have reached them."

"I am sure of it. Now they know just how small ours have become."

"You can hardly blame Diomedes for seeking to learn as much as he could," Mochus said. "We Phoenicians discovered the secret of dyeing cloth with the purple when our people still dwelt upon the shores of the Eastern Sea that looks toward India and the country of the yellow men. We were forced to leave there when the supply of murex grew too small for profitable operation, and if it fails here we will find another way to keep our dyers busy."

"I may have discovered it already." Straton went on to describe how he had come to possess the precious gum called The Dragon's Blood.

"Did you say you stopped at Itanos?" Mochus asked when he finished the account.

"We came directly to Tyre from there."

"Did any of your men go ashore?"

"I allowed the crew to visit the brothels, as I always do. Why?"

"Diomedes inquired just now whether any of our gaouls had sailed the Western Sea south of the Pillars of Melkarth. Some of your men must have talked about the island of The Dragon's Blood at Itanos."

"But we came directly here. Diomedes could not possibly have been at Itanos and reached Tyre before us."

"He told me that he sailed from Itanos," Mochus insisted. "I'll wager he heard you had discovered a new source of the dye and came here to find out about it."

"Any man on my ship will tell you no gaoul has ever sailed faster than ours," Straton insisted.

Mochus shrugged. "When you are as old as I am, you will know that nothing is impossible—especially to the Greeks."

"But they are only men like the rest of us."

"Some men are destined to rise above others—you, for example. In the five years you were away, you became a man and a leader of men."

"I am thirty years old," Straton reminded him. "Manhood came to me long ago."

"I don't mean the kind of manhood you gain by tumbling girls in the Grove of Astarte," the old teacher said. "When you recognized the possible value of The Dragon's Blood, you proved that you have learned to look farther than the pleasures of the moment. One day you might even become king. The line of Mattan has run out in Pygmalion, and there has never been a time when Tyre was more in need of a wise and courageous ruler."

"I have no wish to be king."

"That could be the most important reason why you should be—but you may not yet be ready. Only dire disaster can bring a man really close to the source of all understanding."

"On my first voyage to the West I almost lost my ship when it was cast upon the shore in a storm. That seemed dire—at the time."

"How did you save it?"

"The ocean rises and falls twice daily beyond the Pillars. I set the ship on the shore at the flood of what is called the tide, drained out the water, and patched the hull."

"The way you used the rise and fall of the tide to your own advantage shows how you have matured," Mochus said. "One who would be a leader of men must always think ahead of others; it is the very essence of wisdom."

"Any wisdom I have I gained from you."

"No, Straton. Wisdom comes from a higher source."

"Higher even than Melkarth?"

"Higher than all the gods and goddesses. Perhaps it is but the wishful thought of an old man who sees death approaching. But if a greater god than any we know of yet took the trouble to make the world and all within it, then he must surely have some purpose for many beyond the pleasure and pain of earthly life."

"A Pharaoh in Egypt once had such a thought," Straton reminded him. "I saw the city he built to the Sun God Aton on the banks of the Nile."

Mochus beamed. "You learned your lessons well. His name was Akhenaten."

"Yet Akhenaten's god did not even preserve the city he built. When I was there, it was almost covered by sand."

"In our eyes Akhenaten failed when he tried to make his people serve only one god," Mochus admitted. "But it may only seem that way to us because we do not understand the purpose the One-Above-All has for us."

"With an argument like that, a man could convince himself of anything he wanted to believe," Straton protested.

Mochus clapped him affectionately on the shoulder. "You are still as keen as you were when I taught you. Yes, there is much in the world we cannot understand, Straton, but we must never give up searching. For example, until you brought the gum that drips from trees on the Western Isles, we had no knowledge of another source of the purple dye."

"It still has not been tested."

"Even if you haven't discovered the answer, someone else will," Mochus assured him. "Once the supply of the dye is plentiful, the price will fall. Then the young girls can all wear purple buskins, as Dido did when she was a princess. The poor will be as good as the rich, and the color of a man's robe will no longer mark him as more noble or important than another."

"As well argue that a nation can be made great by reducing its people to slaves, so none will be above the other."

"Not slaves, Straton. But free men, proud of what they make with their hands, instead of what their money can buy. Even in such a city, though, some would be born to rule, for all men are not really the same, even if they wear the same garments. He who is chosen by the gods to lead must not be so ungrateful for their favor that he refuses to play the role given him. Be sure you never forget that."

"What do you mean?"

Mochus, however, chose not to answer. "I am tired and must rest," he said. "Come to me another day and we will talk of the isles in the West from which tin comes—and perhaps of other things."

Straton was halfway across the top of The Rock and still pondering the meaning of Mochus' last few cryptic statements, when he heard a familiar cry of "Master." He turned to see Ares running after him as fast as the little man's somewhat bandy legs could carry him, and even at a distance he could see that his servant was very much excited.

"Come with me to the Egyptian harbor at once!" Ares panted when he came up to where Straton had stopped to wait.

"Why?"

"To see the chariot! The chariot of Juno!"

iv

"What drivel is this?" Straton demanded. Puzzled by the reference of his old teacher to something he did not understand, but which he suspected had to do with the mystery of his recall to Tyre, he found a natural target for his irritation in Ares.

"It's true, Master! I saw it with my own eyes at anchor in the Egyptian Harbor."

"A chariot at anchor? Do you take me for a fool?"

"It is the chariot of Juno—or Hera," Ares insisted. "The goddess who has chosen to favor you."

Straton had never been able to remain angry long with Ares, and he recognized that the little man was more genuinely disturbed than he had ever seen him before.

"I told you the girl is no goddess," he said, somewhat more gently. "Now run to my father's house and fill a tub with hot water. I must bathe before I go to the temple for dinner with the High Priest and Queen Elissa."

"First, come and see for yourself, Master," Ares pleaded. "You can cut off my head if I am not telling the truth."

"I shall cut off something you value more, if this is another of your schemes," Straton assured him. "Where is this vehicle of the gods? Remember, the Queen of Tyre cannot be kept waiting."

"And the Queen of the Gods even less!"

Ares scampered ahead before Straton could question him further, stopping at a craggy overlook jutting from the crest of The Rock and the wall that gave Tyre an additional defense on the landward side. From the elevation it was possible to look down upon the whole of the Egyptian Harbor on the southern side of the island and the warehouse district of the okel at the foot of the wall.

"I saw your goddess at close range only a little while ago," Ares confided, as he waited for Straton to catch up to where he stood. "Such a delectable creature could only be Hera herself come down to earth."

"You must have started drinking wine earlier than—" Straton broke off suddenly as the expanse of the Egyptian harbor opened out before his eyes. For what he saw there so excited his shipmaster's instincts that momentarily he was at loss for words.

"I told you I would show you the chariot of the gods," Ares said proudly. "There it is."

The vessel that had excited the servant's admiration—and his master's as well—was not quite like anything Straton had ever seen before. It was a galley, but such a one as indeed gods might have chosen for a vehicle—as Ares claimed. Long and sleek with trim lines and breathtaking beauty over all, it was in the process of being moved by oars alone across the short distance from the Egyptian Harbor to a quay, where he judged that it would take on a load of goods from the warehouse of Pallas.

With the long oars in the hands of the galley slaves fairly lifting it from the water, the vessel almost seemed to rise above the surface and fly through the air. Nor was Straton surprised to see a slender figure in white standing upon the afterdeck and even without Ares' excited babbling, recognized the girl who, only little more than an hour before, had almost been within his reach in the secluded cove adjoining Mochus' garden.

"Do you know how I recognized yonder galley as a chariot of the gods—besides the presence of the goddess herself upon it?" Ares prompted him.

"You might as well tell me," Straton said resignedly. "Since you will anyway."

"Do you remember seeing the galley before?"

"No."

"That very ship was at Itanos on the island of Crete while we were there."

"That is impossible! No vessel could make the voyage from Crete to Tyre in less time than we did."

"No vessel but one bearing a goddess! You forget that the chariot of the gods flies though the air and takes on any form the driver desires."

Straton, however, was not listening. Instead, he was reviewing in his mind the sequence of events, when he had brought his gaoul to a safe berth at the Cretan port of Itanos a few days before. And as he did, a momentary vision came into his memory, a picture of a lovely galley that had also been approaching the harbor at the same time but at some distance away. Intent upon his own duties, he had barely glimpsed it at the time, yet, even in that brief glance, had been struck by its beauty. But he had forgotten the sleek vessel in the multiple tasks of seeing his own ship made fast to the quay and making arrangements for supplies to be put aboard from the warehouse of Gerlach, while the crew were given liberty for the night.

Now, at last, the pieces of the puzzle began to fall into place in his mind. Diomedes' question to Mochus regarding ventures by Phoenician vessels into the Western Sea; the girl's dive to the bottom of the cove in search of live murex in order to judge their size; the competition of Greek dyers and merchants for the trade in purple—all of it made a pattern of logic that answered every question in his mind save one, the reason for his sudden recall to Tyre. And that, he knew, would be answered by his father in good time.

When Straton looked carefully at the sleek galley, he could hardly blame Ares, with his vivid imagination, for leaping to the conclusion that it must indeed be the vehicle of a goddess disguised as a galley driven by oars and a sail. Once he had rid himself of his instinctive refusal to admit that any ship had been swifter than his own on the journey from Crete to Tyre, Straton's trained seaman's eye had no trouble noting things about the Greek vessel that would make it very fast, whether under sail, oars or both. Moreover, he was already considering how this knowledge could be adapted to the great new vessel a-building upon his father's ways only a little distance from the warehouse of Pallas, against whose quay the galley was now being warped into place.

"You cannot deny it any longer, Master," Ares said triumphantly. "I tell you no man has ever been so favored as you!"

"Come down from Mount Olympus and look at the galley with the eyes of a seaman," Straton ordered. "You have spent much of your life on ships, so you should be able to tell me why it is faster than our gaoul."

Ares studied the smaller vessel carefully. "The sail is larger in proportion to its size, for one thing," he admitted. "But how do they keep it from tearing the mast from the hull?"

"That's what I plan to find out—though I think I know already. Look how the mast slants toward the stern."

"What difference could—"

"I don't know yet for sure, but if I can get aboard her I should be able to find out. Now look to the rowers."

The galley was now being secured against the quay with mooring lines at bow and stern. The girl had disappeared into the small afterhouse rising above the deck, and the overseers were directing the slaves in storing the oars. Even from this elevation, Straton could see that half of them were longer than the rest and, besides the usual set of rowers' benches at deck level, a line of ports had been cut into the hull through which a second row of oars could be handled by men inside it. The ports, however, were staggered, each being located between two of the benches at deck level, so that oars handled through the ports would not strike those being handled on the deck above.

"I see two sets of oars, one longer than the other," Ares said. "And look at the slaves going ashore. Half of them are much taller than the others. They must be the ones who pull the longer oars."

"Two banks of oars have been used before—in war galleys where speed was the only object," Straton said. "Why couldn't we use the same arrangement of rowers' benches in a merchant ship—and leave considerably more space for cargo?"

Ares glanced at the gaoul on the ways of the House of Gerlach not far from where the galley was moored. "The deck on your new ship has not yet been put in. There is still time to make the change."

"And time to step the mast at an angle," Straton agreed. "I must get aboard the Greek galley somehow and learn how they fixed the foot of the mast to the keel."

"The goddess followed you here from Itanos. Surely she will not deny you anything you wish."

"Forget about goddesses," Straton told the little Greek. "The galley belongs to an Ionian merchant named Diomedes. Mochus says he is one of the canniest of the Greek traders. Somehow he must have learned at Itanos about The Dragon's Blood and come here trying to find out more about it." He seized Ares by the shoulders and turned him so he could look into the servant's eyes. "How many cups of wine did you drink in the brothel you visited at Itanos?"

Ares shrugged. "Who keeps count at such a time?"

"And I suppose your tongue was as loose as usual."

The little man drew himself up, affronted. "Do you think I revealed the secret there?"

"Can you swear you didn't?"

Ares collapsed like a sack of meal slit by a knife. "We were all drinking wine," he admitted, "and—"

"You were boasting as usual, I suppose."

"A small man can impress women only in two ways, Master. By boasting and—"

"I know the rest."

Ares looked at him quickly. "Then you are not going to beat me?"

"Why should I beat you?" Straton gave him an affectionate punch on the shoulder. "Because of you, Diomedes was curious enough about The Dragon's Blood to come to Tyre. Now I can study his galley and

55

add any improvements the Greek shipbuilders have made to the new gaoul."

"To say nothing of pressing your claim for the favors of his beautiful daughter." Ares had quickly regained his old impudence.

"As to that, we shall see." But when Straton smiled, the servant knew he was not at all offended by the suggestion.

Four:

*On Tyrian carpets, richly wrought,
they dine,
With loads of massy plate, the
sideboards shine.*

STRATON WAS LATE in getting home and barely had time to dress before accompanying Gerlach to the dinner with Elissa and Sicharbas. The great temple of the Baal of Tyre and his divine spouse was located at the top of The Rock, with its massive back wall looking westward where the long rollers from the open sea dashed themselves into spray against the rocky foundation on which it stood. Of its four terraced stories, the lower was the largest, built of stone quarried from the foothills of the Lebanon range that rose sharply only a little distance back of the shore. Columns of cedar supported the roof that covered a terrace surrounding the entire structure, and above the lower story rose an area containing the quarters of the priests and members of the household, including those of Queen Elissa and her husband.

A staircase of Libyan ebony gave access to the upper stories. At each corner, where the staircase turned to rise to another level, the prow of an enemy ship captured in battle had been fixed. Gratings of bronze protected the windows of the lower floor, which also housed the great hall where the eternal fire of Tyre's god burned within the great image of Melkarth, enabling the temple to be turned into a citadel in case of attack from across the channel or the unlikely occurrence of an uprising among the people of the city. Grateful for the riches the patron deity had granted them, the merchants of Tyre had covered one of the massive pillars supporting the roof with beaten gold and had set another with Tartessian emeralds.

At the entrance to the temple, Gerlach and Straton were met by a shaven-headed priest, whose richly fringed robe of Tyrian purple marked him as more than just an ordinary servant of the Phoenician deity.

"You remember Luli, don't you, Straton?" Gerlach asked. "He is Sicharbas' nephew."

"I arrived from Kition in Cyprus only a few months before the noble Straton left on his last voyage," the priest said. "He would hardly be expected to remember me."

"But I do," Straton assured him. "You took part in the service of sacrifice, when the High Priest invoked the blessing of Melkarth and Astarte upon my voyage."

"I am honored to be remembered." Luli was perhaps five years younger than he, Straton estimated. But though his manner was courteous, there was no warmth in his words and, when Straton looked into the young priest's eyes, he was startled by the look of naked hostility he saw there.

He must ask his father about Luli, he decided, as they entered the building in the wake of the priest and were guided to the private quarters of Sicharbas. It had not surprised him that Mago had been so openly hostile to him that morning, since Mago might well regard the heir of the greatest merchant house in Tyre as his enemy. But he could think of no reason why a much younger priest, whom he remembered seeing only once before, should have such a marked dislike for him.

Athach, the old chief of the Dyers' Guild, had already arrived when Straton and Gerlach were ushered into the luxurious quarters of the High Priest of Baal and Astarte. The carpet, woven on a Tyrian loom, was thick, and the rich purple hangings at the windows shut out all outside sound, giving the apartment privacy from the temple activities. Straton had known the old dyer since his boyhood, when, as a part of his training in preparation for the day when he would take over the direction of the great mercantile empire that was the House of Gerlach, he had been sent to Athach for a rudimentary schooling in the dyer's art. He greeted Athach warmly, having seen him only across the meeting chamber that morning.

Elissa and Sicharbas came into the beautifully furnished chamber a few moments later. The young Queen went immediately to Straton with her hands extended and a warm smile of welcome upon her face. And Sicharbas, far from objecting to her obvious show of affection for a former suitor, seemed to approve, for he embraced Straton in greeting.

Noting again the bony emaciation of the High Priest's body, Straton could hardly put down a sense of revulsion. Seen at close range, the older man's color was even worse than he had thought it to be that morning. The whites of the High Priest's eyes were yellow, as if with rapidly advancing age, though Straton knew he was not more than fifty years old. And he moved slowly and painfully, while his face was lined and drawn with suffering.

It was a strange situation in which Straton found himself—a former lover being greeted warmly both by the woman he had loved and by her husband. Even stranger was the realization that he no longer felt any emotion toward Elissa beyond what he might feel for a childhood friend. She, on the other hand, seemed to assume that nothing had changed and that he was as much in love with her as he had been before sailing for Tartessus. And remembering how easily her temper could be aroused, he decided to walk carefully, for Elissa, the Queen, was far more imperious in manner than had been Dido, the Princess, and obviously even more accustomed to having her way.

"Come sit at my left, Straton," she directed. "You must tell me all about the Western Sea and the islands where you found The Dragon's Blood."

"At the moment I fear they exist only as a sailor's tale," Straton reminded her. "You saw this morning how little the Council of Merchants thought of them."

Moving carefully with Elissa's help, Sicharbas seated himself upon her right. "It is best for a while that only a few think your story more than just a sailor's tale," he said. "That is why we have all come together here tonight."

"First we must celebrate the traveler's safe return," Elissa insisted. "Afterward you men can talk of ships and distant lands. I must confess that I know little of such things."

When Straton saw a quick glance pass between his father and Sicharbas, he was more certain than ever that the presence of all of them here tonight was somehow closely related to the cryptic summons he had received from Gerlach in Gadir, recalling him home. But the servants came in just then with food and wine, so he had no chance to ask his father for information about the reason for the dinner.

The meal was a pleasant one, for all of them were friends of long standing, including Athach, who, though a commoner, had been chief of the dyers in the time of Elissa's father, King Mattan. Only when the massive engraved silver platters on which the food had been served were cleared away, leaving wine cups and an exquisitely fashioned glass bottle of wine from the vineyards of Judah, the Israelite kingdom to the south on the mainland, did Sicharbas speak of the subject uppermost in Straton's mind.

"No doubt, you have noticed changes in Tyre since you have been away," he said. "Has your father discussed them with you?"

"I preferred to let you tell him, Sicharbas," Gerlach explained. "Sometimes even I find it hard to believe what is happening is anything more than a bad dream."

"It is like a nightmare to me, too. When I think that my own brother—" Elissa's voice broke and she did not go on.

"Two months ago an attempt was made on my life by one of my own priests, a man I trusted next to myself," Sicharbas explained. "I am sure he had been promised the place of High Priest if he succeeded in destroying me."

"No man in Tyre is more revered than you are," Straton protested. "If tomorrow you declared yourself king with Queen Elissa beside you, the people would desert Pygmalion."

"Not any longer," Athach said gravely. "The time is past when men like King Mattan ruled here and your father and I were among his most trusted advisers. Mago has the King's ear now and has almost convinced him that we here on The Rock should yield to the Assyrians."

"Is an attack that near?"

"No Phoenician city is as yet under siege," Sicharbas admitted. "But we know a large Assyrian army is moving westward and, if they follow the path other invasion forces from the East have chosen, will soon reach the Sea before Arvad. When Shalmaneser sent an army against Canaan and Phoenicia about fifty years ago, Arvad was the first of our sister cities to fall. Afterward its ships were used by the Assyrians to attack Tyre."

"Why not go to the aid of Arvad for our own protection, then?" Straton asked.

"Your father and I have been urging just such a move," Sicharbas said. "But this morning you heard the Council refuse even to defend Sidon if it is attacked."

"Do you mean King Pygmalion is really considering yielding The Rock?" Straton asked incredulously.

"We don't know. Mago has poisoned Pygmalion's mind even against his own sister, so he may have convinced him that he can make terms with the Assyrians."

"As well nurse an asp and not expect to be bitten!" Straton exclaimed. "This Mago must be in the pay of Nineveh, to advise such a course."

"We suspect just that," Gerlach agreed. "But we cannot prove it. He is too clever to be trapped."

"Meanwhile he poisons my brother's mind against me and against my husband!" Elissa cried.

"Why not depose Pygmalion then and make Elissa the sole ruler?" Straton suggested, but the old dyer shook his head.

"Mago has also poisoned the minds of the younger artisans against the idea of a woman ruler," he said.

"You mean against me, don't you, Athach?" Sicharbas asked.

"It pains me to say it, but some are foolish enough to fear you would rule instead of our Queen."

"I would gladly step down—"

"I will not have it!" Elissa did not let him finish and once again Straton was struck by the change in her since he had seen her last. What had then seemed the natural assumption of the beautiful princess called Dido that her wishes would be obeyed, had now become an imperial will, neither expecting nor brooking opposition. He was beginning to understand, too, something of what lay behind her difficulties with Pygmalion, who must also have inherited some of the same stubbornness from their father.

"Before I would let Sicharbas be humbled by such as Mago and my brother," Elissa said, "I would abdicate and leave Pygmalion as king, with a council of the leading merchants as regents."

"At the moment, Mago has the following to block that, too," Athach warned. "When I was young, both merchants and artisans worked together for the good of Tyre. But he has stirred up those who work with their hands against those who risk their wealth and their lives on the sea."

"What does he want, then?" Straton inquired.

"To see Pygmalion as absolute monarch—which means Mago would rule Tyre."

"Do you have an answer?"

"We had none—until you arrived last night with what you call The Dragon's Blood," Athach admitted. "Fortunately, you were able to deceive Mago into believing it was only a new kind of amber."

"Then, the gum is as good a dye as the purple from the murex?"

"It is better," Athach said positively. "When Gerlach brought me the cloth you and your servant had dyed, I was astonished at the evenness of its color and its sheen, although you knew little of dyeing. This afternoon I tested it upon wool, linen, and even byssus. The result was always the same—a variety of hues and tints I have never before seen equaled."

"How difficult would it be to obtain a shipload of The Dragon's Blood, Straton?" Gerlach inquired.

"Once we reach the islands and record their location, a single ship should be able to bring back enough to supply our dyers for more than a year. Then, as Mochus said, garments of purple could be worn by all men."

"Mochus!" Gerlach exclaimed. "Did you tell him of this discovery?"

"He had word of it already," Straton admitted. "A Greek merchant named Diomedes inquired only today whether Tyre had found a new source of the dye."

"I know Diomedes," Gerlach said thoughtfully. "He is an honorable man—for a Greek—dealing mainly in engraved silverware and ornaments of gold for women."

"How could he have learned about the new purple?" Athach asked.

"In Gadir, the sailor who sold me the gum talked openly of it in the drinking houses." Straton chose not to reveal Ares' part in what had happened. "He even showed me some fabric he had dyed with it. On the way home we stopped overnight at Itanos on Crete for water and food, and the men visited the brothels on the shore. Wine loosens tongues and Diomedes apparently heard of it there. He came directly from Itanos in his galley, no doubt to learn more."

"Are you saying Diomedes outsailed you?" Gerlach asked incredulously.

"By several hours. His galley is faster than any vessel on the sea."

"But how could that be?"

"Diomedes uses two banks of rowers for one thing, and a sail larger for the galley's length than I have ever seen used before," Straton explained. "Tomorrow I start changing the location of the rowers' benches in the new gaoul. Fortunately, the mast has not yet been stepped."

"I can understand a Greek merchant wanting to learn of a new source for the purple," Athach said. "We know the murex beds in the Greek islands are shrinking almost as fast as our own. But is there any chance that he might discover the Western Isles before you?"

Straton shook his head. "The Greeks will not dare venture beyond the Pillars of Melkarth in their cockleshell galleys. For that kind of voyage great ships are needed like the one we are building now, and we of Tyre know how to sail them better than anyone else."

"But if Diomedes can build the sort of vessel you say he has built, what is to keep the Greeks from trading farther west than they go now?" Gerlach asked.

"I think they will eventually," Straton admitted. "That is why we must control trade with distant regions like Tartessus and explore the Libyan shore south of the Pillars."

"It is a dream for young men," Gerlach said, a little dubiously.

"When the Minoans and the Mycenaens were overcome by Grecian tribes from the north, we seized this area at the eastern end of the Great Sea and have held it for centuries," Straton reminded him. "Cyprus is still under our control, and our other trading stations guard the mouth of the Sea of the Aegeans that the Greeks call their lake. If it ever comes to war with them, we could bottle them up there."

"The Assyrians would still be at our backs."

"Then, make a pact with the Greeks leaving them free to trade in their own islands and on the northern shore of Crete. In return they should be glad to let us secure the area west of the land of the Etruscans and our colony of Utica on the Libyan shore. The distant half of the Great Sea would be ours then, plus the Western Ocean beyond the Pillars of Melkarth. And even if the Assyrians should capture Tyre, we could always start anew in the West—as our ancestors did when they left the shores of the Eastern Sea and came here."

"It is a rosy dream," Gerlach said.

"Itanos was only a dream until someone settled there, and so was Tartessus. A little southeast of Utica, I stood not long ago on a headland guarding a fine bay and harbor where a whole fleet could anchor. To the north I could see the great island of the Sicels—the ones the Greeks call the Siculi. They have close ties with our Libyan allies at Utica, and the distance is so short that a fast war galley from either shore could overtake any merchant ship passing to the westward."

"Would you advise placing a trading station there?" Sicharbas asked.

"Not just a trading station but a major city like Gadir." Straton's voice rose in his enthusiasm for the course he was advocating. "With it we could control the entire trade to the west and the Libyan shore eastward to the mouth of the Nile. The strongest native ruler in that region is a prince called Hyarbas, and with our help he could become king of all of Libya. I purchased water and supplies from him on the voyage home and he has even learned to worship Melkarth and Astarte from our people in Utica. I am sure he will see the advantage of having a prosperous Phoenician city with which his people who dwell inland from the shore can trade. Such a city might even one day rival Tyre in greatness."

"This is hardly the time to speak of new colonies," Gerlach said. "In a few months The Rock may be under siege by the Assyrians."

"If King Pygmalion yields Tyre, my lord Sicharbas and Queen Elissa could lead a great fleet westward to found a new city," Straton pointed out. "Then, whatever happens here, the spirit of King Hiram and King Mattan would be preserved."

Busy defending his argument for the establishment of a new city in the West, Straton did not notice that Sicharbas was studying him thoughtfully all the while.

"The most important thing now is to supply Tyre with a source of the purple, so our artisans can be kept busy and less liable to listen to false doctrines," Gerlach argued. "That means we must finish the great gaoul in time for you to return to Tartessus before the winter comes.

Once the storms of autumn are over, could a ship sail southward in the Western Sea even in winter?"

"I am sure it could," Straton said.

"Then we must find the Western Isles and bring back a shipload of The Dragon's Blood," Athach said. "If the members of my guild could be sure of a cheap source of the dye, I believe they would be deaf to Mago when he tells them the merchants have failed them."

"Even at best, I could hardly return in less than a year," Straton warned.

"Leave that to me," the old dyer told him. "When I show the Dyers' Guild what I have already done with only a small piece of your discovery, they will be willing to wait a year—or even two—for control of the purple trade to be regained by Tyre."

"What if the Assyrians attack?"

"If the enemy can be held for even two months at Arvad, it will be too late for them to launch a major attack southward," Sicharbas said. "Then their armies will have to fall back, for the winter at least, into the Valley of the Arantu around Karkar, where they were held fifty years ago by King Ahab and his allies. Or they might even be forced to withdraw east of Mount Hermon. And before they can mount another attack next summer, you will come sailing home with a shipload of The Dragon's Blood."

"With a monopoly of the new dye for Tyre, the Royal Council can levy a tax on both merchants and artisans," Gerlach added. "So mercenaries and machines of war can be hired to defend The Rock."

Elissa reached out to take Straton's hand and press it warmly. "You see, everything depends on you, Straton. I know you will not fail us."

"Tyre will deny you *nothing*, when you dock with a shipload of The Dragon's Blood," Sicharbas added. But only later did Straton recall the emphasis the High Priest had placed on the word "nothing."

ii

The Rock was bathed in moonlight as Straton and his father walked home from the temple. From Palaetyrus faint sounds of revelry floated across the channel but, except for the occasional sound of a woman's laugh from the Grove of Astarte, Tyre itself seemed already asleep.

"Whose idea was it that I should be called back from Gadir, Father?" Straton asked.

"The suggestion came from Mochus, but it was Sicharbas who asked me to send for you."

"The reason couldn't have been The Dragon's Blood, then. None of you knew about that until I arrived."

"It was another matter," Gerlach admitted.

"Since it concerns me—shouldn't I be told?"

"Sicharbas swore all of us to secrecy and the vow still holds. He alone can tell you."

"When will that be?"

"I don't know. Your discovery in the West may have changed the whole picture. Tell me, does it pain you so much to see the woman you love the wife of another?"

"I don't love Elissa, Father."

"But you were betrothed."

"I carried her image enshrined in my heart for five years. But when I saw her again this morning, I realized that she means no more to me than any other woman—except perhaps a Greek goddess Ares insists has fallen in love with me."

Gerlach laughed. "It will be pleasant to have that rascal around again with his tales." Then his voice grew sober. "Are you angry at me for not supporting your vision of a new Tyre rising in the West?"

"Not angry—perhaps disappointed."

"Sometimes the young see visions too bright for the eyes of the old. Tell me more about this Libyan headland of yours."

"From the top of the hill, you look northeastward toward the Isle of the Siculi across a strait as lovely as anything I have seen in all my journeys." Straton's voice kindled with eagerness at the memory. "Utica is only a few hours away and not far to the north is our colony of Nora. With swift galleys stationed at those three points, we could close the entire western half of the Great Sea to any ships save our own and keep most of the Etruscan trade out of Greek hands as well."

"What of the place itself—as a city where people could live?"

"A cape furnishes protection from the winter winds. And a large bay lies just south of the headland, with a nearby lake that could be opened up by a single canal to form a *cothon*. With the cape fortified and the lake as a harbor for ships, all the vessels of Tyre could find haven there in a storm—or sally out to attack an enemy."

"If you are able to extend our trade routes to the Isles of Purple, we will certainly need a station in that area," Gerlach admitted. "And Utica is much too low to fortify."

"No better place could be found than Karthadasht," Straton told him. "It means New Town—a name I gave it in my imagination."

"It is a good name, and I pray that you shall one day see it rise upon your westward headland. But would there be more trade than we already have through Utica?"

"The blacks to the south still use stones for axes and chipped fragments of rock for arrowpoints, so our weapons of bronze should find a ready market among them. Prince Hyarbas, the strongest leader I met among the Libyans, seems to be friendly. And everywhere I went, Libyan merchants begged for more slaves, particularly light-skinned women from the Greek islands and from Lydia and Cilicia."

"King Pygmalion agrees with them there, at least." They had reached the multistoried house overlooking the grove and Gerlach paused before the door. "Are you coming in now?"

"I think I will walk a while and consider the things we talked of tonight," Straton told him. "Besides, I have had no time to inspect the new gaoul at close range."

"When I was your age, other things called for inspection in the moonlight than the ribs of a ship," Gerlach said with a smile. "The servants will let you in when you come to bed. I suppose that rascal Ares is busy earning money for himself in the grove tonight."

"No doubt. As a Greek in the service of a Phoenician, would you expect him to do otherwise?"

iii

The mass of ships berthed along the okel was a forest of orderly shadows in the bright moonlight when Straton descended from the towering ramparts guarding Tyre from attack across the channel to the level of the quays below. A potbellied merchant vessel engaged in the coastal trade with Israel and Egypt was berthed beside a galley that furnished regular service between Tyre, the other Phoenician cities to the north, Kition and Salamis upon the island of Cyprus, and Tarsus, a thriving city located upon a river that cut through the Cilician coast to form a protected harbor. Lined up at the wharves, discharging cargo or taking on new, were other ships from Egypt, Crete, various Grecian ports and Libya.

The wharves and the warehouses were deserted tonight save for a few torches burning in brackets above the water, and a watchman who bowed low before the heir to one of the leading merchant fortunes of Phoenicia. Lights were still burning along the waterfront of Palaetyrus, however, and while Straton watched, a ferry put out from the opposite shore and was rowed across, depositing a returning group of revelers at its debarking point not far from where he stood.

There would be nightlong merriment in the drinking houses of the mainland town, he knew, and, oppressed by a feeling of loneliness, considered hailing the ferryman and asking to be put across the channel to Palaetyrus. But he stilled that impulse before it could be formed into words, sensing that the malaise troubling him was not one to be cured by drink or the embrace of a courtesan.

A swift shadow fled past him along the quay and, glancing upward, he saw a cloud crossing the face of the moon. Was it only his imagination, he wondered—as he shivered involuntarily, although the night was warm—that gave the shadow for an instant the shape of a griffin, the winged lion characteristic of Assyrian heraldry? Or was it portent of the threat hanging over his beloved Tyre, a threat against which only he, with the scant knowledge he possessed of the Isles of Purple in the Western Sea, seemed to stand as a bulwark?

Turning back to the dark-shadowed bulk of the city towering above him, Straton sought comfort in the very solidity of The Rock and the knowledge that, standing at the height of its power as it was now, no city on the shores of the Great Sea could equal Tyre in might and in wealth. Even with his eyes closed and the doors and windows shuttered, as they were tonight, he could name most of the precious cargo stored in his father's warehouses near where he stood. Part of it was for consumption by the people of Tyre, but the greater portion awaited transshipment to other ports and a substantial profit—usually several times over the cost.

Baskets of liparite, the much-prized rare stone found almost entirely on the Isle of the Siculi to the west, were stacked there and, row upon row, thousands of bottles, vases and drinking vessels fashioned by the expert glassmakers of Phoenicia. For the sandy shore of the mainland in this region contained the exact proportion of the chalky ore needed to fuse with pure sand in order to form a clear, white-hot liquid glass that cooled into a thousand shapes in the molds of the glassmakers. Vessels and plate of silver were locked away against thieves, as well as jewelry set with precious stones. Some of the latter had been brought by caravan from deep within the country of the blacks to the south of Libya and shipped to Tyre in the fleet of merchant gaouls that plied regularly through the length and breadth of the Great Sea.

Stacked in long rolls was the papyrus manufactured in Egypt from the pith of reeds growing along the waterways there, but traded for so long by the Phoenicians of Byblus that Greek merchant seamen had given it the name of Byblos. Fine linens from Egypt, byssus from Syrian looms, oil and wine from Israel—all were racked beside armor and weapons of bronze and occasionally of iron. The smelting and forging of this much-sought-after metal had for a long time remained a secret of the Hittites, until the tribes called the Peleset or Philistines—descendants of a vast wave of sea people who had once flowed southward along this very coast—had begun to manufacture it in the vast desert reaches south of the Sea of the Dead in nearby Judah.

Cedar from the mountains of Lebanon was as much desired for making Egyptian coffins and fleet Greek galleys as in the construction of the Phoenician merchant ships constantly being built on the ways within Straton's sight. Gold, lapis lazuli, amber from the far northwest, hemp and rope as cordage for ships, cowhides for tanning into leather —all these and a thousand other articles of trade were carefully catalogued by patient scribes in the Phoenician alphabetic script upon rolls of papyrus.

Slaves captured in the swift raids upon settlements among the Greek islands or farther to the west were also much in demand wherever the Phoenician ships docked. And vast quantities of tin ore, mixed one part with ten of Cyprian copper—also largely a Phoenician monopoly —was constantly being fashioned into bronze tools, weapons, ornaments and armor plate in the shops of the artisans higher up on The Rock, to be sold throughout the teeming world that surrounded this eastern end of the Great Sea.

Leaving the warehouses, Straton walked along the quay to where the great gaoul was being constructed on the ways of the House of Gerlach. The graceful swell of the hull from stem to center and the curve of the prow, with its massive carved head of a battle-proud charger, nostrils flaring and mane flowing like the sea that soon would sing beneath the cutwater, soothed his mind. And when he climbed to the afterdeck, where the planking was already partly in place, he could almost feel the great vessel breasting the long rollers from the west, as she rode the current surging between the stony ramparts called the Pillars of Melkarth and headed out upon the vast reaches of the Western Sea in a voyage of exploration and discovery.

The mast, hewn smooth and already bored for the rigging, lay beside the ways, ready to be stepped. It reminded him of the change in position he had decided upon after studying the galley of Diomedes at long range. And since the warehouse of Pallas, where the galley was moored waiting to take on cargo in the morning, was within his range of vision, he turned toward it.

The Grecian vessel appeared to be deserted, but the broad gangplank connecting it to the quay indicated that it was being loaded, probably for an early departure. With time so short, Straton resolved to make his examination of it now, seeking the secret of how the tall, rakishly slanted mast was secured to the keel. A plank creaked underfoot as he stepped aboard the galley, stiffening him into momentary immobility. But when there was no challenge to indicate that the ship was guarded, he resumed his inspection of the vessel.

The long sweeps by which the craft was propelled when not under sail had been piled neatly beside the benches upon which the rowers sat, ten to a side. When he swung down between the benches to inspect the ports he'd noted cut into the hull, he saw, as he expected, a second row of benches in line with the openings, but staggered so there would be no obstruction when both sets of oars were being handled while the ship was in motion.

The bright moonlight illuminated the interior of the galley enough for him to see the keel. It was slenderer than in Phoenician merchant vessels, but that was to be expected, since the Greek galley carried only a fraction of the load that could be stored within the bulging hulls of the larger ships. The ribs were about what he had expected to see, beautifully hewn in graceful curves, the planking pegged into place against them and the whole caulked and pitched, giving the vessel the dark color that also characterized its Phoenician counterparts.

The prow rose abruptly from the keel and, as he studied it, he remembered hearing Greek seamen in Crete boastfully compare the stempieces of their galleys to the "straight horns" of a bull, which they somewhat resembled. Beyond the prow, he could see the dark shadow of the keel extending forward below the water level as a metal-sheathed projection, or ram, a device which he knew from experience made the swift galleys extremely formidable fighting machines.

The arrangement of the mast differed from the Phoenician construction in only two respects, he decided: the angle at which it was stepped and the heavy timbers forming the socket attaching it to the keel. As he had noted that afternoon from a distance, the mast was slenderer than that of a Phoenician gaoul of comparative length. He saw now that it was less strongly stayed, too, which surprised him, for the sail was much larger in proportion. The mast also differed in character, the lower yard having been left off and the bottom corners of the sail clewed to bollards projecting above the deck rail. All of which, he judged, would give the sail an almost bell-shaped appearance when running before a high wind and enable the Greek vessel to move in a breeze far too light to fill the heavy square sail of a Phoenician gaoul.

Busy deciding how he would adapt what he had just learned to the completion of his own vessel, Straton did not notice a shadow move at the corner of the deckhouse as he stepped up to the gangplank. Only the creak of the planking warned him in time to duck aside, though not quickly enough to evade the blow of a cudgel against his temple.

Desperately clawing at the rail, he slumped over it, but the force of the blow had rendered his hands momentarily powerless. As he tumbled over the side, striking his head a second blow against the gangplank, he found strength enough to cry out once. Then the water closed over his head and he sank into a dark void.

iv

Straton regained consciousness in a spasm of coughing and nausea that left him spent and limp. His head ached and, when he reached up to touch his temple, his hand came away sticky with blood. His last memory was of tumbling across the rail of the Greek galley, following the blow from an unseen assailant, and feeling the water of the harbor close above his head. But since he now lay upon smooth planking that must be the deck of a ship—the quay being built of stone—and was soaked, as well, someone had obviously pulled him unconscious from the water. He could see the rakish mast and spars of the Greek galley silhouetted overhead in the bright moonlight, proving that he had not been carried far. But when he tried to rise upon one elbow to explore further, the effort sent his senses spinning and he fell back to the deck.

"Better lie still; you swallowed half the harbor." It was the voice of Diomedes, the Greek shipmaster. "Breathe deeply until the sickness passes."

Straton obeyed and, as he drew in deep breaths of the cool night air, felt his head begin to clear.

"You have a small cut on your temple," Diomedes added. "Hera is putting on dry clothing, after pulling you from the bottom of the harbor. She will bring some bandages for the cut."

"You are . . . very kind." Straton carefully turned his head until he could see the Greek merchant sitting on a coil of rope nearby.

"I would hardly say that." Diomedes' tone was amused. "Especially after the clout my daughter gave you."

"It was no more than he deserved." The girl emerged from the deckhouse into Straton's field of vision. She was carrying a large towel, some strips of white cloth and a small jar, such as women use for precious unguents. "If I hadn't recognized his voice when he cried out, he would still be at the bottom of the harbor."

"Then I owe my life to you," Straton said, as she knelt beside him and placed the dressings on the deck where she could reach them easily.

"Some might say that makes the two of you even," Diomedes observed in the same amused tone. "Though I must confess that, were I a judge, I would rule my daughter still in your debt."

"Father!" the girl protested indignantly.

"But for the blow you dealt him, the noble Straton would not have fallen overboard and you would not have had to rescue him," Diomedes reminded her. "On the other hand, he saved your life, when your insatiable curiosity led you into the Grove of Astarte last night—where you had no reason to be."

Straton felt a great load suddenly lift from his mind. Ever since the episode in the grove, he had been wondering who the girl had gone there to meet. Now it seemed that, being a stranger to Tyre and its customs, she had merely happened to stray innocently into the grove, where she had been cornered by the caravan drivers.

"The debt will be fully paid, if you let me study the way the mast of your galley is stepped," Straton told the shipmaster.

"So that is why you skulked aboard like a thief in the night?" the girl exclaimed.

"I told you he could hardly have come to steal, Hera," Diomedes said. "The House of Gerlach could buy everything we possess many times over."

"The galley appeared to be deserted," Straton explained. "It seemed a good time to find out how you were able to sail from Itanos to Tyre faster than my ship did."

"It was a good race, a close race," Diomedes admitted. "Even though neither of us knew we were running it."

The girl had been busy while they were talking, cleaning the scalp wound over Straton's temple and applying a pad of cloth saturated with a fragrant ointment from the small jar. He was able to sit up while she expertly bandaged the pad into place.

"There," she said, surveying her work with approval. "Leave the ointment against the wound for three days and it will be healed."

"What is it? A magic portion from Asklepios?"

"What does a Phoenician know of Asklepios?"

"My servant is a Greek. He claims descent from one Podalirius—"

"The physician of our people at Troy?"

71

"So he says. But Ares is such a liar that I suspect he made up the tale." Straton was feeling better all the time. "Except the part about the goddess Juno."

"What of Juno?" the girl demanded.

"Ares insists that you are the goddess in disguise. And he stoutly maintains that this galley is really your chariot."

"It flew faster than that wallowing tub of yours," she said a bit tartly.

"Alas," Diomedes chuckled. "I am afraid my daughter is quite human, even to the point of disobeying me and going about unattended at night—though I think she will not make that mistake again. And my vessel is only a galley, moved by the wind and by the oars of slaves. It was built to my order, but the idea for the angle of the mast that intrigues you so much came from an Egyptian."

"The Egyptians build few ships anymore—and never anything like this."

"This man was a mathematician, not a shipbuilder—a friend of your old teacher, Mochus. He showed me how the force of the sail applied to a mast slanting backward would set the butt of the timber more securely against the keel, instead of tending to tear it from the ship. You must have noticed that we carry a far larger sail in proportion to length than your gaoul does."

"When I saw the size of the sail, I could believe for the first time that your daughter is not a goddess as Ares claimed," Straton admitted. "Until then—especially when I saw her in the cove this afternoon—I had almost come to believe my servant."

He had said it to see what effect the compliment would have on the girl. She sniffed a bit loftily but, as she moved to a seat on a pile of cordage beside her father, he could see that she was not at all displeased.

"I was afraid you had seen through our little scheme to examine one of your murex beds and see if they are shrinking as rapidly as ours," Diomedes confessed.

"What impressed me most was the discovery that your daughter can dive as deeply as I can," Straton admitted.

"In Crete no diver can equal me," Hera said proudly. "I often explore sunken ships."

"That reminds me," Diomedes said. "Bring some cups and pull up the bottle of wine hanging over the side, Hera. We owe our guest at least that much for the way you treated him."

The girl brought silver cups from the deckhouse and pulled up a bottle of wine that had been hanging by a cord over the side in order to cool it. The wine was pleasant and refreshing, warming Straton's stomach and clearing his head.

"You Phoenicians are great traders," Diomedes said. "I will make a bargain with you."

"After your daughter saved my life, how can I refuse?"

"Have you already guessed why we came to Tyre in such a hurry?"

"I imagine it was because your men overheard something babbled by one of mine in a broth—, in a drinking house at Itanos."

"The story was that you have discovered a new source of Phoenician purple in the Western Sea. With the murex growing smaller everywhere, such a finding could improve the fortunes of dyers and merchants both in Tyre and Greece."

"I reported on my voyage to the Council of Merchants this morning," Straton said. "Didn't Pallas tell you about it?"

"He saw nothing except a piece of red amb—" Diomedes broke off suddenly and thumped his fist against the spar beside him. "Of course. I have been a fool—"

"What is it, Father?" Hera asked.

"Pallas said Mago—the fellow who is so close to your king—and the other merchants laughed at you for bringing back a block of red amber and claiming it as a discovery. I should have known the Son of Gerlach would have his father's shrewdness. The gum is a new source of the dye, isn't it?"

"You spoke of a bargain," Straton reminded him.

"So I did. Tell me what discovery you made in the Western Land, and I will let you examine my galley in daylight as long as you wish. In fact, I will even show you exactly how the mast is stepped."

"Done," Straton said promptly. "Athach says the gum is even better than the dye we get from the murex."

"I would gladly buy some of it—at a good price."

"One of the smaller vessels engaged in bringing ore to Gadir from the Tin Islands was blown to another island during a storm," Straton explained. "A sailor happened to pick up the block of gum there and I bought it from him because the color looked very much like our purple."

"Then the islands where the dye is found lie beyond what you call the Pillars of Melkarth and we, the Pillars of Herakles?"

"Far beyond."

"Your secret is safe then. We Greeks have no ships that can sail in those waters."

"That large ship of yours over there," Hera said. "What do you call it?"

"A gaoul."

"You must be building it for a voyage to the islands you mentioned."

"I sent my father the plans for the vessel as soon as I learned about the Isles of Purple," Straton said. "The House of Gerlach should be able to make a fortune with a single shipload of The Dragon's Blood."

"Does it really come from dragons?"

"The sailor didn't know, and I cannot sail there until the autumn storms are over."

Diomedes turned to look at the dark outlines of the partially finished gaoul. "It will be the greatest ship ever to sail the seas," he said admiringly. "But it is still a hard thing to search for a few islands in a trackless sea—even when you follow the Phoinikos—the Phoenician Star."

"To sail in search of something never seen before—and find it!" the girl cried. "If only I were a man!"

"I'll wager you'll find few men to join you in that wish," Straton said fervently.

"You men are all alike," Hera snorted indignantly when her father chuckled, but Straton could see that she was not really displeased. "I can dive as deeply as you, and I'll wager I can outswim you and outrun you—"

"I'll not accept the wager. Remember, I saw you do both this afternoon."

"Then, why don't men treat me like any other man?"

"Don't force him to answer that, Hera," Diomedes warned. "Remember how you are dressed when diving."

"Father!" she cried, blushing, and for the moment was silent.

The wine had cleared most of the remaining dregs of pain from Straton's head. He was enjoying immensely the spirited conversation with the Ionion merchant and his daughter, whose tendency toward independence of thought and speech was something he had never before encountered in so beautiful a woman.

"How can you sail a ship with so small a cargo space and still make a profit?" he asked Diomedes.

"We carry only precious articles of small bulk—plate and utensils of silver and gold, jewelry and fine fabrics," the Greek merchant explained. "I decided to make this voyage so Hera could visit new lands. We Greeks need to be reminded that other people are as intelligent and as skilled as we."

"Our galleys can leave anything I have seen in Phoenicia far behind," Hera said spiritedly.

"For trading east of the Isles of the Siculi and through your Aegean Sea, a vessel like yours is the equal of my gaoul," Straton admitted. "But for long voyages far out of sight of land, we must build even greater ships than the one you see there upon the ways."

"It will be a long time before Greek mariners will be able to dispute your control of the Western Waters," Diomedes assured him.

"Do you Phoenicians wish to own the world?" Hera asked. "Isn't there enough room for all?"

"We rarely seek to control lands and people," Straton explained. "For us it is more profitable to set up trading stations where we can sell the goods produced by our artisans and buy things to be sold elsewhere at a profit. We purchase tin ore in Tartessus and silver mined in the mountains back of Gadir so our own people will have work. And on the Libyan shore we buy hides and precious stones brought by the black men from the south."

"What is King Pygmalion going to do if the Assyrians attack?" Diomedes changed the subject.

"Who can tell? He no longer listens to those his father knew to be wise." Suddenly Straton had a thought. "If you deal in articles of silver, you should know Mago."

"I have bought from him for some time."

"But he only came to Tyre recently."

"This was at Tarsus. I first met him through an Assyrian merchant—" Diomedes gave a low whistle. "Do you think there could be any connection?"

"It would be far easier to take The Rock by treachery from inside than by assault," Straton pointed out. "The Assyrians tried that once— and failed."

"When I first knew Mago, there was talk that he had been a pirate, preying upon ships from harbors on the coast of Cyprus," Diomedes said. "But I never had any real proof of the accusations."

"Where will you be going from here?"

"We plan to visit Dor and Joppa on the way to Egypt. I can always be sure of finding a cargo in any of those places, and I want Hera to see them."

"Would you inquire about Mago and try to find out how many of the silversmiths know him? Or have dealt with him before?"

"Why should we spy for Tyre?" Hera demanded.

"If the Assyrians conquer us, they will use our ships to attack your

Greek cities," Straton explained. "Their armies can even move through the Cilician Gates in the neighborhood of Tarsus to spill out westward and menace your settlements in that region."

"He is right, Hera," Diomedes said. "A threat to Tyre by Assyria is a threat to all of us."

Straton got to his feet. "I will see that a profitable cargo awaits you in the warehouses of Gerlach when you return," he promised. "May I study your galley tomorrow?"

"Whenever you wish," Diomedes assured him. "We will not be sailing until the day after."

"You will never be able to pass us in a race," the girl assured him. "Even without the sail, our oarsmen are better than any others in the world."

"That may be—though I'll not admit it," Straton chuckled. "But I will confess freely that the Greeks have one advantage over us."

"What is that?"

"Their women are far more beautiful than ours—or should I say their goddesses?"

v

A line of slaves extended from Pallas' warehouse along the quay, up the gangplank and across the deck of the Greek galley, when Straton came to the waterfront the next morning to study Diomedes' vessel. The shipmaster was directing the storing of bales containing the cargo in the hold but turned the chore over to one of his overseers, when he saw Straton, and greeted him warmly.

"Hera has gone to purchase food for the voyage," he said.

Straton grinned. "Then it is safe for me to come aboard?"

"I'm afraid I've spoiled her," Diomedes admitted with a chuckle. "She does have a will of her own." Then his face grew sober. "I meant it last night when I said she owes her life to you. If she were younger, I would have taken a cane to her after you left Pallas' house. Where would you like to start examining the galley?"

"The mast first—and the reason you chose to slant it backward."

"The principle is simple, once you see it work. There is a patch of sand at the edge of the quay. Come with me and I will show you what the Egyptian mathematician demonstrated to me."

As they crossed the deck, Diomedes picked up a rod about the length of Straton's arm. When they came to the patch of sand, he knelt and smoothed it over with his hand.

"First we will examine the pull a sail exerts upon an upright mast—as in your vessel." He placed the rod upright in the sand, holding the upper end between his fingers. "Now push against the main part of the rod, in much the same way that a sail exerts its pressure against the mast."

Straton pushed the rod and, although Diomedes held the top firmly, the force of the pressure shoved it forward so the foot was pushed almost out of the sand, digging a shallow trench as it moved.

"You can see that, with a vertical mast, some of the force applied by the sail is spent in lifting it up and does not move the ship," Diomedes pointed out. "It also tends to wrench the foot of the mast loose from where it is set against the keel."

"I never thought of that before."

"Neither did I until the Egyptian proved it to me. Now we will slant the mast backward a little, and I will hold the top, just as I did before, while you apply force once again."

Straton repeated the procedure he had followed in the first part of the experiment, using, as best he could estimate, the same amount of force. This time, however, the lower end of the rod was pushed into the sand and Diomedes had far less trouble in holding the upper end.

"By the fires of Melkarth!" he exclaimed in astonishment. "Why didn't I think of that before?"

"Do you understand what happens?"

"The same force that in an upright position tends to pull a vertical mast from its fixation to the keel presses the lower end of a slanted mast against it."

"Exactly," Diomedes agreed. "But a word of warning. Slanting the mast makes it possible to use a much larger sail with less danger of breaking the mast itself. But the keel must be reinforced with extra timbers where the butt rests upon it, else the force will tend to break the keel or drive the foot of the mast through the hull."

"Think how many centuries we have gone on building ships the same way just because our forefathers always used that method." Straton shook his head in admiration at the simplicity of the device.

Diomedes got to his feet. "We had better examine the keel before the bales cover it. Unless my cargo is stored exactly right, the galley becomes unwieldy. I cannot leave that task to an overseer very long."

The keel of the galley was not quite as heavy as that in Straton's own gaoul, since the Greek vessel was much lighter. And where the foot of the mast was joined to the keel, reinforcing timbers had been added to strengthen the hull against the pressure from the great sail transmitted through the mast. Only in that respect, however, could Straton find any real superiority of Greek shipbuilders over those of Tyre. The joining of the timbers was generally less smooth than in a Tyrian built ship. And the wood, though oak, was not so workable or so fine as the fragrant cedar timbers and planking from the Lebanon that were the hallmark of Phoenician vessels.

He had been dawdling somewhat, hoping Hera would return but, when it was almost noon and she had still not come back, he could find no further excuse to remain. Finally he had an inspiration.

"Did you say you are not sailing until tomorrow?" he asked Diomedes.

"Yes, shortly after dawn. With a good wind we should be able to anchor off the port of Dor by nightfall."

"Would you and your daughter honor my father and me by being our guests for the evening meal?"

"It would be a pleasure to see the noble Gerlach again," Diomedes said. "We have often bought and sold from each other."

"Then we will expect you. The house is not far from the residence of Pallas. I can send my servant—"

"I know where it is. My daughter pointed it out to me."

"How does she—"

"A woman learns much in the shops, Straton. I never cease to marvel at the amount of information Hera brings back from a single buying expedition. We will come at the setting of the sun, but I am afraid we cannot stay very late on account of sailing in the morning."

vi

"That bandage doesn't become you, Master," Ares complained as Straton was dressing that evening. "Let me remove it and put on a better one."

"The bandage stays as it is," Straton told him firmly.

"Why?"

"Would you like someone else to treat a wound you had treated?"

"Did you go to a physician?" Ares demanded indignantly.

"The most beautiful one you ever saw. A goddess, no less."

"The daughter of Diomedes?"

"Yes."

"You lost no time in pursuing her." Ares whistled softly. "Did she promise to meet you in the grove?"

"Of course not. You should know Astarte's counterpart among your people is not Juno but Venus."

"Who has been teaching you about Greek gods and goddesses?" Ares demanded suspiciously.

"Diomedes—and Hera."

"Hera! If you have come to know her that well, why let her escape without paying the ransom of Astarte?"

"The girl is innocent—and a virgin."

"Ha!" Ares exclaimed. "The night she tricked you into fighting her battle for her and ran away, you didn't think her so innocent. Have you found out who she went there to meet?"

"Nobody. It was out of curiosity."

"A likely story. But maybe it is just as well."

"What do you mean by that?"

"Since she did not meet her lover in the grove that night and also managed to escape you, she may still be untouched. Once you demonstrate your superior qualities as a lover to her, she will be certain to prefer you!"

Straton launched a clout at him, but Ares had been deliberately baiting his master and bobbed expertly beyond reach. "I will talk to some of the Greeks among the seamen of the galley," he promised. "Come to think of it, Pallas has a Greek slave. I should be able to learn from him who your rival is."

"Keep your tongue to yourself or I'll have it torn out by the roots," Straton threatened. "What do I care for the girl?"

"A good question," Ares said judiciously. "But if you care nothing for her, why are you trying to convince yourself she just happened to be there?"

Straton chose to ignore the question, for to answer it was to admit what he had not yet admitted to himself—that he was as thoroughly smitten by the Ionian girl as any callow, lovesick youth.

"After she laid your head open last night, I would think a man of your experience would recognize a strong-minded woman when he saw one," Ares continued blithely. "Whoever marries such must keep a firm hand, like driving a high-strung pair hitched to a chariot. For myself, the price is too high, even for a goddess in human form. Besides, goddesses are known to be very fickle when they come down to earth." He shook his head. "No, Master. You will be far better off with some plump Tyrian girl. And besides, it is dangerous for mariners to have beautiful wives. How do we know what they are doing while we are away on long voyages?"

Straton could not help laughing at the impudence of the little Greek. He never managed to remain angry at him very long.

"As for the bandage, I suppose you had better keep it on, since she is responsible for it," Ares admitted. "A woman that strong-minded might lay your head open again if you make her angry."

The sun had barely set when Diomedes and his daughter appeared at the gate of Gerlach's home and were ushered into the inner court, where Straton had ordered the evening meal served. Hera was lovelier than he had ever seen her before, in a long, flowing kiton of pale blue, with a darker cloak of the same hue. Upon her golden hair she wore a small tiara of beaten gold set with blue stones to match her gown. Brilliants of the same shade sparkled from her ears and the necklace about her neck.

Gerlach was quite as taken with her as Straton had been. When he found that she was as intelligent as she was beautiful, the talk surged back and forth across the cosmopolitan world, of which Tyre was a center, ranging from the political problems of the day to the glorious tales of ancient Crete, from which Hera's ancestors had come. The evening sped rapidly by and Straton was given little chance to be alone with the girl. Only when Diomedes begged that they be excused, pleading an early sailing, did he think of a stratagem that might accomplish his purpose—if she chose to cooperate.

"You should not leave Tyre without seeing the top of The Rock by moonlight," he told her. "I will walk with you and your father across to where the street goes down to the quayside."

As he had hoped, Diomedes demurred—but not Hera.

"Let me go, Father," she begged. "Straton will see me safely to the waterfront."

"You may be certain of that, sir," Straton said eagerly, and Diomedes gave in.

Hoping to keep Hera to himself as long as he could, Straton chose a street that crossed the highest point of The Rock. As they passed the dark shadows at the edge of the Grove of Astarte, the girl moved closer to him and took his arm.

"Is it true that every young woman in Tyre must give herself to a man in the grove?" she asked.

"Astarte demands it, but most arrange to meet their betrothed there."

"As you did Princess Elissa?"

"Who—" Straton gulped. "Who told you that?"

"Pallas—after you came to his house the other night."

"You know how gossip spreads and how little truth there is in most of it."

"Pallas said you and Princess Dido were betrothed when you sailed away five years ago, and that she met you in the grove before you left, but King Mattan forced her to marry the High Priest Sicharbas."

"It was a move to preserve the kingdom. Sicharbas is the strongest and richest man in Tyre."

"Was it because of her that you stayed away almost five years? The servants in Pallas' household say you only came back because she sent for you."

"They are wrong," he assured her, but was not at all displeased to discover that she had asked about him.

"I think you were sent for because you are needed here—if all the things they say about King Pygmalion are true."

They had reached the overlook, where he and Ares had stood the afternoon before and watched the galley below. When she started to descend the winding street toward the waterfront, he took her hand and drew her back. She made no move to withdraw it but turned to face him.

"I'm glad I did come back just now," he confessed. "And that my servant boasted about The Dragon's Blood at Itanos."

"Why?"

"But for that I might not have seen you."

"Or be wearing a bandage on your head."

"Ares wanted to remove it tonight," he told her. "He is very jealous of his medical skill and assured me that he could apply a better one."

"Why didn't you let him?"

"Because you put it on. From this very spot yesterday Ares showed me what he insisted was the chariot of a goddess, the galley that brought you here. Now I know he must be right, for only a goddess could so completely enchant me in so short a time."

A little smile softened her lips and, when he put his arm about her, she did not resist. Her mouth was warm, soft and trusting against his own, as her arms tightened about him. But though he was intensely conscious of her lovely body through the soft folds of her kiton while she clung to him for a long moment, he did not resist when she pushed herself gently away. With an arm about each other's waist, they descended the street to the quay where her father's galley was moored.

"When will I see you again?" he asked at the rail of the ship.

"We should return from Egypt in a month or six weeks."

"Good. I will talk to Diomedes as soon as you return."

81

"About the cargo you promised him?"

"No. About the bride price."

He saw her eyes suddenly twinkle in the moonlight and she leaned down from the deck, where she was standing, to kiss him quickly before moving to the door of the afterhouse, where she and her father lived aboard the ship.

"I thought you had already paid that." Her voice floated back to him. "The other night in the Grove of Astarte."

Five:

*She poppy seeds in honey, taught
to steep,
Reclaimed his race, and sooth'd
him into sleep.*

DETERMINED THAT HIS NEW vessel should be ready by the month Hera had estimated their voyage to Egypt would last, Straton spent the next week working from sunrise to sunset. He rigged the great mast in the new position Diomedes had shown him, reinforced the keel so it could take the thrust of the great sail, and put in a second bank of oars. During this same period he was supervising the shipwrights as they finished putting in the deck and began the laborious task of caulking the seams with long, thick strands of cordage soaked in pitch. Finally, both caulking and planking were covered with still another layer of the black bitumen obtained from the region around the strange lake in eastern Judah, whose waters were so salty that nothing could live within them and a man could float standing upright.

It was vitally important that this ship should be as near perfect as possible, in order safely to explore waters where no such vessel had ever sailed before, so almost every detail of the final fitting-out required Straton's personal attention. The hull had long since been launched from the ways and was now moored beside the quay before the warehouses for the final details of putting in the rowers' benches and fitting the great sail—far larger than anything that had ever driven a Phoenician gaoul before—to its spars and rigging. Each night Straton fell upon his couch exhausted, only to be on the quay again shortly after dawn, personally supervising the thousand and one details connected with preparing the great vessel for the sea.

If the news from the ship was good, that from the north was not. Assyrian armies were reported to be moving steadily closer to Arvad, and travelers from that city told of preparations for a siege, though without much hope of being able to hold out very long. The major deficiency in the defenses of the northernmost city of the Phoenician coast was its lack of an ample supply of water, the only source other than rainfall being a spring that burst from the floor of the sea between the island and the mainland. And while the spring alone was ample to supply Arvad's needs, an enemy had only to capture it to bring the city quickly under submission.

Busy fitting out the big ship, Straton had quite forgotten his talk with Gerlach after the dinner in the palace with Elissa, Sicharbas and Athach, and the still unanswered question of why he had been called back to Tyre. He knew Athach was busy spreading the news of his discovery of a new source of the purple dye and the significance of that discovery for everyone in Tyre. And so he was not surprised to receive a summons from Pygmalion shortly after the new gaoul was launched from the ways.

He was ushered into a private chamber where, besides the King and the ever present Mago, the only other person present was a shipmaster named Hamil. This rather unsavory individual was known to be in the employ of Mago and to act as his agent in such nefarious ventures as supplying female slaves to beguile the fancies of the youthful King.

"Why did you withhold the secret of the new purple from the Council of Merchants?" Mago set the tone of audience at the outset. "You know such discoveries are the property of all, not just of one man or one house."

"I showed it to you in the presence of the Council," Straton reminded him. "It was you that named it only red amber."

"But you kept its value secret."

"None of us knew just what it was worth then. Athach tested it later."

"You also kept secret the location of the islands where the gum is found."

"Could they be the same as the Tin Isles?" Pygmalion asked. "Our people have been going there for centuries."

"The seaman who sold me the gum was uncertain of the exact location," Straton said, truthfully enough, for the only real bearing the man had given him was the observation that, in its rotation, the paws of the Great Bear, when viewed from the island, almost dipped into the ocean. But to one trained in navigation, this fact alone placed the islands well south of the Pillars of Melkarth. And with the fiery mountaintop on one of them visible as a beacon a considerable distance away, he was confident that he could find the spot for himself.

"You were intending to keep the location of the islands to yourself," Mago accused him. "And make Tyre pay you tribute."

"I am descended directly from King Hiram, who sent ships eastward to Ophir centuries ago and brought back ivory, apes and peacocks,"

Straton snapped. "Where were your ancestors then that you can lecture me on my loyalty to Tyre?"

Straton had expected Mago to be angered by the question. But when he saw a thoughtful look come into the other man's eyes, he regretted reminding Mago that the blood line of another royal house of Phoenicia flowed in his veins.

"Be careful how you speak in the presence of the King," Mago warned, but in a strangely mild tone. "Even the richest merchant in Tyre is not immune from punishment."

"I was not speaking to King Pygmalion but to those who thrust themselves before men who were loyal to his father when your ancestors were brigands," Straton said coldly.

Hamil scowled and his hand dropped to the long dagger he wore at his belt, but Pygmalion spoke before the quarrel could develop any farther. "The Son of Gerlach need not defend his family before the throne of Tyre." The note of firmness in the young monarch's voice seemed to hold some promise that Mago had not yet gained complete control over him. "What did the tests made by Athach show about the new dye?"

"It imparts a color to any fabric equaling our finest murex tints," Straton admitted.

"By the fires of Chemosh!" Mago exclaimed. "That is a miracle."

Straton looked away quickly, lest the excitement that had suddenly swelled within him be revealed to the others. For with the one explosive oath, Mago had revealed much about his own ancestry, Chemosh —though a counterpart of Melkarth—being the particular god of people on the mainland to the eastward beyond Israel, notably the Amorites and the Assyrians. And though the reference to an Assyrian god was not in itself proof that Mago was a traitor in the pay of the enemy, it was at least suggestive.

"I have no proof that the Western Isles contain enough of the gum to be of any real value," Straton warned. "The large gaoul my father and I are building is almost finished, and before the end of summer I hope to sail to the Western Sea and search for them."

"Suppose you cannot find them before the storms?" Mago asked.

"Then I will make Gadir my base for the winter and search again as soon as the autumn storms are over. With luck, I should return in the spring with enough of the dye to free Tyre from dependence upon the murex."

"Whoever takes the trade in purple away from the Greeks entirely will be rich beyond belief!" Hamil exclaimed.

"And with Tyre in control of the purple, we should be able to hire mercenaries to defend ourselves against the Assyrians," Straton pointed out for King Pygmalion's benefit. "Then there will be no need to pay tribute to the enemy."

"The number of the Assyrian horde is like the sands of the sea," Hamil growled. "As well try to hold back the waves with your bare hands."

"It has been done before," Straton retorted. "And it will be done again."

"How soon can you sail westward?" Pygmalion asked.

"The new gaoul will be ready in about a month," Straton told him. "I plan to make a trial voyage to Arvad, while I am waiting for the merchant Diomedes to return from Egypt. His daughter and I are going to be married and I shall take her with me to the Western Land."

"If what I am told of the Lady Hera is true, you are indeed the most fortunate of men," the young monarch agreed, and got to his feet, signifying the end of the audience.

ii

The Temple of Melkarth and Astarte was not far from the palace, and Straton decided to make what he had learned about Mago known to Sicharbas, so the High Priest and Elissa could pursue it farther if they wished. But when he inquired at the temple for Sicharbas, he was shown into a room where the priest called Luli was working on some documents with the aid of a scribe.

Straton had no reason for any particular feelings where Luli was concerned, aside from what he had judged to be a look of dislike in the priest's eyes when he had first seen him about a month before. Nevertheless, he could not help feeling his hackles rise when he was left to stand before the table like a petitioner or a servant, while Luli—deliberately, he was sure—leisurely finished the work he was doing and dismissed the scribe before acknowledging his presence.

"My slave informs me that you asked to see the High Priest," Luli said at last. "My lord Sicharbas is resting at the moment."

"I will speak to him another time, then." Straton turned on his heel to leave, but Luli's voice sounded behind him.

"If your business is urgent, I can arouse him. Or I shall be glad to help you myself."

"What I have to say can wait," Straton said brusquely. "I will request an audience later."

"The High Priest will be informed that you were here."

86

Having made the point that he had the say over who could or could not see Sicharbas, Luli had now chosen to be gracious, but the oily politeness in his tone did not deceive Straton. Obviously the priest was determined to keep him from seeing Sicharbas, perhaps for no other reason than that of any petty official exercising his small amount of authority for his own satisfaction, but it happened that Straton had no reason to delay his audience. As he was hurrying through the corridor toward the entrance to the temple, Sicharbas himself came out of a door opening upon it.

"Straton!" he exclaimed warmly. "What brings you to the temple?"

"I came to see you, but Luli said you were resting."

"My nephew is like an old hen these days where I am concerned," the High Priest said. "Come inside and tell me why you are here."

The chamber into which they entered contained a couch, from which Sicharbas had evidently just arisen, for the pillows with their coverings of fine linen were in disarray. As the High Priest poured glasses of wine from an exquisitely molded decanter, Straton noted that he seemed to have lost more weight in the weeks since the dinner here in the palace on the evening after his arrival from Gadir.

"This wine is from the vineyards of Israel across the Lebanon hills," Sicharbas said as he handed Straton a glass. "But I am afraid that source may be cut off from us soon."

"By the Assyrians?"

"Yes. Even if they should leave us alone here on the seacoast, they will almost certainly descend the Hollow of Syria between the Lebanon and the Anti-Lebanon Mountains to attack northern Israel. And, unfortunately, King Ahab is not alive to form a coalition of the Canaanite people and fight the battle of Karkar again."

"Then you think we are in for really serious trouble?"

"I know it," Sicharbas said soberly. "Just this morning a vessel arrived from Arvad with news that advance parties of the enemy are seizing galleys along the coast opposite the city. And they have already captured a vast number of logs drying there."

"I wonder why the logs, unless they are going to bring up machines for laying siege to the walls."

"The catapults are moving westward already," Sicharbas confirmed. "In another week, or perhaps two, they will be on the shore."

Straton realized fully the significance of what Sicharbas had said. During the usually brief winter, the farmers who tilled the fields in warmer seasons went into the forests back of the shoreline to cut cedar logs. Dragged by teams of oxen to the shore, the logs dried in the sun and were then bound into huge rafts. These were guided to cities farther south along the coast and even up the Nile to Egyptian centers, where they were prized for the construction of fine buildings and for making cabinets and furniture.

In the hands of an enemy, however, the dry logs could fulfill another function. Rafted together they could serve to transport the great catapults with which the Assyrians traditionally carried out the siege of any city they sought to capture, battering down the walls of even such a sea-girt citadel as Arvad or Tyre.

"Do you think Arvad will be able to hold out?" Straton asked.

"My informant said King Aziru is keeping all his larger ships in port, lest the galleys of the Assyrians attack and capture them one by one. That means the enemy forces will have only the smaller vessels they are able to seize along the mainland shore to use in making up an attacking fleet. But when they get enough of them together, they will no doubt make the attempt—with every chance of success."

"And then use the Arvadite fleet to attack Tyre?"

"Why not? It was done once before—successfully."

"Meanwhile what do we do?"

"I have tried to convince Pygmalion that we should send a fleet to help Arvad in order to help ourselves. But lately he had been listening to voices other than mine or Elissa's." Sicharbas grimaced, as if with pain, and pressed his hand against his right side.

"Luli was right," Straton said, suddenly concerned. "I should have waited and come another time."

"No! Stay!" Sicharbas rang a small silver bell beside him. To Straton's surprise—and, judging from the High Priest's expression, to his also —Luli himself answered the bell.

"The crushed poppy seeds," Sicharbas gasped. "Bring me a potion."

Luli disappeared through some draperies which Straton was sure covered the doorway to another chamber. He did not doubt that the younger priest had been eavesdropping but, with Sicharbas in so much pain, did not trouble the older man by pointing it out.

Luli returned in a few moments, bringing a small portion of brownish powder upon a piece of papyrus. Sicharbas seized the parchment and upended it, spilling the powder into his mouth with trembling fingers and washing it down with a glass of wine. The younger priest turned to Straton, his eyes hot with anger. "Even the noble Straton has no right to intrude upon a sick man," he said sharply.

"Nay, Luli," Sicharbas said. "Straton did not intrude. I met him in the passage outside and asked him to come here."

"Perhaps I had better go," Straton suggested, but Sicharbas shook his head. The lines of pain upon his face were already beginning to erase themselves, though he still kept his hand pressed to his right side. "I was going to send for you tomorrow anyway," he said. "Elissa learned from an Egyptian physician how to steep powdered poppy seeds in honey to relieve my pain, but I sometimes forget to take the potion regularly. The dose I just swallowed will soon act."

"But you should rest," Luli insisted.

"Perhaps I have already rested too long." Sicharbas pushed himself up on the pillows into a half-sitting position. "Leave us now, Luli. You have work of your own to do and I promise not to overexert."

The younger priest departed by way of the hangings through which he had come with the medicine. Straton hesitated to open them and verify his suspicion that the door behind them was not closed and that Luli was still close by. Instead, he pulled a stool near the couch, so he and Sicharbas would not have to speak loudly. Crushed poppy seeds he knew to be a specific for pain of whatever cause, for Ares always carried a supply of the powder in the chest from which he dosed the members of the gaoul's crew and dressed their wounds. But Sicharbas' near collapse seemed to indicate more than simply an attack of pain.

"You did not tell me why you were seeking me," Sicharbas said.

Straton gave a rapid summary of his interview with Pygmalion, Mago and Hamil. When he finished, the High Priest's expression was grave. "I was sure Mago would realize the importance of your discovery, even if Pygmalion did not," he said. "Hamil is only a tool."

"Then you think Mago understands all that the new purple means to Tyre?"

"Both he and Hamil. Athach saw to that."

"Why reveal it to them, if they are enemies?"

"It is part of a plan," Sicharbas explained. "I intended to tell you earlier, but I didn't realize time would be so short."

"I still don't understand."

"We were trying to protect you by making you indispensable. After all, only you know how to find the Isles of Purple in the West."

"I only have what the sailor told me to go on—and that was little enough."

"Little enough to an ordinary man perhaps, but not to you. Besides, even the purple trade, valuable though it is, is not the most important thing to Tyre right now."

Straton shook his head. "I was never good at riddles, sir. Ares can fool me every time."

"Then your father hasn't told you the real reason why you were brought back to Tyre?"

"No. Except that it was Mochus' idea—and yours."

"You may blame me, though I hope to earn your gratitude. You see, I know of your love for Elissa. And since I am High Priest of both Melkarth and Astarte, I naturally learned that you two sacrificed to the goddess together the night before you sailed for Tartessus five years ago."

"But—"

"For a while after Elissa became my wife under the terms of her father's will, I even envied you your youth," Sicharbas admitted. "I have loved her since she was a slip of a girl called Dido. But I was an old man then and I am an older one now."

Straton didn't know what to say—so said nothing. Obviously, his father had not told Sicharbas of his own confession that his love for Elissa had faded during the five years of absence. Nor did this seem to be the time to reveal that he loved another woman with a passion that burned far more brightly than his love for the Princess of Tyre had ever done.

"Elissa loves me." Sicharbas' voice brought Straton out of his reverie. "Though perhaps not quite with the same feeling she had for you."

"She must have forgotten that long ago, sir."

"I am not so sure," Sicharbas said. "But her loyalty and affection for me has at least pushed it into the back of her heart, where it will stay as long as I am alive."

"May that be many years," Straton said fervently.

"That question, at least, is settled. I am dying, Straton. All of Tyre will know it soon—many suspect already."

"You could be wrong," Straton protested, but remembering his shock at seeing Sicharbas again on the day after his arrival in Tyre, he knew the High Priest was speaking the truth.

"Give me your hand."

When Straton obeyed, Sicharbas pressed it against his side, where he had supported himself against the pain a few moments before. Even through the older man's clothing, Straton could feel a stonelike mass beneath the ribs, a thing so shocking and evil by its very feel that he instinctively drew his hand away.

"You see, even you recognize its nature," Sicharbas said.

"But there are physicians—"

"As soon as the hardness appeared I went to Egypt. A wise physician in the Temple of Imhotep at Memphis told me its growth could not be stopped. It was he who showed Elissa how to grind poppy seeds and steep them in honey to relieve the pain I was already experiencing. But for the drug, I could not go on."

"Does she know?"

"Only that I am ill—not that the sickness is mortal."

"The Greeks have fine physicians. Ares claims they are the best of all."

"After I came back from Memphis I sent to the Temple of Asklepios at Cos for one of their wisest priests, but he gave me no hope. That was over a year ago and the hardness has increased steadily, just as the Greek priest and the Egyptian physician said it would. You must have noticed before how the creature growing within my body has wasted away my substance."

"Surely Dido—Elissa—must suspect."

"I paid both the Egyptian and the Greek physicians to lie to her, but she must be told the truth soon. You see, I was hoping to live until winter, when the Assyrians would be forced to withdraw on account of the weather, since they prefer not to winter away from the Valley of the Two Rivers. Then Tyre would have been safe for the better part of a year and you would have had time to seek the Isles of Purple. With the profit from a single shipload of The Dragon's Blood we could hire an army to defend Sidon and Palaetyrus."

"I was telling King Pygmalion and Mago the same thing this morning."

"It is too late for that now. The physicians give me not more than a month, and Mago has gained control over Pygmalion more rapidly than I realized."

"A sick man should not be troubled by traitors," Straton protested. "Let me charge him with being a spy in the pay of Assyria and have him arrested."

"He may well be in the pay of the enemy," Sicharbas agreed. "But we have no proof."

"Perhaps I have." Straton recounted the story of Mago's oath in the name of Chemosh, but when he finished, Sicharbas shook his head.

"An oath to a god worshiped only a few days' journey away in the Amorite lands across the Jordon is suggestive, but certainly not proof. We must fight Mago another way."

"I can always challenge him to single combat to prove his innocence or guilt," Straton suggested.

"You must not take the risk," Sicharbas said. "In fact, I forbid you to take it."

Straton threw up his hands in a gesture of futility. "What course is left then—except to surrender Tyre to them?"

"The course for which I asked Gerlach to call you back to Tyre. I shall die in a few more weeks, Straton. The hand of Moth, the God of

Death, is already upon me. When I am dead, you must marry Elissa and seize the kingdom."

"B-but."

"This is no time to trouble yourself about custom or precedent. Elissa loves Pygmalion deeply and cannot see his faults, as you and I do. For the past year I have been the only barrier keeping Mago from complete control of the boy and of Tyre. With no firm hand left to rule after I die, all will be lost."

"But why me?" Straton stammered. "I am not even of the House of Mattan."

"You are more than that, though I had forgotten it, until Mochus reminded me of it. The blood of Tyre's greatest ruler is in your body, and when you marry Elissa at my death the two lines will be joined together. My own treasure will go to Elissa, and together you will control the greatest fortune in all of Tyre."

"But the people."

"You are already a hero through your discovery of the new source of the dye in the Isles of Purple. Besides, the people love Elissa more than they do Pygmalion, and the important merchants fear Mago's control over the boy. With Elissa beside you and with my fortune and Gerlach's at your command, you can easily buy the favor of the rabble by giving them free grain and enough wine to stay drunk for a week. By that time your control over Tyre should be complete."

"What about Pygmalion?" The question was spoken in order to gain time to think, not in agreement with the plan. Sicharbas, however, took it as his answer.

"Do what you wish with him. The boy is not strong enough to be the kind of king Tyre needs and demands in such times as these, but Elissa will not let him be destroyed. You may have to banish him to one of our islands, with plenty of wine and women to keep him occupied."

Straton felt like a drowning man, seized by a current he could not control. And, like a drowning man, he grasped at anything that seemed to offer support. "But it is an evil thing to usurp a throne," he protested.

"Not when the throne is rightfully yours. Your ancestor, Phales, was the last king in the line of Hiram the Great. He was murdered by Ithobaal, ancestor of Elissa and Mattan, so, when you seize the throne you will only be restoring the rightful ruling house once again in Tyre."

"But—"

"You cannot refuse, Straton." Sicharbas' tone was stern now, the voice of a High Priest delivering a divine edict. "Your duty to Tyre is greater than any personal feeling. I command you to obey in the name of Melkarth."

Straton found himself in the bright sunshine outside the temple, still a little dazed by the import of that final command. Now that he thought of it, however, the whole course of recent events obviously fell into a pattern. His father's cryptic summons; the alarming situation he'd found upon his arrival, with the youthful Pygmalion controlled by a man who was almost certainly an agent of the enemy—everything fitted, except the chance that had sent him to the grove the night Hera was attacked by the ruffians.

But for the encounter that first evening, he might feel entirely differently now about the offer Sicharbas had made to him. But since he had found the golden-haired girl in the Grove of Astarte, the whole course of his life had been changed. Even the opportunity to become King of Tyre—which he could almost certainly be with the immense power and wealth of Sicharbas and the affection of the people for their beloved Dido behind him—offered no lure. Somehow he had to find an answer to the problem of avoiding the wrath of the gods with which Sicharbas had threatened him and, at the same time, choosing his own course. In his dilemma, he instinctively sought the advice of the one man he respected most in Tyre after his father—Mochus.

The old teacher was in his usual place under the ailanthus tree in the garden, with a cluster of students gathered around him. When he saw the look upon Straton's face, he dismissed them and nodded for the younger man to take one of the benches beside him.

"I take it Sicharbas has spoken to you of his plan," he said without preamble.

"Yes. I just came from the temple."

"The High Priest has been weakening fast. I fear the growth within his body will soon choke out his life."

"Then there is really no hope for him?"

"None save through the gods—and he is their servant. It seems the will of Melkarth and Astarte that he must die."

"Sicharbas said you thought up this plan," Straton accused the old man. "Why didn't you warn me?"

"He swore both me and your father to secrecy—as was his right."

"Now he says it is the will of the god that I marry Elissa after his death—and name myself king."

Mochus gave him a keen look. "Don't you agree—when agreeing will make you ruler of Tyre?"

"It is no small thing to overthrow your country's ruler and set yourself up in his place. A man would have to be absolutely convinced about the rightness of his purpose before he would even attempt it."

"And you are not convinced?"

"Everything in me cries out against it."

"Because it would be wrong? Or because you love the Greek girl?"

"How did you know?"

Mochus laughed and clapped his hands for a servant to bring refreshments. "You should know my students discover everything that goes on in Tyre and seek my favor by telling me the news each morning. I know who slept with whose wife; what highborn maiden lost her virginity, and to whom; which merchant made a fortune with a shipload of silver, and who he lost it to at the gaming board. Nothing happens in Tyre that does not eventually reach the ears of its sage." He grinned wickedly. "How else do you think I got my reputation for wisdom?"

Straton smiled in spite of the troubles weighing upon him. "Then, I have no secrets from you either?"

"None," Mochus assured him. "For example, on the night you brought the green necklace as a gift to the goddess, you also fought three men in the grove for Diomedes' daughter. You broke the jaw of one of them, but the girl escaped you and ran to the house of Pallas. Later, you almost drowned when she clubbed you for snooping aboard her father's galley. But on the evening when you entertained her and Diomedes at your father's house, you and the girl kissed on the crest of The Rock and walked down to the quay with your arms about each other. Had Diomedes stayed in Tyre another week, my students would have been wagering among themselves on when the marriage-maker would be approaching her father."

"Does Elissa know any of this?"

"Some, I imagine, though not all. My students are more eager than most and more intelligent, but I imagine one of her maids has already spoken to her of it." Mochus drank a cup of wine and wiped the rich purple droplets from his beard with a sweep of an already wine-stained sleeve. "Anyway, it would make no difference."

"In Astarte's name—why not?"

"Dido was your first love. It is hard for any woman to believe the man who deflowers her is not thereby bound to her for life by a bond dissoluble only at her whim. Remember, she has known the embrace of no other man except Sicharbas and, considering the difference between you in age and build, I imagine you came out much the best as a lover. Besides, Sicharbas has not been capable of exercising a husband's duty for some time."

Remembering the warmth of his welcome by Elissa when he'd first seen her on his return from Tartessus, Straton could not dispute the truth of Mochus' words.

"Of course," the old teacher added, "Dido is a queen. She will hardly consider a slip of a Greek girl a serious opponent."

"But I love Hera!" Straton protested. "Doesn't that mean anything?"

"Ordinarily—perhaps, yes," Mochus said reflectively. "Though, mind you, I believe such a disorderly emotion should generally be reserved for moments of pleasure and diversion, after the real business of living has been accomplished. It is hard for a man to think intelligently when his loins are throbbing with desire. In fact, when I was younger and capable of such things, I discovered that my thoughts always flowed most freely immediately after passion had been sated."

"I didn't come here to talk of passion," Straton said a little shortly. "Why did you bring up the question of the Greek girl, then?"

"Because I love her and want to marry her."

"You once loved Dido, didn't you?"

"Yes—or thought I did."

"Is that passion entirely stilled now?"

"Yes."

Mochus shrugged. "It always saddens me to see desire addle the wits of an intelligent man. Let us forget about women and talk about what is good for Tyre. If you remember what I taught you, our greatest glory came in the time of King Hiram, when our ships were sailing not only to Tartessus and the Tin Isles beyond the Pillars of Melkarth, but also to the land of the people who dwell beyond the Eastern Sea. Can you see in Pygmalion such a king as Hiram the Great was?"

"No."

"Do you also admit that these are perilous times, perhaps the most perilous in all our history?"

"Of course."

"Then Pygmalion should be replaced, and who in Tyre is more qualified to replace him than yourself?"

"I have no right to answer such a question."

"You have every right. In fact, it is your duty to look inside yourself and find the answer."

"Simply because the blood of Hiram the Great flows in my body."

Mochus shook his head. "Blood lines tend to weaken in most families, which is why Tyre has always required that the son must be approved by the Royal Council before he can succeed the father. Who should know better than I, who taught you, that you are everything Tyre needs in a king, Straton? You are just, fair and strong. Above all, you can think and are not afraid, except where a man should be afraid—when the odds are against him and his fear will lead him to judge wisely instead of act impulsively."

"How long ago did you arrive at this scheme to have me rule Tyre?"

"Perhaps when you first came to me and asked questions I sometimes found hard to answer. Or when you were able to dive deeper in the cove than any other of my students. The fact that you recognized the importance of the new dye, when others saw in it only a piece of red gum, proves you have the qualities that have set Tyre above the other cities of our people."

"Then you, too, say it is the will of the god that I should rule?"

"I suspect that gods have more important things to do than meddle in the ordinary affairs of men," Mochus said. "After all, they set the sun and the moon in the heavens to give us day and night. They made the courses of the sun longer and its elevation more directly above us at one season than another, so the warmth will make crops grow and give us food. They put cedars upon the hills to furnish timbers for our ships and placed the southing star in the heavens, so we can move about upon the face of the waters. And they send floods like those that pour fresh soil over the valley of the Nile in Egypt, so the crops will never lack for food upon which to grow."

Mochus paused to empty another cup of wine. From long experience Straton knew his thirst usually grew with the opportunity to talk to one whose intelligence he considered on a par with his own.

"But I suspect that when it comes to the day-to-day problems of living between men and men and between men and women, the gods leave us to work out our own destinies," Mochus continued. "Though sometimes they send storms and tribulations to try a man's spirit and sharpen him into a fine weapon, as the smith does the iron in his forge. No, Straton, I do not say that Melkarth orders you to be King of Tyre, thought I can see no one better fitted. Nor will I tell you where your particular destiny lies, since that is something you must seek for yourself."

"What of happiness? Doesn't a man have a right to that?"

"Not only a right but a duty, for when sorrow clouds his mind he no longer thinks clearly. If you love this Greek girl enough to think only of her, then take her when she returns from Egypt and go back to Tartessus."

"Why can't I stay in Tyre?"

"Even with the Greek girl as your wife, could you watch Tyre be captured by the Assyrians and see its king become a vassal or its people made slaves, without cursing yourself for failing to prevent it when you had a chance?"

Straton got slowly to his feet. "You leave me as little choice as Sicharbas did," he accused his old mentor. "He names it the will of Melkarth that I do as he says. By what god do you order me?"

"By a god who has no name, yet may be stronger than all the gods man has devised to blame for his own wrongdoings—the one who dwells deep within your own soul."

iv

Gerlach stood looking out a window in the quayside countinghouse that served as the center of the vast mercantile empire he controlled. He seemed lost in contemplation of the dockside activities beyond the window, where the final details of fitting out the great gaoul were going on apace, but Straton knew his father was listening intently to every word, as he told of his talks with Sicharbas and with Mochus. Only when he fell silent did Gerlach speak.

"What do you want me to do?" he asked.

Straton lifted his hands in a gesture of futility and let them fall to his side. "When the storm threw my ship upon the shore at Gadir, I knew what must be done to make it sail again. I know how to fight a tempest at sea and how to drive off pirates when we seek to approach a new port for trade. But in this matter of political affairs—how does a man know what is best?"

"By searching his heart."

"I have searched and still find no answer."

"Don't you mean that your heart refuses to accept the answer others would thrust upon you?"

Straton gave his father a startled look. "How did you know?"

"You are my son. A part of me went into your making."

"The best part, I am sure," Straton said warmly. "Then you were not wholly in favor of this scheme of Sicharbas' from the beginning?"

"To someone other than you, a man who loves power, I can see how it might be feasible, perhaps even admirable and attractive," Gerlach admitted. "But if even a descendant of Hiram the Great seized the throne of Tyre, the loyalty of people would be divided—for a while at least. And Tyre needs all its strength now in a time of crisis."

"Don't forget that, if I made the attempt and failed, all you have worked for would also be lost," Straton reminded his father.

"I would willingly risk that to see you fulfill your real destiny."

"But you are not sure my destiny lies in this venture?"

"I told Sicharbas as much when he asked me to send for you. But I also promised not to influence you until he could talk to you about it. A new power is rising in the East, Straton—or rather an old power taking on new life. We Phoenicians are but a small people caught between Assyria and Egypt in a struggle that may go on for centuries. The Greeks, too, are gaining power and may one day embark upon a program of conquest for themselves. I have been thinking much lately about the Libyan headland you described to us, and you may be right. The real future of Tyre and all of Phoenicia could lie far from these shores, perhaps in the West with a new city at the spot you discovered near Utica."

"Why can't Sicharbas see that?"

"He is thinking of Dido," Gerlach explained. "She loves being Queen of Tyre and, knowing your love for her, he naturally thought of you as her consort after his death."

"He says it is the will of Melkarth that I obey."

Gerlach smiled. "Gods are divine, but their priests are only human. I suspect that much of what we are told about the will of the gods exists only in the minds of priests."

"What shall I tell Sicharbas, then?"

"Why tell him anything, until you return from Arvad?"

"The ship will have to be blessed before we sail. You and I may doubt the power of the gods, but the crew would be afraid to leave the harbor without the blessing of Melkarth and Astarte."

"I will talk to Sicharbas and explain that we want the gaoul ready, in case anything should go wrong, so the trial voyage to Arvad must be made. He can hardly object when you will be gone no more than a week—or perhaps two. That way, you can find out the truth of what is happening in the north."

A great load had been removed from Straton's mind by the talk with his father, and he turned all his energies once again to the task of making the new gaoul ready for the formal ceremony of dedication to Tyre's god and goddess, performed whenever a new addition was made to its fleet. But if he had thought to keep the substance of his talks with Sicharbas and Mochus secret, he was disillusioned a few days later, while Ares was dressing him for a dinner to which he and his father had been invited at the home of Athach.

"They are saying in the drinking houses that you can be king if you wish, Master," the servant said as he was lacing up Straton's sandals. The tone was casual but knowing the little Greek as he did, Straton understood that Ares was fishing for more information.

"Who speaks such foolishness?"

"One of the priests told a dyer that the High Priest cannot live much longer. He fainted yesterday while performing the weekly sacrifice and the priest Luli had to continue with it."

"Sicharbas is growing old."

"And he is married to a young and eager wife. Who knows better than you what a strain that puts on him?"

"One of these days you will find yourself without ears as a punishment for your impertinence," Straton threatened, but Ares prattled on, though maintaining a weather eye for the first sign of a blow.

"Did you know he had sent for a priest from the Temple of Asklepios at Cos?"

"Yes, I did."

"Oh ho!" Ares' eyes widened. "So it is true that Sicharbas would have you marry the Queen upon his death and seize the throne? Now is the time to use the potion I obtained from that poisoner in Memphis, Master. Unless you act quickly, word of this will get to Mago and Hamil. You can be sure they will know what to do."

"Who would you have me poison? King Pygmalion?"

"It may come to that later, though it would be a merciful act to put my lord Sicharbas out of his misery." Ares nodded sagely. "Yes, that must come first. Then, when you are the husband of Queen Elissa, you can seize the throne and send Pygmalion away. After all, he has enough female slaves to keep him happy—and busy."

"Mind you, I'll have no part of what you are suggesting," Straton warned. "But how do the artisans and the sailors feel about my being king?"

"They have nothing against you, Master," Ares assured him. "In fact, you are far more popular than King Pygmalion, especially since you brought word of the new dye from the Western Isles. But the workmen don't like the idea of anyone seizing the throne of Tyre whenever he wishes."

"Then, they would be against me?"

"Not against you. In fact, they would probably even cheer you, if you won out over Mago and his ilk. But they could never be certain someone else would not seize the throne from you, and in such a struggle every man is forced to choose. If his side loses, he can wind up a slave—or a corpse."

"Have you heard them say this?"

"All of it—and more. Some even argue that it would be better to yield to the Assyrians and pay a tribute. Then the Assyrians would say who ruled in Tyre and see that he held his throne. Rebellion is not good for trade, Master, and what is not good for trade is not good for Tyre."

"Where do you stand on this suggestion?"

"Behind you—where else?"

"But if the decision were yours alone?"

"There are better things than being king—and wondering every time you pass a dark spot whether a knife will be thrust into your back. Besides, if you married Queen Elissa, you would have to give up the beautiful Greek."

"I could have more than one wife."

"A man with a goddess for a mistress can have no other!" Ares cried, aghast at such blasphemy. "Even Neptune obeys Juno, so you don't want to lose his favor. It would be a pity to lose that fine new gaoul because you angered the Mother of the Gods and she told Neptune to destroy you."

"You know as well as I do that Hera is only a woman!"

"Alas, there's none of the poet within you, Master." Ares shook his head sorrowfully. "I am beginning to think you deserve something less than the beautiful Greek, maybe no more than a plump merchant's daughter who will stir with heat once a month and conceive every year. Have you no pride, to seek no fitter vessel for the seed of one who is the descendant of kings?"

"Go find a harpist and set your lies to music; you Greeks seem to have a talent for such things." Straton pulled a purple cloak over his kiton and set it upon his broad shoulders with a shrug.

"Will you be needing me, Master? There is a matter—"

"Of some urgency in the Grove of Astarte," Straton finished the sentence for him. "Go earn your pay, you male harlot. I'll undress myself when I return."

Gerlach had gone on to Athach's house earlier and it was already dark when Straton left the house. He had gone only a few paces when he saw a shadow move in the shrubbery beside the house and, tensing himself, dropped his hand to his belt, where his dagger hung in a sheath of polished silver lined with leather to protect the point and the tempered double edges of the blade.

"Come out!" he ordered, drawing the dagger.

Two men moved into the circle of light cast by an oil lamp burning before the building. Both were in full armor, with swords at their belts and spears in their hands.

"Tarquin! Acestes!" Straton exclaimed.

Tarquin, an Etruscan, was captain of the soldiers from Straton's own gaoul. Acestes was a Greek and his lieutenant. Both were mercenaries hired to help protect the vessel from attack by pirates and launch reprisal expeditions ashore whenever they were refused the right to land and trade. He knew them both as doughty warriors, completely loyal to him—or so he had thought until this moment.

"The noble Gerlach commanded us to follow you, sir," Tarquin explained. "Our intention was to keep hidden, but we are not accustomed to skulking in doorways."

"Then skulk no more," Straton told them. "If my father ordered you to watch over me, it was with good reason. And I could not want two braver comrades at my side, should trouble occur. Come, we will march together to the House of Athach."

But as the three strode through the darkened streets he could not help feeling a sense of foreboding, for never before had he hesitated to walk wherever he pleased in Tyre, no matter what the hour. And the fact that his father had deemed it necessary to post guards to protect him from possible attack by an assassin seemed as much a threat to the city's security as to his own.

Six:

Then oaks for oars they fell'd; or as
they stood,
Of its green arms despoiled the growing
wood.

As THE DAY FOR the formal dedication of the new gaoul approached, speculation concerning the illness of the High Priest Sicharbas began to mount in the city, along with rumors of an impending seizure of the throne upon his death. Busy as ever, Ares kept his master informed about public gossip. And, yielding to his father's fears for his safety, Straton kept Tarquin and Acestes beside him whenever he went abroad, ostensibly as companions but actually as guards. Using the size of the new ship as an excuse, he also augmented considerably the company of mercenaries who normally formed the complement of fighting men on a Phoenician gaoul, placing them under Tarquin's command.

To two tasks Straton gave his personal attention. One was that of cutting stout shafts of oak in the forest and directing the shipwrights in hewing them down to form the extra-long oars required by the upper banks of rowers in order to clear the lower banks, while the ship was being rowed. Unusually tall and powerful slaves were required for this chore, too, and these had to be carefully selected and trained lest, in a moment of danger, a rower fail to keep the pace and throw all into turmoil.

The other—and far more pleasant—task was the construction of a large afterhouse on the new ship as quarters for himself and his bride. It was a far more luxurious structure than the usual sparse living quarters of a ship's commander, and he was busy supervising the final stages of its construction one day, when Ares brought word that a priest waited on the quay to come aboard the ship. To his surprise, Straton saw that it was Luli, arrayed ostentatiously in a robe of rich cloth fringed with purple and wearing a gold chain around his neck.

The change in the priest's manner since Straton had seen him last was remarkable. Today Luli exuded confidence and assurance and his manner was affable. When the workmen bowed low in deference to the man everyone knew had been chosen as successor to the ailing High Priest, Luli returned them to their work with a casual wave of his hand and a blessing from the god. Straton, too, greeted the priest courteously but kept on his guard.

"This is indeed a great ship," Luli said unctuously. "Surely nothing like it has ever sailed the seas before."

"Our seamen who were in the service of King Solomon of Israel long ago heard tales of greater ships in the land of the yellow men beyond the Eastern Sea," Straton said. "But nothing larger has ever been seen in our part of the world."

Luli glanced up at the peak of the rakishly slanted mast, where the great square sail was being rigged and the lines by which it was handled, when under way, secured to stout pegs set into the heavy rail surrounding the deck.

"Will it not be difficult to handle such a great vessel as this?" he asked.

"Actually, we think not." Straton walked to the rail and leaned over to point out the apertures in the hull through which the shorter sweeps were handled. "By placing the rowers in two banks, one above the other, we gain considerable rowing force. And the sail is almost twice the size of that in my other gaoul.

"With a heavy rail like this one, we have been able to place brackets just inside it," he added, pointing them out to the priest. "In battle each will hold the lower edge of a shield, forming a rampart that will protect both the deck rowers and the fighting men from arrows and spears. And since this ship is considerably higher than anything we are likely to encounter, it will be almost impossible for anyone to shoot down upon us, except perhaps from an overhanging cliff on the shore."

Luli's shrewd, appraising gaze moved to the stern, where the giant sweeps that would steer the ship were already in place, with a heavy bar attached to the upper end of each enabling the combined strength of four men to be applied to it when a quick change of course was necessary. Crossing the deck, he looked into the afterhouse with its luxurious cabinet work, furniture and the smaller bedchamber, which could be shut away from the rest of the structure by rich hangings sliding upon a smooth rod set close to the ceiling.

"The House of Gerlach seems to have spared no cost here," he observed.

"The voyage I anticipate may be quite long."

"To the Western Isles?"

"Yes."

Luli's eyes narrowed. "Quarters such as these would be fit for a princess—or even a queen."

Straton was certain now that Luli's visit was actuated by more than just casual curiosity about the ship which had aroused so much interest in Tyre. He could have appeased at least a part of it by revealing his plan to marry Hera when she and her father returned from Egypt. But a perverse impulse told him to keep the other man in suspense a little longer, if for no other reason than to punish Luli for eavesdropping when Straton had talked to Sicharbas in the temple not long before.

"I hope the High Priest is feeling better," he said, without rising to the bait Luli had cast out.

"My uncle's infirmity leaves him quite weak," the priest said. "In fact, I came here this morning to beg of you the favor of holding the ceremony of dedication for your new ship on the portico of the temple rather than here at the waterfront. I fear that a journey even this far would not be good for my lord Sicharbas."

"Is he so much worse, then?"

"The High Priest is dying," Luli said flatly. "Only yesterday I sacrificed a sheep and examined the liver, but the omens gave no hope."

"Perhaps it is too much for him to preside at the ceremony—"

"He insists upon being there himself, but I shall perform the actual sacrifice. It will be Sicharbas' first appearance in public for a month."

When Luli made no move to leave the ship, Straton was convinced that his purpose in coming to the waterfront that morning was still something more than merely to bring him the message from Sicharbas, since a servant could easily have performed that small chore. Still seeking to corner his elusive visitor, he said, "I trust that Queen Elissa is in good health."

"The Queen is very devoted to her husband and tires herself needlessly by insisting upon doing things for him that his servants and the physician could do." Luli paused for an instant. "She has made a vow upon the altar of Astarte to remain celibate, since the goddess often rewards such devotion with her favor and might save my lord Sicharbas from death in return for so great a sacrifice."

Now, at last, the real reason for Luli's visit had been revealed. The plump priest had come to the quay that morning, on the pretext of an errand from Sicharbas, for the sole purpose of warning Straton against any hope he might have of persuading Elissa to become his wife after the death of her husband. Only the High Priest could release anyone from such an oath. And, being in love with Elissa himself, Luli had taken advantage of her distraught condition and cleverly persuaded her to take a vow that would deny her to any man until, in his capacity of High Priest after the death of Sicharbas, he chose to release her from it.

Both the planning and the timing of the scheme were very clever, and Straton decided that he would have to watch Luli a little more closely in the future. At the moment, however, it was important to find out just how complex this whole affair was.

"No doubt the pain of dying is somewhat eased for my lord Sicharbas by his knowledge of the Queen's fealty." Straton spoke on a casual note, but the sudden guarded look in Luli's eyes warned him that his suspicions concerning the part the priest must have played in Elissa's vow were correct.

"The Queen thought it best to withhold knowledge of the vow from her husband at the moment," Luli admitted. "She would rather not disturb him when he is so ill."

"But surely it could have been made only to the High Priest—"

"Fortunately, my lord Sicharbas had already named me to act as High Priest in his stead," Luli informed him. "I was therefore able to receive the Queen's vow in the name of the goddess, and the High Priestess has also given her approval, making it a sacred bond."

"Which cannot be broken?"

"Not without incurring the wrath of both Melkarth and Astarte—unless, of course, she is released from it by the High Priestess and myself."

"What of the regency?"

"The Queen has decided to turn all power over to King Pygmalion, upon my lord Sicharbas' death." Luli lifted the tasseled hem of his robe and stepped carefully over the sill of the afterhouse. "May the blessings of Melkarth and Astarte attend you and your vessel during your endeavor," he said sonorously, lifting his hands in a gesture of benediction. "I will meet you at the temple on the morning of the day of dedication."

Straton stood in the still unfinished doorway of the afterhouse and watched the priest make his way fastidiously across the littered deck and down the gangplank to the quayside. A luxuriously upholstered sedan chair borne by four slaves moved from the shadow of the warehouse building and Luli stepped inside, seating himself before the slaves lifted the handles of the chair and bore it away.

One thing was certain, Straton decided, as he watched the chair disappear up the street leading away from the quay. Luli had made his own bargain with Mago and, in return for influencing Elissa to relinquish her rights under her father's will, had insured for himself the support of the others for his tenure as High Priest and his eventual campaign to win her for himself. It was an alarming development in the grim game being played out for the control of Tyre and the great fortune Sicharbas was known to possess. Straton was on the point of going to the countinghouse to discuss the matter with his father, when a cry from Ares drove it quite out of his mind.

"Master!" the little Greek cried. "Look yonder to the southeast. It is the Chariot of Juno returning from Egypt!"

ii

The mast of the gaoul had already been stepped and Straton quickly climbed to the peak. There he perched with one leg wrapped around the wooden shaft, for the small platform upon which the lookout stood while the ship was under way had not yet been affixed to the top of the mast.

Ares was right, he saw at once. Perhaps a half hour's sail to the southeast, a sleek galley with familiar lines was approaching. And although he could not see her at that distance, he was sure Hera herself was standing like a lovely living figurehead beside the prow, the wind whipping her light kiton about her body until she resembled nothing less beautiful and less queenly than the goddess Juno—for whom she was named.

Straton had planned to remain on the quay until Diomedes' galley tied up before Pallas' warehouse. But as he stood watching the sleek vessel approach, straining his eyes for his first glimpse of Hera, a messenger came from his father instructing him to go at once to the Royal Palace for a meeting of the Council of Merchants.

It was common knowledge upon the waterfront that a galley from Arvad had arrived that morning. But the fact that only a few hours had elapsed between its arrival and the summoning of the council seemed to indicate that the news from the north was even worse than expected. When Straton came in with his father, every merchant of importance was already in the large audience chamber of the palace, along with fully as many artisans, grim proof that the guardianship over the affairs of Tyre was already threatened by a group who took none of the risks assumed by the merchant seafarers who had made the city great.

The royal party came in just then, so Straton had no opportunity to confer with Gerlach. Elissa took one of the three ivory chairs arranged in a row upon the front of the dais, with Luli just behind her. Mago lounged beside Pygmalion, while Hamil stood back of the dais. The look of bored confidence on Mago's face seemed to promise that, in his opinion at least, all this was a mere formality to be gone through with as quickly as possible.

The emissary from Arvad was a distinguished merchant of that city named Hagemon, a friend of Straton's father whom he had known for a long time. Pygmalion gave the visitor the formal welcome due so distinguished a representative from the second most important member of the loose confederation of Phoenician city-states.

"May the Baal of Tyre, illustrious Melkarth, and his spouse, the divine Astarte, give long life to King Pygmalion and Queen Elissa," Hagemon said ceremoniously when he took the floor. "And may the greatness and strength of Tyre never be diminished."

Without pausing, the ambassador went at once to the matter that had brought him southward. "All of you know how the forces of the Assyrian King have ravaged our shores from time to time, seizing tribute and seeking to enslave our people. When I left Arvad three days ago, enemy troops were once more encamped on the shore opposite our city. Unless their progress southward is stopped, they will soon seize Palaetyrus and besiege The Rock itself. Already, the Assyrian general is gathering a vast fleet of galleys upon the shore opposite my own city and building great rafts to carry engines of war. I bring you the urgent plea of King Aziru that Tyre come to our aid with ships and men, lest you find yourselves left alone against the enemy.

"Hardly a generation ago an Assyrian army captured Arvad," Hagemon continued. "In order to save our women and children from torture by the enemy, we were forced at that time to lend them ships and seamen for an attack against other Phoenician cities. In all of Phoenicia, only Arvad and Tyre possess fleets today that could be of use against the Assyrians and, acting together now, we might preserve both The Rock and my own city. Acting separately, both will almost surely fall."

Mago leaned forward. "Is the noble Hagemon threatening that the ships of Arvad will be used against us?"

"Not threatening." Hagemon spoke over a ground swell of angry murmuring, particularly from those who lived in Palaetyrus on the mainland. "I came here to warn you that, if we fail to stand together now, what happened once before will almost certainly happen again."

"What if we are both defeated?" Mago asked.

"We will lose nothing that would not have been lost anyway."

As soon as Hagemon took his seat, Hamil rose to speak. "Would Arvad be of more help to us than the people of The Rock would be to Palaetyrus if it were attacked?" he demanded. "I say, let the merchants who have profited long enough from the sweat of the artisans, farmers and herdsmen pay tribute to the Assyrians. We little people have no quarrel with them or with anyone else. Being poor, we have nothing to lose."

Straton could not sit still and let this crude attempt to turn the two classes in Tyre against each other go unanswered. "Have I the King's permission to speak?" he asked, rising to his feet.

"You may speak," Pygmalion said, in spite of Mago's scowl.

"I will answer Hamil first," Straton said. "All of us in Tyre have only two things to lose, our freedom and our lives, and I would as soon lose one as the other. I am proud of being a Tyrian, but I would not be proud of being a slave." A burst of applause interrupted him and he waited for it to subside.

"I have been away from Tyre five years and only returned about two months ago. Because of my stay in another land to the west, I am able to view our problems from a distance, as one studies an entire coastline from the sea and is able to realize its vastness while, if he were in a small cove, he might think the walls had closed in around him. From Tartessus I brought silver and tin ore to be worked by the artisans of Tyre, so they could earn their bread and a place to live.

"To many of you it may seem a small thing to raise a sail before the wind and be blown across the sea. But if my crew were not highly trained and loyal, our ship could have been cast upon the rocks in many places between here and Tartessus. And if that ship had been lost, many artisans here in Tyre would have no bread for themselves and their children because tin and silver were not available to be worked." He paused and studied the audience for a brief moment, finding no lack of interest anywhere except in the scowls Mago and Hamil turned upon him.

"The artisan who mixes tin with copper to produce bronze and hammers it into a weapon or a shield deserves to be paid for his labor. But if the shield or the weapon cannot be sold, who will pay him? Since ancient times the merchants of Tyre have risked their wealth and their lives, building ships and sending them to the far corners of the world, carrying the products of our artisans to be sold in other markets and bringing back raw materials like tin, so these same artisans will have work to do."

"What does that have to do with the Assyrians?" Hamil growled.

"If the artisans of Tyre are turned into slaves, the things they produce will move eastward into Assyrian markets," Straton answered. "Then the enemy will profit, not the men who work in the forges, the looms or the dye vats. You, Hamil, have traded with the Assyrians and know what they are like. You, more than any other, should be advising the people of Tyre against yielding and becoming slaves."

The implication that Hamil might be in the pay of the enemy brought a murmur from the crowd and Straton decided to strike while he could.

"I am sure that Mago has traveled in Assyrian lands, since a few days ago I heard him swear by the Amorite god, Chemosh, who is known also to be an Assyrian god. Mago, too, should be advising us not to yield, when the threats to Tyre may be avoided by helping Arvad."

The ground swell of anger from the crowd was growing stronger now. Hamil looked uneasily about, as if seeking a place to retreat, but Mago chose to brazen it out.

"Since the noble Straton has an answer for everything else," he blustered, "perhaps he knows how to keep the Assyrians from our gates."

"Any answer would be better than the slavery you suggest," Straton retorted. "I have known Hagemon since childhood. He is a brave and honorable man who would not have been sent here by King Aziru if the need were not great, and I would listen to him twice before I would listen to newcomers to Tyre about whose past we know nothing."

"Tell us what you think should be done, Straton," Athach, the dyer, said. "We who are old need now to listen to the young."

"Yes," Mago sneered. "Give us the benefit of your wisdom, O Seer. Tell us how you would save Tyre from its enemies."

Straton turned toward the artisans, knowing that, if he could gain their support for the course he was about to suggest, the merchants would be on his side.

"Let us begin to gather a fleet here at Tyre, since, even if we do not send it to Arvad, we will need it to defend The Rock. Meanwhile my new gaoul will be dedicated in two days and, as soon as we can take on food and water for the short voyage, I will sail north and study the situation there."

"Are we to take your word for what is found in Arvad?" Mago demanded. "You just admitted that Hagemon is an old friend, so you will naturally be prejudiced."

"I will take with me whatever observers King Pygmalion may select," Straton offered. "You may even go yourself, if you are not afraid."

Before Mago could answer, Elissa spoke. "Has the council forgotten that I am Queen by the terms of my father's will and co-regent with my husband until my brother reaches his majority?" Her voice was sharp and her cheeks flushed with anger. Pygmalion looked startled and Mago's mouth dropped open in astonishment, as she swept on imperiously without waiting for an answer.

"My husband is in great pain and could not come here today, but he has not lost interest in the welfare of the state. The noble Hagemon came to us immediately upon his arrival in Tyre, and we have listened with sympathy to his story of the plight of Arvad."

Straton was seeing a new Elissa. As a princess she had been strong-willed, but there was truly a queen, speaking in a queenly manner, as was her right, and confident that her subjects would listen and obey.

"I bring you a message from the High Priest Sicharbas, who alone speaks for the gods of Tyre, and from myself as your Queen," she continued. "We are the strongest and richest of the Phoenician cities. But, as the noble Straton has said, unless we come to the aid of our fellow people, we shall all go down in defeat."

A cheer broke out among the merchants at her words and, after a moment's hesitation, it was swelled from the artisan side of the chamber. Though Mago sat gnawing his lip, Pygmalion made no attempt to silence the crowd. Only when the cheering began to die away did he speak.

"I join my sister in thanking the noble Straton for his offer," he said. "Let those who own ships begin to gather a fleet at once and make ready for whatever need arises. Meanwhile, we will wait for news from Arvad, when the first voyage of the new gaoul has been completed."

As the royal party filed from the chamber, Straton pushed through the crowd toward the door, certain that Diomedes' galley would already have docked and Hera would be wondering why he was not there to meet her. But as he was leaving the chamber he was stopped by a slave.

"Queen Elissa bids the noble Straton join her and my lord Sicharbas in the chambers of the High Priest," the man said.

It was a royal command and he had no choice except to obey. Noticing Ares standing with a crowd of townspeople just outside the chamber where the council had met, Straton beckoned to him and the servant hurried over to where he stood.

"The Queen and my lord Sicharbas have sent for me," he said. "Hurry to the quay and tell the lady Hera why I have been delayed."

"I will tell her you were sent for by the High Priest," Ares promised. "After all, a goddess would not be pleased to learn that you neglected her for a mere queen."

iii

Though Sicharbas was lying upon a couch, he seemed somewhat better than when Straton had last seen him, an appearance which, Straton knew, could be explained by the pain-relieving effect of the poppy leaves he apparently took quite frequently. Elissa was already in the chamber, striding up and down, her face flushed and her eyes stormy.

"You were there, Straton!" she cried when he came into the room. "My brother and those two—" For a moment her indignation would not let her go on. "They were not even going to consult me—me, the Queen of Tyre!"

"Mago and Hamil were trying to have things their way," Straton agreed. "Fortunately, your brother did not let them do it."

"Pygmalion would have yielded to them if you had not spoken out when you did!" she cried. "He has deserted us for our enemies."

"Tell me what happened, Straton," Sicharbas said.

When Straton finished giving a brief account of the meeting, punctuated every now and then by an angry outburst from Elissa, the face of the High Priest was grim. "By daring to name Hamil and Mago the traitors they undoubtedly are, you have set yourself up as a target," he warned.

"I don't think I am in danger," Straton said. "After all, they think I know the secret of finding the Western Isles, where the new purple can be found. They would hardly risk losing that, just because I wrecked their plot this morning."

"Events may be moving too rapidly for even that knowledge to protect you any longer," Sicharbas said. "Hagemon is an honorable man and I am sure he spoke the truth. When you return from Arvad you will confirm it, so Mago and Hamil must destroy you before you sail."

Elissa paused in her pacing. "Surely you don't think my brother would stoop to assassination!"

"I don't know what he will do—with those two advising him," Sicharbas said. "But whatever it is, we cannot take any chances now. Straton's life has been in danger ever since he arrived in Tyre."

For a moment Straton was afraid Sicharbas might be about to reveal the scheme for which he had been recalled from Tartessus. The High Priest continued, however, before Elissa could ask a question. "I was counting upon your knowledge of the new purple to protect you, but Hamil and Mago know now that they can lose Tyre for their Assyrian masters if we send a fleet and break up the attack upon Arvad. They will have to act soon—or not at all."

"I have been guarded by my own men for several weeks," Straton assured him. "I still don't think I will be in any great danger."

"You must add to your bodyguard and never be without them," Sicharbas insisted. "Who knows better than I that even someone you trust may turn out to be an assassin?"

A message from one of Elissa's ladies-in-waiting that her dressmaker was waiting for a fitting seemed to offer Straton a chance to get away. But as he started to leave with the Queen, Sicharbas called him back and he had no choice except to obey.

"I am sure we will have to send a fleet to help Arvad," the High Priest said. "And it should be as soon as possible, before the Assyrians can gather any ships."

"Perhaps King Pygmalion will send help if you assure him it is the will of Melkarth and Astarte."

"The boy has some strength and, with some proper guidance, might even one day make Tyre a good king," Sicharbas agreed. "But as long as he is under the influence of our enemies, it is not safe to risk waiting to see what he will do. We must be sure that you get safely to Arvad and back with news of the situation there. Then Pygmalion will have no choice except to place you in command of the fleet that goes to help King Aziru. And with strong forces supporting you, it will not be difficult for you and Elissa to take control here."

Now, if at all, Straton realized, was the time to tell Sicharbas of Elissa's vow and of his own determination not to join in the plan to usurp the throne. And yet he hesitated to bring further pain to an already sick man.

"Have you spoken to the Quee—"

"She must have no inkling of this before my death," Sicharbas said firmly. "But I have left a letter with Luli for her, outlining my wishes."

Straton gave a start of surprise which—fortunately—Sicharbas did not notice. For if his suspicions concerning Luli's relationship with their enemies were correct, then Sicharbas had unwittingly played directly into their hands and perhaps signed Straton's own death warrant as well.

"You seem better today." He changed the subject deliberately. "Perhaps your illness is not as severe as you thought."

Sicharbas shook his head. "Nothing is changed. A ship from Egypt last week brought me a fresh supply of poppy seeds, so I was able to increase the dose I take daily. I have seen that word was spread through the city, though, saying that I am recovering from my illness and will soon resume an active role in governing the state."

"You are only inviting them to attack you," Straton warned.

"I am well guarded, as long as I stay in the temple." Then Sicharbas' face brightened. "Perhaps Mago and Hamil will attack you, and your men will destroy them."

Straton left the temple on that note, but he felt none of Sicharbas' hope that, by using himself as the bait, so to speak, he might destroy the spies who were trying to turn Tyre over to the Assyrians. Mago and Hamil, he felt sure, were the kind who would send assassins under the cover of darkness to do such a job, with no risk to their own lives.

As Straton had expected, by the time he reached the waterfront, Diomedes' galley was already moored to the quay before the warehouse belonging to Pallas. A line of slaves was carrying packages and bales of goods from the ship, but as he hurried up the gangplank to the deck, Hera opened the door of the quarters she shared with her father and came out.

She wore a kiton of Egyptian linen that accentuated the slender beauty of her body somewhat less than the soft clinging garment she'd worn when he had first seen her. But with her skin burned a pale brown from the sun, she was as lovely as ever. And when her eyes met his, the warm light of happiness in them was more than he had even dared to expect.

"I have been counting the days," he said breathlessly. "It seemed you would never come."

"There was much to see and do in Egypt," she said. "Besides, a prince of that land insisted upon entertaining me. He wanted to make me one of his wives."

"Surely you gave him no encouragement."

"He was of royal birth and very rich. They say in Memphis he might one day become Pharaoh!"

"I am descended from Hiram the Great, whose ships went where no Egyptian would dare to go. Come, I want to show you something."

She let him take her hand and lead her across the deck and down the gangplank to the quay where the new gaoul was moored. A line of slaves was loading blocks of stone cut from the mountainside back of Palaetyrus and transported across the narrow channel on log rafts, one of which was moored just beyond the gaoul.

"I sail for Arvad as soon as the ship is dedicated the day after tomorrow," he told her. "We are loading ballast now."

"Are you going on to seek the Isles of Purple?"

"This will be only a short voyage to determine what the fate of Arvad is likely to be. It is already under siege by the Assyrians."

"We heard of it at Dor," she said. "Father took on part of a cargo of silver plate in Egypt, to be sold in Arvad. He is anxious to reach there, too."

They ascended the ladder leading to the after portion of the gaoul's deck and came to the sturdy house set between the great steering sweeps overhanging the stern. Straton opened the door and stood back for her to step over the low sill that kept water from running in when the spray from a rough sea swept over the deck.

He heard her catch her breath at the beauty of the pumice-rubbed cedar planking and the rich hangings drawn back to expose the small but exquisitely furnished cabin occupying one side of the deckhouse. The rich smell of cedar permeated the room and everything was complete, even to a polished silver mirror on the wall over the small dressing table of ivory, with a bench of the same material. On one side of the table stood an exquisite figurine carved from ivory, a lovely woman whose majesty of feature and form was apparent, even in so small an image.

"It is the goddess Juno!" She turned to face him, her eyes shining. "My namesake."

"Ares found it in the warehouse of another merchant here. Being a Greek, he recognized it at once."

"But Astarte is your goddess."

"From now on I worship only one called Hera."

"Then all this—"

"Was built for you. After all, one doesn't have a goddess every day as a passenger—or as a bride."

She pretended surprise, but the warm light in her eyes as he put his arm about her and drew her close in the privacy of the small chamber assured him it was only pretense. "How do you know that I—"

"You said once you could imagine no greater thrill than seeing new lands and new people. Here is your chariot. In it we will search together for the Isles of Purple."

Her mouth was soft and clinging and he could feel her heart beating strong and regularly against his own. Only when a voice spoke from the doorway of the cabin did they break apart, in some embarrassment at being caught thus in an intimate moment.

"You two certainly seem to have come to a meeting of the minds," Diomedes said with a chuckle. "I didn't realize what I was intruding upon—until it was too late."

"I was going to send a marriage broker to you tomorrow," Straton said.

"Then we can both be happy at saving his fee." Diomedes stepped across the threshold. "I don't have to ask how the new ship goes. I trust your father is as well."

"He is," Straton said. "About the marriage settlement—"

"Gerlach and I can talk that over tomorrow. You and Hera seem to have reached an agreement already."

"Straton is going to take me with him to the Western Isles, Father!" Hera cried. "He built this cabin for us."

"And a beautiful piece of work it is," Diomedes agreed. "When do you wish the wedding to be?"

"The sooner—" Straton remembered suddenly that he could not announce his betrothal as long as Sicharbas was alive, but fortunately Hera did not notice his hesitation.

"I couldn't possibly be ready for a month or more," she protested. "And I want to be married at home in Crete. Straton can stop there on the way to the Western Isles."

Straton drew a deep breath of relief. "Hera tells me you are going to Arvad," he said to Diomedes. "I leave for there in a few days on a test voyage. Perhaps we can sail along together."

"Why not make it a race!" Hera cried.

"My new ship will probably not even be as fast as the old one," Straton demurred. "The Western Sea is more stormy than the protected waters inside the Pillars of Melkarth, so I had the prow covered with heavy plates of bronze to protect the hull. If we are not able to find a suitable harbor we can drive the ship on the shore."

"I was just admiring it," Diomedes told him. "You have stepped the mast well and I shall be surprised if you don't find it faster than you think. By the way, I may have discovered something of worth to you on the voyage southward."

"About Mago?" In the excitement of seeing Hera again, Straton had forgotten about his request to the Greek shipmaster.

"A merchant at Joppa remembered him. He said both Mago and Hamil once owned caravans and traded in slaves with the Assyrians."

"But he knew of no more direct connection?"

Diomedes shook his head. "It is little enough, I know. But it does prove that they have connections with Assyria."

"It may not matter now," Straton told him. "King Pygmalion has agreed to be guided by what I find at Arvad. If they need our help there, a Tyrian fleet will sail northward to help break up the Assyrian attack."

"Then you may be delayed in sailing to the West," Hera protested. "Am I to be left at the altar before I am even a bride?"

"Whatever happens at Arvad will be decided quickly," Straton assured her. "The fate of the entire world may hang upon whether Tyre stands against the Assyrians—or falls."

Like all ships built at Tyre, the newest gaoul from the ways of the House of Gerlach was to be dedicated to the goddess Astarte, whose favor was sought by all mariners of Phoenicia. Straton had not yet stocked the ship with supplies and cargo for the long voyage to Tartessus, since the visit to Arvad was expected to be very brief. But the full complement of the crew was ready, including the doubled number of fighting men, armed with brazen shields, helmets, spears and arrows, the points of the latter two fashioned, at considerable extra cost, from the Hittite metal, iron.

Because even the great temple of Melkarth and Astarte could not accommodate the huge crowd expected for the ceremony, it was to be held—like all major ceremonials—upon the broad portico, where all who wished might witness it. Straton had not seen Sicharbas since the day he had visited the quarters of the High Priest at Elissa's request. Somewhat to his surprise, no attempt had been made to harm him, though Mago was in Tyre and reported by Ares, who kept himself informed on every subject, to be in constant attendance upon King Pygmalion. Straton did not doubt that Mago was trying to influence the young ruler against going to the aid of their sister city to the north, but as yet there had been no public change in Pygmalion's decision that he should go to Arvad and assess the situation there. Hamil, Ares reported, was mysteriously absent, having gone, it was said, to the mainland across the channel from Tyre itself.

By midmorning of the day for the ceremonial, a vast crowd had gathered before the temple, filling all available space except a place of honor reserved for Straton and his ship's complement. As was usual on such occasions, the great brazen image of the goddess had been brought out of the temple itself and now stood upon the highest level of the portico, with the crowd filling the open space in front of the temple steps and extending as far as the edge of the Grove of Astarte, facing it.

The goddess was seated upon a throne, beneath which were the rollers that enabled it to be moved outside for important ceremonies. To either side of her were Egyptian sphinxes, relics of an earlier day when Tyre had been under direct control of Egypt. Squat and broad of hip, the Earth Mother held between her knees a large bronze bowl, or laver, whose rim lay beneath the nipples of her massive, pendulous breasts.

Straton and his crew—except Ares who, since he was not a worshiper of Astarte, had chosen to be only an observer, and Amathus, the pilot, who had remained aboard the gaoul with the galley slaves, completing the final taking on of food and water for the voyage to Arvad—had formed a column at the edge of the grove. There they waited for a signal from the platform where Luli, in priestly robes, was presiding over the introductory portion of the ceremony.

Gerlach stood beside his tall son and, as they watched, four stalwart slaves appeared from inside the temple, bearing a table-like altar upon which glowed a large shallow brazier filled with coals. Guided by a priest, the slaves carefully deposited their burden in front of the image on the next step below it and partially beneath the edge of the great bowl resting upon the knees of the Goddess.

"Diomedes and I worked out the terms of the marriage settlement last night," Gerlach told Straton as they stood waiting to march to their assigned positions. "I will travel in one of our galleys to his home at Herakleon on Crete for the wedding. The galley will return afterward, while you and Hera sail in search of the Isles of The Dragon's Blood."

"I did not dare ask you to make the journey, for fear you would feel it was your duty to go," Straton said. "But I am glad you will be there for the wedding."

"Have you told Sicharbas about Hera?"

Straton shook his head. "I could hardly speak of her without revealing that I cannot carry out his plan—so I said nothing."

"It was the better course," Gerlach agreed.

"Luli tells me Elissa has sworn a vow of celibacy to Astarte, hoping the goddess will make Sicharbas well again. I wonder how he managed to convince her that she should swear it."

Gerlach gave his son a startled look. "Are you sure of what you are saying?" he asked.

Before Straton could answer, four slaves appeared on the portico of the temple before the squat image of Phoenicia's patron goddess. They bore an open chair in which Sicharbas sat and, at the sight of the High Priest, who had not appeared in public for more than a month, the crowd broke into a cheer. The four slaves deposited the chair almost against the brazen flank of the image and stepped back, as priests standing on either side lifted the traditional curved trumpets of ram's horn preparatory to sounding the signal for the ceremony to begin.

"I am sure Luli loves Elissa and hopes to marry her himself," Straton said in a low voice. "He knows of Sicharbas' plan, so he naturally hates me."

"Did you tell him you refused to have any part of it?"

"I pretended to know nothing. But he also said that, if Sicharbas dies, Elissa will abdicate the regency and leave Pygmalion to rule alone."

"You did well," Gerlach approved. "While you are away at Arvad I will see what I can learn for myself. A few debenweight of silver in the right place sometimes loosens tongues remarkably."

From the elevated portico of the temple, twin blasts of the ram's horns sounded the signal for the ceremony to begin. Father and son began to march along the aisle that had been left for them by the crowd, with the members of their own column following behind them. When they reached the steps leading up to the temple portico they began to ascend toward a space reserved for them before the image of Astarte near the chair in which Sicharbas sat.

The shoulders of the High Priest drooped as if the ceremonial robes were too heavy for his painfully thin body to bear. Elissa stood beside the chair, with one hand resting upon her husband's shoulder, while King Pygmalion lolled upon a portable ivory throne on the other side of the goddess. Mago stood just back of Pygmalion, one step in front of a file of palace guards, who appeared to be more numerous than Straton remembered from previous occasions. They were fully armed, too, with helmets, breastplates, swords, spears, and shields. Mago was also armed, though he did not carry spear or shield, but Hamil was nowhere to be seen, as had been the case now for almost a week.

Diomedes and Hera were standing at the front of the crowd near the aisle which had been opened for Straton and his party to pass through. In a white kiton, with her golden hair shining in the sunlight, she stood out among the women of the crowd like a jewel among baser stones.

Straton was at the lowest of the temple steps, when Ares darted from the crowd and fell into place just behind him. The little man was panting and his face was flushed.

"Master," he whispered loud enough for Straton to hear but not those in the crowd. "I have new—"

"This is no time—"

"Hamil landed early this morning with fifty Amorite mercenaries. He has been training them at Dor, so he could bring them here in a day's voyage."

"Where are they now?"

"Some are up there behind Mago. Hamil had new palace-guard uniforms made for them."

They were almost at the section of the temple steps reserved for Straton and his party now and it was much too late to do anything to counteract whatever action Hamil and Mago planned. Straton's only course was to be constantly on the alert until he sailed tomorrow for Arvad, but he wished now that he had been warned in time to arm himself with something other than the jeweled dagger at his belt. Fortunately, he had hired additional mercenaries to make up the enlarged complement of the new vessel, and all who marched behind him were fully armed.

"Did you hear?" Straton asked his father in a whisper.

The older man nodded but continued to march, bearing before him a small model of the gaoul which would be ceremoniously sacrificed to the goddess, invoking her favor for the ship and its crew upon future voyages.

"We heard, too." Tarquin and Acestes, who had been Straton's constant bodyguards over the past several weeks, were just behind him as always. "But one of us is a match for two Amorites anyday."

The sun was shining brightly upon the colorful scene, and the brazen statue of Astarte had been polished until it shone like gold. Straton's party filed into place on the steps just below the altar which, with its bed of coals glowing, stood almost between the knees of the squatting figure of the Earth Mother as she held the large bowl beneath her breasts.

The ram's-horn trumpets sounded again and from inside the temple came the sound of feminine voices, high-pitched yet melodious, chanting a ritual hymn as the High Priestess appeared at the side of the image, leading a column of the sacred women of Astarte.

The High Priestess wore a ceremonial robe of white and purple and her face was covered by a mask of the yellow metal called electrum, extending upward to form a high-tiered headdress. A shaven-headed priest followed her, bearing a carved bowl of electrum filled with wine. Behind him came others, bearing fruit, grain and acacia flowers which they deposited upon the altar before the image, on either side of the brazier in which the coals glowed.

At the appearance of the High Priestess, Sicharbas rose from his chair, with the help of Luli and Elissa, and moved into position beside the image. He was still an impressive figure, for the frailness of his tall body was hidden by the ceremonial robes of his office. And in spite of his illness, the voice of the High Priest of Melkarth and Astarte was still sonorous as it rolled out over the vast throng:

> I summon the gods, generous and beautiful,
> Children of princes, come savor the offerings we
>   give thee.
> Bless this new work of thy people to thy glory.

At the first words, Gerlach stepped forward to kneel before the altar, holding out before him the wooden model of the gaoul. And at a gesture from Luli, a priest moved down the steps to lift the small ship from Gerlach's outstretched hands. Twice the priest lifted it high above his head before the brazen image of Astarte and lowered it again. But on the third uplifting, he cast the small image of the ship upon the glowing coals covering the center of the altar.

A cry rose from the crowd when a burst of yellowish flame seemed almost to leap up and meet the sacrifice. And, where a moment before the coals had been without flame, they now crackled as if they had suddenly come alive, licking smoking tongues to encompass the bowl held upon the knees of the image and blot it momentarily from sight.

From each side of the altar, other priests quickly cast first the grain and then the flowering branches of acacia upon the coals. And each time the flames leaped up again to devour them and lick at the brazen bowl. To the onlookers it must have seemed as if the eager flames were alive, but Mochus had explained to Straton long ago that the trick was accomplished by means of packets of powdered brimstone which the priests cast upon the flames along with the offerings. He was not surprised when the flames rose again to envelope the whole front of the image and the acrid smell of brimstone met his nostrils.

"The gods are present!" the thunderous tones of Sicharbas announced. "Let everyone fall down before them and await the sign of favor from divine Astarte."

Though he had participated in such ceremonies often enough to know just how the mummery was accomplished, Straton could not but share some of the breathless anticipation that gripped the crowd, who prostrated themselves upon the steps of the temple and the ground outside wherever there was room, or bowed their heads when there was none. From the corner of his eye he saw Hera and her father bow with the rest and, though he knew well just what the next step in the ceremony would be, the mood of the crowd gripped him, too, as he waited like the others for the final miracle indicating the favor of Astarte for the ship represented by the now charred model.

A deep silence fell momentarily over the waiting crowd. Then it was broken suddenly by a sound Straton had never heard in such rituals before—the high-pitched scream of a woman.

Seven:

*Then strife ensued, and cursed gold
the cause.*

THE VOICE WAS ELISSA'S, and Straton was upon his feet at once, shouting to Tarquin and the men-at-arms behind him to rise. But when his eyes moved to the spot where the Queen had been standing, he saw only the tall form of Sicharbas tumbling forward down the steps.

"The goddess has rejected the offering!" a man shouted, and he was not surprised to recognize Mago's voice. "She has stricken the High Priest with her own hand as a sign that this ship should not sail to Arvad."

As if a clouded window had suddenly been wiped clean, Straton understood why Mago had waited until today to launch this bold stroke. If successful, it would rid him of the restraining influence Sicharbas and Elissa had maintained over the young King and at the same time insure that no fleet would be sent northward to help defeat his Assyrian masters. And even before he saw the red stain upon Sicharbas' robe as the tall, frail body of the High Priest crumpled upon the steps, Straton was certain of the course the rest of the plot would take.

The priest who had cast the small gaoul upon the altar was straining now at the handles by which it had been carried. Obviously a part of the plot, his purpose was to tumble the coals down the steps, driving back the crowd if they tried to intervene. Even more important, the heat of the flames must be quickly removed from the great bowl resting upon the knees of Astarte if the whole scheme were to succeed. The altar was heavy, however, and the priest failed to overturn it on the first try, giving Straton the chance he needed to block the clever scheme Mago had devised to gain control of Tyre.

"Tarquin!" he shouted. "Stop the priest there at the altar."

The twang of a bowstring sounded at Straton's shoulder by the time he had finished speaking the command. As he raced up the steps he was near enough to the priest to see his mouth gape open with surprise when an iron-pointed arrow transfixed his chest. A glance told Straton that Sicharbas was dying, but, though a red stain was already dribbling from the corner of the High Priest's mouth, he struggled to speak when Straton knelt beside him.

"Hamil!" The word was barely audible. "Elissa saw him, so they will kill her, too."

Straton started to rise but the dying man held his sleeve and pulled him back. "Swear on your life to save her from Pygmalion and Mago," he begged.

"I swear it," Straton said without hesitation.

"Melkarth protect you both!" Sicharbas' mouth went slack and Straton thought he was dead, but he spoke again, though only in a whisper. "My treasure." The words were barely audible. "The ca—" A fit of coughing cut the words short. "Melkarth," he gasped and was suddenly silent.

Straton needed no second glance to know that Sicharbas was dead. What was more, the High Priest had died believing he would marry Elissa and seize the kingdom. And, even though both Elissa's vow of celibacy and his own reluctance to take the throne meant that the plan would not be carried through, he was still obligated to save Elissa and avenge the death of her husband.

Searching desperately in his mind for a key to the riddle of where he should start in both these endeavors, Straton thought of Luli. Only Luli could have planned the details of the dedication ceremony, so Hamil would have an opportunity to assassinate the High Priest on the first occasion in months when Sicharbas had shown himself to the people. Luli would have known, too, that the death of Sicharbas at the height of the ceremony would be seized upon by the people as a sign that the patron goddess of Tyre did not look with favor upon the city's joining in the defense of Arvad. And finally, from his familiarity with temple ceremony, Luli could have arranged for the priest who had presided over the sacrifices to overturn the altar before the flames could heat the brazen image of Astarte enough for the final miracle of the traditional ceremony to occur.

These thoughts were racing through Straton's mind as he lowered Sicharbas' body to the steps and rose quickly to his feet. Around him was the clash of arms, as the guards who had been standing behind King Pygmalion, led by Mago, moved down the steps to attack Straton's men.

"Keep them from the altar at all cost," Straton warned Tarquin. "The fire must burn on!"

The Etruscan was busily occupied at the moment thrusting his spear into the belly of an Amorite mercenary. Twisting the double-bladed point, he wrenched it from the body of the screaming soldier, almost tearing the victim in half, and stood erect to acknowledge the order. Ares, too, realized the import of Straton's words and ran quickly to the body of the priest who had sought to overturn the altar. Fumbling momentarily in the man's robe, he rose with a handful of the brimstone packets and cast them into the fire. At once the yellow flames leaped high again and a cry of wonder arose from the crowd, who had not yet realized fully what was happening in the area around the image.

Straton did not wait to see the effect of the fire upon the image, however, for he had just seen Luli appear in the spot where Sicharbas had been standing before he was stabbed. The priest's face was as white as the robe he wore, and he held his left arm with his right hand while a stain of red crept from beneath his fingers.

"Straton!" he called. "Hamil has seized the Queen!"

Silently cursing his own ineptness in failing to arm himself that morning with a better weapon than the jeweled dagger at his belt, Straton looked desperately about him. When he saw the body of one of his own mercenaries, struck down by an enemy spear, lying nearby, he quickly seized the man's sword and shield, choosing the latter over a spear for the sort of close fighting he might have to do inside the temple, where Hamil had apparently taken Elissa. Thrusting his left arm through the tough leather thong of the shield—a plate of bronze fastened to a framework of wood—he carried the sword in his right hand as he ran up the steps to where Luli was leaning against a column for support.

"How badly are you wounded?" he asked.

"Only a cut." Luli was trembling with fear but managed to gain control of himself with an effort. "I tried to stop Hamil, but he slashed my arm."

"Where is the Queen?"

"Hamil took her into the temple. He will surely kill her and then all will be lost."

"He could have slain her when he killed Sicharbas, so he must have taken her as a hostage—for Sicharbas' treasure. Does she know where it is?"

"I don't think so. None of us knew!"

"Then, we have a chance to defeat them," Straton said. "Listen carefully and do as I say, or you will answer to me with your life. The flames are still heating the image, so the miracle may occur at any moment. The people know you were chosen by Sicharbas to be High Priest after his death. Announce the miracle when it happens and part of Mago's plan will be defeated."

Luli nodded, showing that he understood the strategy Straton had chosen. "Go after the Queen," he said. "I will announce it."

Tarquin and his mercenaries had been successful in holding Mago's forces away from the altar, Straton saw as he surveyed the situation quickly, before turning to the entrance to the temple, whose great doors had been thrown wide when the image of Astarte was wheeled out upon the portico. Behind him he heard a sudden shout from the crowd as Luli announced:

"A sign! A sign! The goddess has spoken!"

Straton did not need to be outside to know that the very thing Mago had been fighting to prevent by removing the fire from the altar had happened, when the heat had finally melted the stoppers of wax closing the openings in the brazen nipples of the goddess. From a reservoir in her head, filled before the ceremony through an opening in the back, milk had poured down to spurt from the pendulous breasts into the bowl she held between her knees in the traditional sign of favor from Astarte that was the culmination of the dedication ceremony.

Coming from the bright sunlight of the portico into the relative shadow inside the temple, Straton was half-blinded for an instant that could have cost him his life but for Elissa's cry of warning. Reacting instinctively to the sound, he cast himself forward upon the floor, the bronze shield clanging like a gong as it struck the stone. Even then the heavy spear, driven with all of Hamil's strength at close range, almost nicked him in passing. So great was the force behind the weapon that, when it struck the floor a few paces beyond him, the impact split the bronze point and shattered the shaft.

Straton saw Hamil now. He stood just inside the temple door, with the point of his sword at Elissa's throat.

"Try to free her and she dies," he warned. "She only lives because she knows where her husband's wealth is hidden."

"Sicharbas told me where the treasure is." Straton moved to the other side of the doorway, ready to thrust anyone through who might come to Hamil's aid. "Let the Queen go and it will be yours."

"A likely story!" Hamil obviously judged other people's honesty by his own.

"The goddess has spoken against you, too. Didn't you hear the crowd just now?"

"What are a few spurts of milk from the teats of an image? The people know the priests use such miracles at will."

"Your Amorite mercenaries aren't very good fighters either." Straton was talking to gain time, hoping his own men would break through the forces led by Mago and follow him into the temple. "My Greeks and Etruscans are cutting them to pieces."

He saw by the sudden flicker of apprehension in Hamil's eyes that the thrust had gone home. Being a brigand, Hamil was quite familiar with the fighting qualities of the Greeks and the Etruscans, who were known for their bravery and love of warlike pursuits from one end of the Great Sea to the other.

"Your scheme has already failed," Straton added. "But if you free the Queen, I swear to let you and Mago sail away unharmed."

"Leaving you as King of Tyre? We know all about the scheme you and Sicharbas were hatching.

"You have been listening to idle gossip." Straton spoke quickly, before Hamil could reveal more, but the Assyrian spy was far from yielding yet. Holding the blade at Elissa's throat, he had been inching toward the outer door all the while, obviously seeking to learn how the fighting was going outside. Straton, however, could make no overt move for fear of causing Elissa's death, so his only hope was to hold Hamil in conversation until help arrived, or some change in the situation occurred.

"The Queen will renounce her claim to the throne and leave King Pygmalion as sole ruler," he offered Hamil. "Then you and Mago will have won the fight without stirring up the people to take sides."

He could see Hamil considering the offer as he moved toward the open doorway, through which sunlight was reflected into the temple from the polished stone floor of the portico outside. "Would you still go to Arvad?" he asked.

"Let her go free and I will sail for the Western Isles directly from Tyre," Straton said, willing to pay even the price of abandoning Arvad to the Assyrians in order to fulfill that part of his promise to Sicharbas specifying that he would protect Elissa. But, fortunately, the sudden change he had been hoping for happened just then. A small figure shot through the doorway of the temple, moving so fast that it could not change direction in time and went barreling into Hamil's flank, knocking him off balance and forcing him to release Elissa in order to hold on to his sword and stay on his feet.

Straton had never been more glad to see Ares, but there was no time to thank the little man now for running into the temple to help his master. Leaping across the open doorway, he engaged Hamil with his sword before the other man could seize Elissa again, capitalizing on the brief advantage the sudden appearance of Ares had granted him. But though Hamil had suffered a momentary backset in the loss of his prisoner, he was still a deadly opponent and, regaining his balance, moved eagerly into the task of cutting his attacker to pieces.

Straton found himself wishing he had spent more time as a youth training in warlike pursuits and less in studying philosophy, nature and navigation at the feet of Mochus, but it was too late to remedy that lack now. Like his own, Hamil's sword was of iron rather than the considerably softer bronze, but Straton's, unfortunately, was shorter than the other man's weapon. And, though possession of the shield gave him an advantage at the outset, it disappeared with the first blow Hamil landed directly upon the metal.

Being softer than iron, the bronze plate of the shield split in half and Hamil's sword went on to cut through the framework as well, forcing Straton to leap back in order to keep from losing the arm which had been thrust through the thongs. With a desperate effort, he disengaged the thongs from his left arm and flung the two halves at Hamil's head, forcing his opponent to give ground momentarily. The delay was brief, however. Pausing only to kick the fragments of the bronze shield aside, Hamil advanced forthrightly to attack and, by virtue of superior swordsmanship, forced Straton to give ground steadily.

Though half-stunned when he had struck Hamil with his head, Ares had now managed to pick himself up from the floor. Calling encouragement to his master, the little Greek drew his dagger and began to circle Hamil warily, watching for an opportunity to flip the small weapon through the air and bury it in the spy's back. And realizing the danger of a simultaneous attack from both front and rear, Hamil now redoubled his attack upon Straton, who was at a considerable disadvantage because of the shorter length of his sword.

Forced to give ground by the slashing attack of his more skilled opponent, Straton did not see the remains of Hamil's spear upon the floor, until his foot came down upon the broken shaft. Losing his balance when the smooth wooden cylinder rolled beneath his foot, he went down with such force that his right elbow struck the stone-paved floor of the temple, paralyzing his arm momentarily and causing the sword to drop from suddenly nerveless fingers.

With a shout of triumph, Hamil leaped forward, slashing downward at his now seemingly helpless opponent. Straton, his right arm still numb from striking the stone-paved floor, reached out desperately with his left hand, seeking the sword he had lost, but his questing fingers found only the splintered fragment of Hamil's spearshaft, over which he had fallen. Though the partly shattered bronze point was still attached, it was a poor weapon with which to defend himself against a skilled swordsman, but flailing desperately with the broken handle, he somehow managed to deflect Hamil's blade away from his body. A second stroke would surely have dispatched him, however, had not Hamil made the mistake of being overconfident of destroying him as he lay helpless on the stone floor.

As it was, the broken spear handle slid off the edge of Hamil's blade and the partially shattered point struck the side of his neck, almost knocking the weapon from Straton's grasp. He clung to it instinctively as, reacting to the pain, Hamil tried to twist himself away and clear of the jagged metal fragment. But the Amorite lost his balance instead and fell, jamming the broken shaft into a crevice between two of the paving stones and literally spitting himself upon the razor-sharp remainder of the bronze point. Almost decapitated as the metal tore through the flesh of his neck, Hamil was dead before he struck the floor.

Still trembling from his close call with death and the shock of the fall, Straton managed to push himself to his feet just as Elissa threw herself sobbing into his arms, almost bowling him over again. And as his arms closed about his former sweetheart—as much to keep himself from falling as to support her—he looked up to see Hera standing in the doorway of the temple, staring at him in startled disbelief.

ii

To Straton, still hardly able to believe he was alive, when death had been so very near only moments before, the temple vestibule seemed suddenly to be full of people. They were members of his own party, he saw, but some were wounded and the weapons most of them bore were red with blood, testifying to the character of the battle that had raged outside. Nor was he surprised to see that—like the Greek goddess Diana, of whom Ares had told him—Hera was carrying a bow, which she must have picked up on the steps outside, and a partially filled quiver of arrows slung over her shoulder. Her eyes met his for only a moment, however; then she went to stand beside Diomedes, who had entered with the others.

For once, Straton was glad to see Luli and, when the priest moved to Elissa's side, willingly gave him custody of her. While Luli led the still sobbing Queen to a bench beside the wall, Tarquin and several of the mercenaries pushed the great doors of the temple shut. And, with the noise from outside shut away, the temple was suddenly strangely peaceful and quiet.

Straton had not realized that he was wounded, until he felt blood trickle down the side of his face. But before he could wipe it away, Hera was beside him.

"You are hurt!" she cried.

"I must have broken the skin of my temple when I struck the stones," he said, warmed by her concern for him. "Most of the blood is Hamil's."

She looked down at the inert figure of the spy, lying at their feet, and shivered a little. "I did not prostrate myself before Astarte, so I saw the whole thing. Hamil stabbed the High Priest, then seized Queen Elissa and pulled her back inside the temple doorway just before Mago led the guards down the steps to attack you and your men."

"They were trying to overturn the altar and keep the wax in the image of Astarte from melting," he explained. "Mago wanted to convince the people that the goddess did not favor our helping Arvad."

"One of them aimed an arrow at you, as you knelt beside the High Priest. A tall mercenary in your band struck him down with a spear but was killed a moment later."

"That would have been Acestes," Straton said. "I was hoping you and Diomedes would not become involved in this affair."

"We were in the crowd when the fighting started," she said. "We couldn't stand by and see you killed."

"It may cost your father the loss of his galley—if any of us manage to escape with our lives. But I am glad you are here and safe." He reached out to take her hand, but Hera drew it quickly away.

"Shouldn't you see about Queen Elissa?" she asked.

"I suppose so. Sicharbas left her in my care."

Later Straton was to wish he had explained to Hera more clearly the exact relationship between himself and Elissa. As for Luli, who was hovering over the Queen solicitously, in the excitement of the fight with Hamil, Straton had forgotten his suspicion that the priest had been more intimately involved in the whole affair than his presence here would seem to indicate. And at the moment it seemed that nothing would be gained by voicing such doubts to Elissa, who appeared to trust Luli completely. Later, if they escaped and there was time for such things, he would demand an explanation from the priest himself.

"Are you all right?" Straton asked.

Elissa nodded. "Hamil planned to torture me into revealing where Sicharbas' personal fortune is hidden." She took a deep breath. "Is my husband dead?"

"Yes. I was with him on the steps of the temple when he died. His last thought was of you."

She seized his hand and buried her face against his sleeve until her spasm of grief was over. From outside, shouts were occasionally heard, but the fighting in the area of the temple steps and portico, where the brief foray had occurred when Sicharbas had been slain and Elissa seized, seemed to have ended with the retreat of his own forces into the temple.

"I was hoping your brother would stop Mago," Straton said. "But it seems I was wrong."

128

Elissa lifted her head, grief displaced, for the time being at least, by indignation. "Pygmalion wanted me killed for the same reason he let them kill Sicharbas—my husband's wealth." Too angry for further speech, she did not go on, but Straton could see that she was in control of herself and turned to more pressing matters.

"Tarquin," he called to the Etruscan, who was watching the portico outside through the partially open door. "What is the situation out there?"

"They have fallen back. Mago's Amorite mercenaries fled as soon as the battle turned against them."

"Can we fight our way to the harbor and the gaoul?"

"If we move at once and surprise them," the Etruscan said. "Mago still has more fighting men than we do, but he is probably content at the moment to keep us bottled up here. In a bold move, the element of surprise would be in our favor."

"We will try to reach the gaoul then," Straton decided.

"What is your plan, Straton?" Gerlach had retreated to the temple with the others.

"First, we must get the Queen safely away from Tyre," Straton said. "Mago knows that as long as she is alive and in the city she is a menace to his control of Pygmalion. He has to destroy her if he is to gain full control of Tyre."

"But where can you go?"

"To Arvad—as we had planned."

Elissa spoke, her voice sharp. "Am I not to be consulted about my own fate?"

"Our first concern is to keep you alive and get you safely away from Tyre," Straton explained.

"And leave everything here to my brother and Mago?"

"We are too few to fight them long, but if we make a dash for the harbor now we may be able to get the gaoul under way before they can stop us."

Diomedes gave the answer to the immediate problem of Elissa's safety, an answer Straton had not considered until that moment. "I would be honored to take Queen Elissa to Arvad," he said. "My galley is lighter and can get under way much faster than your gaoul."

"No ship in Tyre can catch you, if Mago tries to pursue," Straton agreed. "It may be the answer we need—if the Queen will accept." He did not add that getting Diomedes' galley under way would also insure Hera's safety, a particularly important consideration.

"What choice do I have?" Elissa said dejectedly. "With my husband dead and my brother in league with those who killed him, I no longer have any control over my own destiny."

"Are you going with us, Straton?" Hera asked.

He shook his head. "I'll not willingly leave my new gaoul as a prize for the enemy. But I should catch up with you easily at Arvad."

The decision having been made to try and reach the waterfront, nothing was to be gained by delay. With Elissa surrounded by a cordon of Straton's own fighting men, the column emerged from the temple and started toward the okel. Fortunately, Mago had been so confident of being able to keep them bottled up in the temple, to be destroyed at his pleasure, that he had posted only a few guards outside. These retreated immediately at the sight of Tarquin and the grim-faced mercenaries, but Straton had no expectation of getting away unscathed. The logical place for Mago to launch a counterattack would be on the quay, while Straton and his crew were occupied in getting the huge gaoul under way. And he did not doubt that it would happen there.

At the waterfront, Straton escorted Elissa aboard the Greek galley, while Diomedes busied himself with preparations for sailing. She was fairly composed now, enough to be concerned about the future.

"What shall I do in Arvad?" she asked.

"Luli is High Priest of Astarte. He can arrange refuge for you there."

"But I have nothing. All my husband's wealth is hidden somewhere in the temple."

The words rang a bell in Straton's mind and with it came the beginning, at least, of a plan whereby he might still take a major step toward wrecking Mago's plan for control of Tyre and at the same time make Elissa secure for the future. Hamil, he knew, had seized the Queen because he thought she could lead him to the treasure. But, though Luli had said neither he nor Elissa knew its location, Straton was fairly sure now that Sicharbas had revealed it in his dying words.

"Did Sicharbas ever tell you where the treasure is hidden?" he asked Elissa, but she shook her head.

"He promised to tell me if it ever looked as if his life were in danger. But he never expected things to happen as swiftly as they did this morning."

"None of us did," Straton agreed. "But I think he told me the answer just the same."

"Where is—" Luli asked eagerly, but Straton cut him off.

"I want you to think hard," he told Elissa. "Try to remember whether Sicharbas ever gave you even the slightest hint of where he kept his wealth."

"I don't remember any—" She stopped suddenly, and frowned. "Wait! He did pose a riddle about it once to me—but I never discovered the answer, so it couldn't help you much."

"It might help a great deal," Straton told her urgently. "What was the riddle?"

"I'm not sure that I recall it exactly. Let me see. I remember he said there are greater riches within the earth than in the sky." She hesitated, then went on, "But that whoever sought them must not fear the sea." When Straton gave a pleased chuckle, she looked at him hopefully. "Does it mean anything?"

"It means Mago shall not have your husband's treasure," he assured her jubilantly. "And before the week is out you may well be the richest woman in the world."

"Straton!" Diomedes called from the afterdeck of his galley. "We are ready to cast off and I think I see soldiers approaching the quay."

"Cast off! And may the gods of both Tyre and Greece speed you on your way." Straton took Hera by the shoulders and kissed her quickly in farewell, then leaped across the narrow gap between ship and quay as Diomedes' galley slaves used their oars to push the sleek vessel out into the harbor, where the sail could be raised.

Gerlach had been directing the preparations for sailing from the quay while, on the gaoul, Amathus drove the slaves as they broke out the oars and prepared to cast off the lines holding the great ship against the quay.

"Did you hear, Father?" Straton asked.

"I heard—but I did not understand."

"As soon as we are under way, I will tell you." He raced along the quay to the ladder leading upward to the deck of the great gaoul. The grizzled pilot stood at the head of it, shouting commands to the slaves and to the topmen who were busy freeing the mooring lines.

"How much longer do you need, Amathus?" Straton asked.

"Only a few moments more." The pilot's glance went to the northern end of the quay. "But you may have to fight for it."

"Keep ladders in place for us to get to the deck. We will give you whatever time you need."

A glance at the open harbor told Straton the Greek galley was safely under way, the sail already filling out as Diomedes set a course for the open sea. And, relieved that his worries about Hera and Elissa were over, he turned his whole attention to the threat of which Amathus had spoken.

As Diomedes had warned, when he suggested that Elissa make her escape on his own ship, the great gaoul could not be gotten under way nearly so easily as the galley had been. Yet, working desperately, Amathus and the men under his command had already accomplished a near-miracle. The oars stored in the nearby warehouse had been brought aboard and fitted against their tholepins, ready for the rowers. The eight men who handled the great steering sweeps when under way stood ready with extra oars in their hands now, waiting to use them as poles with which to thrust off as soon as the order was given. Meanwhile others of the crew were busy breaking out bronze shields and securing them in the brackets along the landside rail to form a metal-sheathed bulwark against the arrows and spears that would come raining aboard when Mago's forces, now closing in from both ends of the quay, came within range.

Tarquin, Straton noted approvingly, had needed no command to deploy his forces as a shield against attack. Part of the mercenaries were guarding the section of the quay used by the House of Gerlach, utilizing the protection afforded by the walls of the warehouse as cover against attack from either direction. Furthermore, to guard against attack from the city above by the way of the streets that descended to the waterfront, Tarquin had sent aboard the gaoul several of his men who were especially skilled with the bow, ready to pick off with swift-flying arrows any who might try to shoot down upon the deck and disrupt the frantic pace of the activities going on there.

The commander of the two attacking columns took no chances, however, having already suffered severe casualties in the fighting at the temple. Halting his men well out of fighting range, he sought to parley.

"In the name of King Pygmalion, Straton, Son of Gerlach, is commanded to deliver the person of the lady Elissa," he announced. "This is the word of the King: Obey and you will be allowed to sail in peace for whatever port you desire."

"The Queen is already safe from the murderers of her husband." Straton shouted the words, so the crowd watching from the higher levels of The Rock overlooking the waterfront would be sure to hear. "She is now on her way to Arvad to seek refuge with King Aziru, since King Pygmalion no longer rules in the city but has turned it over to the Assyrian spy, Mago."

The captain of the attacking forces was obviously reluctant to give the order to attack. But, when a swelling murmur of anger floated down from the crowd above, he finally drew his sword and shouted the command. Tarquin let them approach near enough to loose the first flight of arrows from their bowstrings in a futile attack against Straton's mercenaries, who were protected by the corners of the warehouse building.

Then he shouted an order to the bowmen stationed behind the bulwark of shields erected upon the rail of the ship, who aimed downward carefully from the high deck of the gaoul at the same moment that his own soldiers launched a flight of arrows.

Perhaps a fourth of the attackers were wounded or killed by the first volley, throwing the enemy into confusion and forcing a retreat. Those on board had been working desperately all the while and the last hawser was now ready to be cast off. Straton was still on the pier with the fighting men, but when Gerlach called down that they were ready to cast off, he gave the order to fall back to the ship, under the protection of the bowmen on the deck. These held the attackers back with a steady rain of arrows while the fighting men climbed the ladders leading to the high deck of the gaoul. Meanwhile, the galley slaves who handled the lower bank of oars within the hull pushed them through the openings and helped the steersmen shove the ship away from the quay. Only when the vessel was a safe distance from the mooring did Straton order the deck rowers into place and, with a double bank on each side driving it, the gaoul began to move out of the harbor.

iii

Certain that no vessel would dare pursue such a strongly defended ship, Straton did not set a course northward, as Diomedes had done. Instead, he headed south with the sail still furled, since the wind was blowing from that direction, and with the two tiers of rowers pulling steadily to the rhythm of the pacemaker drum. Gerlach had remained in the safety of the afterhouse during the brief battle on the pier. But when he heard Straton give the steersmen a southwesterly course that would partially circle The Rock of Tyre, he could contain his curiosity no longer.

"Why this course?" he inquired. "Have you decided against going directly to Arvad?"

"We will head north in good time," Straton assured him. "But first I want to refresh my memory about the Cave of Melkarth."

"Is there really such a cave? I always thought someone had imagined it."

"The cave is there, and I suspect it holds the key to Sicharbas' fortune. Elissa will need it—especially if we establish a new city at Karthadasht."

"What makes you think the treasure is hidden in the cave?"

"Sicharbas tried to tell me how to find it as he was dying. I didn't realize what he meant, until Elissa spoke of the riddle."

"Things were happening so fast in the temple, I'm afraid I don't remember."

"Sicharbas tried to say 'cave' when I knelt beside him as he lay dying, but a fit of coughing interrupted him and I didn't understand. His next word was 'Melkarth,' but I didn't realize then that he was using the two words together. The riddle he posed to Elissa gave me the key to that. Remember? He told her there are greater riches within the earth than in the sky, but whoever seeks them must not fear the sea."

"He could have meant that the treasure is buried somewhere." Gerlach frowned. "But why the reference to the sea?"

"Sicharbas was trying to tell me that its hiding place could be reached through the Cave of Melkarth. He intended that Elissa and I would use it together when we seized the throne."

They were rounding the southern point of the base upon which Tyre stood now. Gerlach looked at the waves dashing themselves upon the rocks and shook his head doubtfully. "Once or twice, when I was approaching port in calm weather, I thought I could distinguish what looked like a cave with its mouth open to the sea," he admitted. "But I have never been sure, and everyone knows the area is forbidden, under pain of displeasing the god."

"Do you remember when this belief was first voiced?"

"No."

"Did you hear it when you were a boy?" Straton insisted.

Gerlach combed his beard with his fingers. "I think now that I heard it first when I was a young man."

"Perhaps after Sicharbas became High Priest? If he wanted to keep his treasure secure, what better way could he take than to hide it where people would be afraid to go, for fear of displeasing the god."

"I cannot argue the point," Gerlach admitted. "But do you know that a Cave of Melkarth really exists?"

"I swam into it once when I was studying with Mochus," Straton explained. "I was so paralyzed with fright when I saw an image of the god inside the cave that I swam right out again, but I think I remember seeing a door cut into the wall of the cave." He spoke an order for a change of course, and the steersmen leaned upon the great bars controlling the sweeps that extended down into the water on either side of the stern.

"Keep a close watch, Amathus," he called to the pilot, who was perched above the brazen prow of the ship in his usual place. "I want to swing as near to shore as I can."

Amathus nodded, but did not remove his eyes from the furrow being opened by the prow, with its reinforcement of bronze plating forged in the furnaces of Tyre. Although the wind was now at their backs, Straton did not yet order the great sail raised, for he wanted to keep the gaoul moving as slowly as he could without the risk of being driven upon the rocks, against which the thunder of the surf could now plainly be heard.

"Half speed!" he called to the overseer pounding out the rhythm for the rowers upon the drum and, as the great ship slowed, he studied the rocky shore carefully.

"That dark spot among the rocks," he called to his father. "Could it be the open mouth of a cave?"

"I—I'm not sure."

"It's in the right place. Directly beneath the west wall of the temple."

"But how did Sicharbas find boatmen skilled enough to enter such a place?" Gerlach asked. "And how could he keep them from revealing the secret afterward?"

"I suspect that the cave was never intended to be anything but a possible route of escape, in case Sicharbas needed to remove his wealth because of an enemy attack or treachery in Tyre itself. I'll wager there is a passageway in the foundation of the temple that leads down to it."

"Surely you are not thinking of—"

"If we sail northward to Arvad, who would expect us to come back for it?"

"When will that be?"

"Tonight—before Mago starts looking for the treasure himself." Straton spoke quietly to the steersmen and, as the prow slowly swung toward the rocks, Amathus gave a quick glance of warning over his shoulder. The ship had moved nearer the western side of the craggy outcrop upon which Tyre was built, but was still a safe distance from the reef, when Straton suddenly saw what he had been searching for.

Located just at the water's edge in an area shunned by both fishermen, who each night cast their nets from the boats well beyond the rocks, and mariners, who gave the reef a wide berth when entering one of Tyre's two fine anchorages at the north and south end of the island, the opening of the cave was just as he remembered it. Low-roofed, it was largely hidden from view by the breakers that rushed upon the shore, but each time the waves receded the opening was revealed to sharp eyes that already knew where to look.

It was quite impossible to see inside the Cave of Melkarth, but Straton remembered it well from the one occasion years ago when, his heart beating excitedly, he had swum into it and found to his surprise that the water was shallow enough for him to wade out on a narrow beach lining the perimeter. He had spent only a few moments inside, however, for the corroded bronze image of Melkarth set into a niche in the farthest limits of the wall had been enough to send him plunging out again in terror. But he still recognized the narrow opening through the reef that gave access to a pool at the mouth of the cave, and a second glance confirmed his belief that a boat like those used by fishermen could be brought into that small area of quiet water, though probably not into the cave itself.

Eight:

*Last, to support her in so long
a way,
He shows her where his hidden
treasure lay.*

DARKNESS HAD FALLEN several hours earlier, when the gaoul silently approached the western side of The Rock that night. The torches of fishing boats could be seen here and there and from time to time the voices of fishermen working at the task of hauling in the night's catch floated across the water. On Straton's orders, a strict silence was maintained aboard the gaoul, as the fishing boat he had bought at a village on the shore north of Tyre that afternoon was drawn by its towing line into a position beside the larger vessel. Small but sturdy, the craft was like hundreds launched from the beaches each night to set huge circular nets and harvest the catch trapped within them.

Straton had carefully picked those who would go with him on the hazardous expedition to seek the vast treasure. Each man was a good swimmer, against the possibility that the fishing boat might be smashed upon the rocks as they sought to find the entrance to the Cave of Melkarth in the darkness. Half of them were also skilled bowmen, in case they were surprised and had to fight their way back to the cave and the boat. And all were volunteers, for he would not order anyone to join in a venture that might well bring death to all.

The lights had been doused aboard the gaoul lest they betray the size of the ship, but he did not hesitate to take torches in the smaller boat, since many similar lights burned from the fishing fleet scattered here and there at their nightly work. In addition, a pot of coals glowed in the bottom of the boat, to be used for igniting several unlit torches that were wrapped in cloth to keep them dry.

The buoyant craft rode the waves well as Straton handled the steering oar, guiding it toward the massive dark shadow of The Rock looming ahead of them in the faint moonlight. Though the breeze was not very strong, the waves still broke against the rocks ahead and the rowers were forced to backwater with the oars in order to keep the craft from being crushed against the reef. Turning the steering oar over to Ares, Straton moved to the bow and lifted a flaming torch to search the rocky face of the outcrop upon which stood the dark mass of the temple.

From time to time, he gave low-voiced commands which were relayed back to the rowers and to Ares.

A half-dozen axes, some with bronze blades, but a few of far more precious iron, were stored under the thwarts, along with swords enough to supply each man with a weapon, if it came to a fight. But Straton was fairly certain that Mago would not easily discover the hiding place of Sicharbas' fortune and was hopeful of securing it without causing an alarm.

On the boat's first trip across the face of the rock on which the temple stood, Straton was not able to make out the mouth of the cave in the darkness. But on the second trip, he identified the break in the reef before it, with the dark mouth of the cavern just beyond. A whispered command to the rowers directed the boat through the rocky breach, giving access to the reef-enclosed pool that he remembered just in front of the cave. It was close going, and at one point he was forced to reach out with his hand and fend the side of the boat off the rocks guarding the entrance. But once they were inside the small pool before the cave, the water was much quieter, though it rose and fell with each long swell breaking upon the shore.

Like the others, Straton had stripped to a loincloth before leaving the gaoul. Now he dropped over the side of the boat into the warm water, searching with his toes for the bottom as he held to the gunwale. Only when the prow was almost at the entrance to the cave itself did his feet touch sand, giving him enough footing so he could steady the craft and guide it forward. He had hoped to be able to take the boat into the cave, but the rise and fall of the water level, as the breakers dashed themselves upon the rocks, plus the low curve of the arch giving access to it, made that maneuver impossible.

Following a prearranged plan, the tallest among the party dropped overside to steady the boat while Straton ignited another torch from the first and waded into the mouth of the cave, holding it above his head. The water here was no deeper than his armpits and, once he was safely beyond the arch of the opening, the whole of the cavern was illuminated by the light of the flaming torch. Moments later, Ares' head broke the surface beside him. The little servant clutched an ax of iron in his hand as he scrambled for a footing on the bottom in the shallowest part of the cave.

At another time, Straton might have paused to study the cabalistic symbols chiseled into the walls of the cave. He'd only glimpsed them on his previous visit, but even then he had recognized them as being from another and earlier age, perhaps chiseled into the dripping rock by people who had occupied this area long before the coming of the Phoenicians. The bronze image of Melkarth revealed by the light of the torch was at the same spot where he remembered it being before. But it was covered with slime now and not nearly so intimidating as it had been to the boy who had waded into the cave on trembling limbs long ago.

"By the thunderbolts of Zeus!" Ares' voice broke the silence. "You Phoenicians have an ugly god."

"Hand me the ax," Straton told him. "Then go back and send the others inside."

"Do you see a door?"

Straton pointed the torch to a spot just to the left of the image of Melkarth. The heavy planking was so covered with marine growth that it was barely distinguishable from the rocky wall of the cave. But when he exchanged his torch for Ares' ax and stepped forward to draw the blade down across it, the slimy growth was stripped away, revealing the cedar planking behind it.

While Ares went outside to bring others into the cave, Straton located a crevice in the rocks and stuck the torch into it, leaving both hands free to use the ax. At the first blow, the door shuddered a little, but there was no sign of weakening. Obviously Sicharbas had made sure his riches were well guarded, and the door would virtually have to be chopped to pieces in order to gain access to the passage beyond it.

Tarquin and several of the most powerful among the mercenaries waded into the cave, each bearing an ax. Behind them Ares came in a second time, holding high another torch. Working in shifts with fresh hands ever ready to take the axes, they soon cut through both the planking and the bars that held the door, revealing a narrow passage beyond it, apparently hewn from the solid rock on which Tyre and the temple stood.

Straton was first into the passage, his pulse quickening with anticipation and excitement when he saw, at its farther end, a set of steps leading upward toward the foundation of the temple itself. At the top of the steps another door barred the way, but its timbers were much less formidable than those at the entrance to the passage from the cave. A few strokes of the heavy iron ax demolished this barrier and, when Straton stepped into the room beyond, he gave a gasp of astonishment.

Stacked row on row against the wall were chests of cedar. And when he crossed the room to lift the lid of one of them, he saw that it was filled with bars of silver, just as they had come from the smelter ovens, each with its weight in *deben*—the unit of measure used for precious metals—stamped upon it.

Ares had come into the room behind Straton and gave a low whistle of astonishment at what he saw.

"Truly, Master," he said. "This makes you the richest man in the world."

"Everything belongs to the Queen." Straton turned to Tarquin. "Start the men carrying the chests down and putting them into the boat," he ordered. "Someone inside the temple may have heard us chopping at the doors."

The chests were heavy but, with two men to each, they were able to carry them down the steps to the cave and wade through the shallow water to the boat outside. The first few chests Straton examined contained only silver. Others, however, were filled with plate and vessels of gold, much of it richly engraved, and several contained precious stones and jewelry. The common belief that Sicharbas was the richest man in Tyre had been well founded, Straton decided. And with all this wealth at her command, Elissa would indeed be the richest woman in the world, with no need for his protection any longer.

As soon as the boat was loaded, Straton left Tarquin to direct the men not required for rowing in the task of bringing down other chests and placing them on the sandy beach outside the cave, where they could be loaded easily for the second trip. Meanwhile he piloted the fishing boat to where the gaoul waited and supervised the transfer of the treasure to it.

On the second trip shoreward, he had no difficulty locating the mouth of the cave, for the torches burning inside it shone through the opening like a beacon at the water level. The loading went easily and soon the boat was alongside the gaoul once again, being unloaded for a second time. Altogether, three trips were required to transfer the treasure from its hiding place to the gaoul, necessitating hours of back-breaking toil.

Dawn was just breaking in the east over the green-clad Lebanon range and the chalk cliffs of the Ladder of Tyre, when the sail of the gaoul was finally hoisted and the great vessel began to plow its way northward toward Arvad. The fishing boat was under tow again, to be released farther up the coast and allowed to wash ashore, where the use to which it had been put would not be suspected.

Looking back at the white houses of Tyre taking form from the morning fog as it was dispelled by the sun, Straton could not help feeling a little sad at the thought that this view of the city might be the last he would ever have, a memory he would carry to whatever new world awaited him in the West. But his melancholy was tempered by the knowledge that he had kept his vow to the dying Sicharbas and, with the vast treasure beneath the deck of the gaoul in her possession, Elissa need never lack for anything.

As for himself, he was now free to seek his own happiness with the beautiful girl waiting for him in Arvad.

ii

Seen from the south as Straton's gaoul approached it a few days after the daring removal of the treasure, the city of Arvad was very impressive. Though smaller than Tyre, its houses rose to a greater height, giving it a striking silhouette against the northern sky. Of all the Phoenician cities, it alone was completely enclosed by a wall, built upon the extreme outer ledge of the reef surrounding the island. Constructed from heavy blocks of stone, the wall gave Arvad a formidable defense not possessed by the other Phoenician city-states.

For the past several hours they had seen signs of considerable activity on shore. Carts were moving along the roads, presumably carrying supplies for the Assyrian army, and fleets of small boats were scuttling back and forth along the coast. Even the fishing craft, which normally put out from the villages along the shore every night, appeared to have been pressed into service, for only occasionally did they see one of them drawn up on the shore, where normally there would have been hundreds.

Hagemon had not exaggerated at all, Straton decided, in reporting that Arvad was besieged. And, in order to get as close a view as possible of what was happening on the mainland shore, he ordered the great ship to be steered close to the beach. From the masthead he counted nearly a hundred galleys which had been taken over by the Assyrians, but what interested him most was the strange sort of activity going on in one section of the shore.

Swarms of men were at work there, building huge rafts of the cedar logs that were cut each winter in the forest of the Lebanon and dragged to the shore where they were allowed to dry. Rafted together, they were customarily floated to ports along the coast and even as far south as Egypt, so at any other time he would have thought nothing of their presence in the shallows next to the water's edge. Today, however, a much more sinister purpose was apparent, for beside each waited one of the great catapults which the Assyrians always used when besieging a city by land, battering down defending walls by hurling great stones against them.

"What do you make of it?" Gerlach asked when Straton climbed down from the masthead.

141

"Obviously, the Assyrians plan to float catapults near the walls and batter them down," Straton said. "Galleys will be used to push the rafts into place, I imagine, and for landing troops after the walls are breached."

"Then Arvad is lost?"

"Perhaps. But there may be a way to defeat them."

"Pray Melkarth you find it," Gerlach said fervently. "Else that flotilla and the Arvadite ships, too, will be launched against Tyre next and our homeland will be no more."

"Arvad is the keystone."

Straton was voicing a truth he had long since learned at the feet of Mochus. To the north and south of Arvad, the coastline in the immediate area was studded with villages into which the excess population of the island city had overflowed through the centuries, very much as Palaetyrus had spread out upon the mainland opposite Tyre. Beyond the towns lay a fairly flat strip of very fertile land known farther south in Israel and Judah as the *shephelah*. And behind this easily tilled zone to the eastward rose the mountain range of the Lebanon with the vast forests from which came the famous cedars, prized for ships, furniture and buildings even as far south as Egypt.

The whole Phoenician coast shared in this natural wealth, but what distinguished Arvad from the other cities was the presence nearby of a rift in the Lebanon range through which flowed the most important river in that region, affording by way of its narrow gorge a gateway to the Hollow of Syria. This great valley, lying between the Lebanon range nearer the shore and the Anti-Lebanon range farther to the east, was, historically, a broad highway leading southward to central Canaan and Israel and a favorite route for invaders from the north.

The Hollow of Syria had naturally been chosen by the Assyrians for their latest attempt to drive southward toward the lush green delta of the Nile. Following the route favored by invaders for thousands of years, they had flowed southward along the valley of the river Arantu until they reached an opening westward through which they could move to gobble up the rich prize of Phoenicia and gain a fleet to use in subduing other coastal cities. Fortunately for the Assyrians, and unfortunately for the Arvadites, they had chosen the natural route to the sea through the gorge near Arvad. And since further movement southward would be militarily dangerous with such a formidable sea-girt bastion and its fleet in the rear of their armies, the Assyrian generals had decided to reduce the Phoenician center first.

As the gaoul approached an anchorage in the northernmost of the two basins formed by stone jetties projecting from the east side of the island upon which Arvad stood, Straton's heart was gladdened by the sight of Diomedes' galley already moored to the quay. But he was also troubled by a feeling that something was wrong, though he could not decide what it was—until Ares pointed out a change in the situation of Arvad since their most recent visit.

"The spring, Master!" he exclaimed. "The Assyrians must have stolen the leather pipe from the spring."

The spring to which Ares referred was a bubbling fountain of fresh water bursting from the sea bottom perhaps a third of the distance between the city and the mainland shore. Like Tyre, Arvad obtained much of its water from cisterns, stone-lined tanks into which the rain falling upon the rooftops drained. But the rocky island on which the city stood was smaller in proportion to population than Tyre, so the Arvadites were not able to drain off enough water to supply their needs and would have had to bring water from the mainland, but for the spring.

Many years earlier the Arvadites had devised an ingenious mechanism whereby they were able to obtain an ample supply of water from the spring in a pure form. A bell or cone of lead large enough to cover the main "boil" of the spring had first been molded. To the top of it they had next fitted a pipe made by sewing together a large tube of leather and pitching the seams—in the same way the hulls of the ships were pitched—to make it reasonably watertight. When the funnel-shaped bell had been let down over the spring upon the bottom of the sea, the water surging upward through the tube of leather was easily gathered and carried to the city in a fleet of boats built for that purpose. But now the leather pipe seemed to have disappeared, probably seized by the enemy, Straton surmised, as a means of cutting off the vital water supply to the besieged city.

The gaoul had been forced to make a wide swing in order to reach the northern anchorage, where Diomedes' galley was moored. In doing so, they sailed almost directly over the bubbling geyser of fresh water, which not only rose above the surface but, where it came into contact with the salt water was marked by a difference in color. But though he could have dipped water from the spring as they passed over it, Straton could still see no sign of the leather pipe which, on his previous visits, had projected above the surface, with a group of the small waterboats always gathered around it while their containers were being filled.

Drawn by the great size of the gaoul, easily the largest craft ever to dock at Arvad, and hopeful that the coming of the vessel might represent the first installment of the help Hagemon had pleaded for in Tyre, a considerable crowd had gathered on the quay. Straton saw Diomedes and Hera among them and, while the ship was still being moored under the expert direction of Amathus and the skilled topmen, seized a line hanging from the boom of the great sail and swung out to drop to the quay.

Fending off the crowd who called questions to him from all sides, he pushed through toward where he had last seen his betrothed and Diomedes. But when he was still a few paces away, he was startled to see Hera turn and flee through the crowd without waiting to greet him. Unable to understand her strange behavior, he started to follow her, but a restraining hand on his shoulder held him back and he looked around to see Diomedes standing beside him.

"Have I suddenly become afflicted with a plague?" he demanded angrily of the Greek merchant.

"In my daughter's eyes, yes, I'm afraid," Diomedes said. "I keep telling her there must be another side to the story than the one she has heard, but you know how impulsive women are."

"Just what has she heard that would make her shun me?"

"Queen Elissa was very gracious and spent much time with my daughter on the voyage from Tyre. They talked of many things."

"Including me?"

"You were one of the main topics. The Queen recalled your growing up together—and your worship at the shrine of Astarte."

"Hera knew about that! Besides, it was five years ago and Elissa became the wife of Sicharbas a few months later."

"But now she is a widow and it was her husband's wish that she marry you after his death and that you should rule together in Tyre." Diomedes' expression was grave. "I am very fond of you, Straton. But was it fair to deceive He—"

"I deceived no one! Unless perhaps it was Sicharbas."

"Then the story is not true?"

"Sicharbas was dying from an incurable illness and knew he could not last many months more," Straton explained. "He tried to make me believe it was the wish of Melkarth and Astarte that I marry Elissa after his death. I am a descendant of Hiram the Great, and Sicharbas was convinced that I could be King of Tyre."

"You might still be."

"I wanted none of it," Straton said emphatically. "The idea came from Mochus, when he thought I was still in love with Dido—with Elissa. They persuaded my father to recall me from Tartessus, but when I saw her again it was almost as if I were looking at a stranger."

"Five years would dim your memory, I suppose."

"More was involved than the passage of time. The night before I saw Elissa again, I found a goddess in the Grove of Astarte. And as Ares says, 'How could even a queen hold the love of one smitten by a goddess?'"

"What answer did you give Sicharbas?"

"He was dying and troubled about Elissa's fate, when he could no longer protect her," Straton explained. "I discussed the whole thing with my father and we agreed that he should be left to die in peace. Then Hagemon arrived with the request for aid from King Aziru, and both Elissa and Sicharbas supported my move to help, so Mago and his followers had to act quickly."

"Then you think they only let the Queen live because of her husband's treasure?"

"I'm sure of it. Enough wealth is stored beneath the deck of my gaoul to set any man afire with greed."

"Where did you find it?"

"In the Cave of Melkarth, where Sicharbas said it was. When I turn it over to Elissa tomorrow, my responsibility for her will be ended. Besides, she took a vow before Sicharbas died."

Diomedes frowned. "What sort of a vow?"

"A pledge of celibacy to Astarte, hoping to obtain the favor of the goddess in healing Sicharbas. Didn't she tell Hera about it?"

"No."

"Did she tell Hera how she learned of her husband's plans for us to rule in Tyre?"

"The High Priest might have told her before he died."

"That could be," Straton admitted. "Sicharbas knew he could live only a few weeks longer, at most. But if Elissa has decided to keep her vow secret, how am I going to convince Hera that weeks ago I gave up a chance to become King of Tyre because of my love for her?"

Diomedes stroked his chin thoughtfully. "You are the first man my daughter ever loved," he said finally. "At the moment she feels hurt and betrayed, but if you explain to her just what has happened, I think she will believe you. Besides, Queen Elissa may acknowledge the vow if you remind her of it."

"Even though at the moment she appears to have put it out of her mind?"

"She may feel that Astarte failed her in letting her husband die," Diomedes suggested. "Or she may think returning to Tyre and ruling there is more important. Would the size of her fortune allow you to hire mercenaries and go back to seize the kingdom?"

"I am sure of it," Straton said. "But from the way the situation looks here at Arvad, the Assyrians will soon take care of that for us."

"I suspect you are right," Diomedes agreed. "Queen Elissa tells me you suggested that she build a new city on the Libyan shore and rule there."

"I did, before all this happened, but now may actually be an even better time. With the Assyrians moving westward in force, Tyre has probably passed the summit of its greatness. There is a spot near Utica where I am convinced that a resolute people could control all except the eastern shore of the Great Sea."

"No doubt Queen Elissa would expect you to rule there with her too."

Straton threw up his hands in a gesture of angry frustration. "I saved her life and risked my own to secure her husband's treasure for her! What more could anyone ask?"

"Elissa is a queen," Diomedes reminded him soberly. "Queens don't ask. They simply order their subjects to obey."

Nine:

*At once the brushing oars and brazen prow,
Dash up the sandy waves, and ope the depths below.*

THE KING OF ARVAD was a tall man with the sharply etched profile of a Phoenician aristocrat. His ancestors had settled there many centuries before, when they had been forced to flee from Sidon during the same period of political turmoil that had led to the settlement of Tyre nearer to the ancient Sidonian capital. Aziru was related to many of the great merchant families of Tyre and distantly to Elissa and Pygmalion, as well as to Straton himself. He listened gravely to Straton's account of the recent events in Tyre. When it was finished, he stood for a long moment, looking out of a window overlooking the harbor and at the activity on the shore before turning back to those in the room.

"Then we can expect no aid from Tyre." It was a statement rather than a question and required no answer.

"Just what is your situation here, my lord King?" Straton asked.

"You must have seen for yourself when you approached the harbor." Aziru smiled wryly. "I am sure many of my people wish there was room on your fine new gaoul for them."

"I noticed that the enemy is building rafts for moving catapults."

"They are almost finished, but the Assyrian general knows how little water we have left and is in no hurry. I may be forced to sue for peace without his even troubling himself to bring the siege machines against us."

"What happened to the leather pipe from the spring that bubbles up between Arvad and the mainland?"

"The Assyrians cut off that source of water almost from the beginning. By putting lines around the top of the pipe at night, two of their galleys were able to tear it loose from where it was connected to the leaden cone covering the spring on the ocean floor."

"What of the pipe itself?"

"The leather slipped out of their lines and floated ashore. We have kept it safe, but it does us no good here."

"Have you tried to attach it again to the leaden cone?"

"We tried—once. All our best divers were killed when the Assyrians

147

sent galleys to pick them off with arrows, as they rose from the bottom of the sea, and we were barely able to keep the leather pipe from falling into the enemy's hands. Fortunately, it rained about that time and our cisterns were filled, but the weather has been dry ever since and now they are almost empty again."

"How soon do you expect the main attack?"

"My spies among the fishermen on the mainland tell me the enemy is waiting for a fleet of heavy galleys to arrive from Tarsus, so it may be a week, perhaps longer. But we have water in our cisterns for only a few more days."

"And the prospect for resistance?"

"The walls of Arvad are thick and, even with the catapults, we might be able to fend off the first attack. But the Assyrians would only withdraw to the mainland and, with our cisterns empty, we would eventually be forced to capitulate."

"Unless their galleys were destroyed. I saw no large vessels on the shore."

"We withdrew all of our larger vessels to the island before the enemy reached the sea," Aziru said. "But they have scoured the coast for fishing boats and smaller galleys and now have more than enough to transport their troops and maneuver the rafts."

"Unless a much larger vessel smashed the enemy attack by crushing the frailer craft," Straton said crisply.

King Aziru had turned to the window again. He wheeled sharply now, and a sudden light of excitement and hope blazed in his eyes. "It would have to be the largest vessel ever to sail these seas," he said with almost a note of awe in his voice. "Have you the bronze sheathing—?"

"Perhaps not enough, but we could add more. Two hundred men can loose arrows and spears in volleys behind the protection of shields raised above our bulwark. And from the height of the deck, others can cast down flaming brands dipped in brimstone and pitch to set fire to the flimsy hulls of the galleys."

"It would be a great fight—but a daring gamble. I could not ask a friend to risk his life for a city that is not even his own."

"If Arvad falls, your fleet will be turned against Tyre by the enemy," Straton reminded him.

"Would you save a city that made all of you and its Queen fugitives?"

Gerlach gave the answer. "Kings will come and go, but as long as The Rock remains in the hands of our people, Tyre will be Queen of the Seas. Pygmalion and those who control him have won the first skirmish, but we refuse to believe they have also won the battle."

"Then I welcome you as allies," King Aziru said warmly. "I will issue a decree at once naming Straton of Tyre commander of our fleet and of the defenses of Arvad by sea. If your plan fails and any of the enemy reach the walls, I will lead my people in destroying them." Then his face grew sober. "But the Assyrian general will not attack until the galleys from Tarsus are added to his fleet and his strength is at its peak."

"Unless we draw his attack earlier, before he is entirely ready," Straton said.

"By what means?"

"Arvad needs water. Under the protection of my gaoul and your fleet, we should be able to attach the leather pipe once again to the leaden cuff over the spring. When the Assyrians see us laying in a supply of water against the siege, they will have to move against us, even if they are not ready. And that will be to their disadvantage."

"You forget that our best divers were killed," King Aziru reminded him.

"I can dive deeper than any man in Tyre," Straton said. "Have the leather pipe prepared and I will attach it for you tomorrow. Even if we are not able to draw the enemy out for a premature attack, your city will at least have a supply of water for the siege."

ii

The audience with King Aziru finished, Straton was eager to hurry back to the waterfront and find Hera. But he was foiled by Luli, who was waiting when he came out of the King's audience chamber.

"The Queen wishes to see you at once," the priest said peremptorily. "She sent me to bring you to her."

"Where is she?"

"Here in the palace. King Aziru has placed an apartment at her disposal."

Straton had no wish to see Elissa, until he could talk to Hera and find out to what degree the Queen had managed to convince his beloved that things were still as they had been five years ago. But he had no choice, with Elissa waiting for him to report what he had accomplished in the Cave of Melkarth. Besides, something about Luli's manner warned him to walk softly. In Tyre, Luli had been apprehensive, but now there was an air of assurance, almost of contempt, in his manner, as if he were well aware that his status had changed—for the better.

The apartment assigned to Elissa was adequate, though not as large as the quarters she had occupied in Tyre, since Arvad was considerably smaller and the houses had to be compact in order to use every possible amount of space on the rocky island. It was luxuriously furnished, however, and Straton could see no reason why Elissa should find fault with it. Nevertheless, he found her in a petulant mood.

"Why didn't you report directly to me?" she demanded imperiously.

"King Aziru sent Hagemon to the waterfront to bring me to the palace," he explained. "It would have done no good to give offense to one who has given us refuge."

"Refuge? When the Assyrians will take the city any day?"

"Arvad has a chance—if it is defended properly."

"If you see any chance of survival with Assyrian catapults waiting to batter down the walls, you are a fool!"

Straton shrugged and changed the subject, since there was obviously no point in arguing with her in her present mood. "I secured the treasure for you," he said.

Elissa wheeled to face him. "How much?"

"I did not count it. But you are now one of the richest women in the world—perhaps the richest."

Straton heard a quick intake of breath, but it came from Luli, not Elissa.

"I shall use the treasure to regain the throne of Tyre," she said. "With it we will hire ships and mercenaries to besiege The Rock, while those still loyal to me in the city rise up and destroy Mago and my brother."

"Would you see Pygmalion killed?"

"Why not, when he sought to kill me? How soon could we attack Tyre?"

"Not before Arvad is safe—if it seems best to attack at all."

"I will decide that," Elissa spluttered angrily. "Am I not still Tyre's Queen?"

Straton could have reminded her that, Queen or not, she had no domain at present, but he could see that nothing was to be gained in arguing with her. Somewhere between Tyre and Arvad, Elissa's naturally imperious will, subdued briefly by the assassination of Sicharbas and her own close brush with death, had been fired anew. Nor did he need to look far for the reason.

Her vow of celibacy quickly forgotten, Elissa had obviously refused to believe any man could choose another woman over her and had embarked upon a campaign to humble him in order to prove her point to all. Diomedes, he realized now, had sought to forewarn him concerning all this. But with little experience in the changing wills of women, Straton had not been able to anticipate Elissa's determination to bring him publicly to heel.

"I realize fully how much I am in your debt, Straton." Suddenly gracious now, in a complete change of mood, she moved to a cushioned sofa and, indicating that he was to sit beside her, sent Luli to order wine brought for all of them. "But when I remember that Pygmalion tried to have me killed and assassinated my husband, you can hardly expect me not to punish him."

"By taking your husband's treasure out of Tyre you have already won over all your enemies."

"How could I win—and lose my throne? What is it worth to be Queen —with no country to rule?"

"You are rich enough to build a new Tyre. I described the place to you once—on a hilltop not far from Utica."

"It would be no more than Pygmalion deserves, if I did build a city to rival his." Her eyes took fire at the thought. "But I would rather see him deposed."

"Just now you wanted him destroyed."

Elissa smiled as she took the glass of wine handed her by a servant. Luli, Straton observed, also took a glass from the tray and picked a cushioned seat not far away, leaving Straton to serve himself.

"I am but a woman and subject to a woman's whims," Elissa said cajolingly. "Who should know that better than you, Straton? After all, you knew me well when I was still only a carefree princess called Dido."

"I am sure you will know those days again." Realizing that she was expecting from him some sort of protestation of affection—or at least of unquestioning support—and conscious that he must walk a narrow line, Straton was careful to keep his tone noncommittal.

"No. I am a woman now and a queen—with responsibilities to my people. How soon do you really think we can return to Tyre?"

"Tyre must wait—at least until the fate of Arvad is decided," he told her. "If this city falls, so will Tyre, no matter who rules there."

"But you have seen the Assyrian host encamped on the shore. How can one small kingdom on a rock not much larger than the temple and the grove at home hope to stand against them?"

"King Aziru and I believe there is a way to save Arvad."

"And if you fail?"

"I will take all the people I can crowd aboard my new gaoul and set sail for the Libyan shore."

"What of my treasure? Will you risk it in a hopeless battle against the enemy and perhaps have them capture it?"

"I intend to use the gaoul in battle; without it we cannot hope to succeed in the plan we have devised. But your treasure can be transferred to another ship." He had a sudden inspiration. "Why not put it into Diomedes' galley? Being a Greek, he is under no obligation to fight the Assyrians. And, if it appears that Arvad is going to fall, he will take you to Cyprus or to one of our ports on the island of Crete. There you can charter a ship for the journey to Libya."

"And if I do not choose to follow your plan?" Elissa's eyes had grown stony while he was speaking.

"I have promised King Aziru that I would help him and he has made me commander of Arvad's defenses by sea. I have no choice except to stay here and fight."

"You had no right to make such a promise without my consent!" Her hand shot out and, since he was not expecting the blow, he had no time to dodge. The emerald ring on her finger raked him across the side of his face, bringing blood.

"Go!" she commanded in a choked voice. "Leave my presence, until I send for you again!"

iii

"You are wounded!" Hera cried at the sight of the blood on Straton's face when he stepped aboard the galley. He had made no attempt to wipe it off since leaving the palace, counting on her instinct as a healer to bridge, for the moment at least, the gap that Elissa had managed to drive between them on the journey from Tyre.

"It is nothing. Only a scratch."

"Let me look at it." She guided him into the small deckhouse, where she and her father lived when on board, and he managed to kick the door shut when they were inside. "Sit here on this stool."

"Not until you kiss me." He reached out for her, but she darted away.

"Have you no shame?" she cried indignantly. "I can never kiss you again."

"Why?" he demanded as she bustled about, opening the doors of cabinets and putting a piece of cloth, a small silver bowl of water, and one of her many jars of healing ointments on the table where Diomedes' sailing directions for the voyage from Tyre to Arvad were still spread out. Being a sailor, Straton stole a look at them, but they were written in Greek, which he did not read, so he learned nothing.

"You know why." She began to bathe the scratch on his temple with the damp cloth, causing it to smart for the first time. In his anger at Elissa and Luli, he hadn't noticed the pain before.

"You loved me when you left Tyre. Why not now?"

"I am no wanton—to come between a man and the woman he has promised to marry."

"I haven't promised to marry anybody but you. And nothing Elissa has told you is going to change that."

"I don't blame you for loving her." He did not miss the hurt note in her voice, or the way her fingers suddenly pressed hard against his temple, where she was applying a fragrant ointment with the scent of balsam. "She is very beautiful—and a queen."

"You are even more beautiful." In his irritation at Elissa, and at Hera for listening, he did not realize that he was almost shouting. "When I first saw you I thought you were a goddess."

She put her fingers to his lips, but drew them away quickly when he kissed them. "Shh! Do you want all of Arvad to hear?"

"I want even the Assyrians to hear, if it will convince you there is nothing between Elissa and me. I promised Sicharbas when he was dying to see that she was safe. She is here and I brought the treasure to her, so that promise has been fulfilled. I'm free now to marry you."

"Queen Elissa explained the whole thing to me," Hera said.

"Then she sold you a crippled slave!"

"Do you deny that her husband wanted you to marry her as soon as he died—and put her on the throne of Tyre?"

"That was Mochus' plan. I never agreed to it."

"But Sicharbas died, thinking you had."

"I was only trying to keep from bringing sorrow to a dying man."

"You are still obligated."

Straton threw up his hands. "Do you know where I got this wound on my face? Elissa gave it to me, because I told her I am going to help defend Arvad. I've had enough trouble from her—without having you suddenly tell me you don't love me anymore."

"I didn't say that."

"Then you do love me?"

She straightened her shoulders proudly. "I love you enough to give you up for the good of Tyre." But her lips trembled a little as she spoke and, when he saw how much it cost her to speak the words, all of his exasperation with her went out of him.

"Listen to me, Hera," he said. "Whatever was between Elissa and me five years ago is over. I told you that in Tyre, and I tell you again now. She tried to poison you against me on the way here, because she wants me to put her upon the throne of Tyre and depose her brother."

"Wouldn't that be best for Tyre?"

"Who can say? But if I took Pygmalion's throne, I would be just as guilty as Mago was in killing Sicharbas to get his treasure."

"What are you going to do?"

"I can help Tyre most by doing what I can to keep the Assyrians from taking Arvad. King Aziru has put me in command of the city's defenses by sea."

"Does Queen Elissa know this?"

"I told her. That's what got me this cut on my face. She didn't think I should have accepted without consulting her."

"I will not stand between you and the welfare of the people of Tyre who trust you," Hera said, but he could already see that she was weakening in her resolve to give him up.

"Talk to Ares," he suggested. "He will tell you that the little people of Tyre have no liking for the throne's being seized by anyone. They say that if one does it, another will, and there would be no such thing as a stable government anymore. Besides, Elissa cannot marry again. Even before her husband was killed, she had already sworn a vow to give up her rights to the throne and become celibate."

"Why would she do that?"

"In the hope of gaining Astarte's favor to heal Sicharbas."

"But she said nothing to me of any such vow."

"Luli received the vow as High Priest of Astarte—or so he said." Straton had a sudden thought. "I wonder if he was lying."

"Why would he do that?"

"At the time he still thought I wished to marry Elissa and seize the throne. Besides, I'm sure he was in league with Mago and the others, at least for a while. But when they seized Elissa, he realized that they had played him false."

"How can you find out the truth?"

"I will talk to Elissa about it again after we settle this matter with the Assyrians."

"Do you really think you have a chance to win?" she asked.

"A chance—if things work out as I have planned them." He told her in detail of his plan to draw an Assyrian attack before the reinforcement from Tarsus arrived and while the great rafts were not yet completely finished.

"You are risking much—for a city not your own," she said doubtfully. "Why?"

"Perhaps because I think people should be left to live in peace, as long as they don't harm others. We Phoenicians are not interested in conquest, but in carrying knowledge and the products of our skill to less advanced people wherever we trade. After all, look what we have done for writing by spreading the use of the alphabet abroad."

"Father says you did the whole world a service there," she agreed.

"Even what might seem so useless a thing as the sale of purple cloth in garments spreads knowledge, for those who buy it also buy other

154

things. My main purpose in helping King Aziru is a selfish one, though. If the threat is removed from Tyre this year, it may not come again for some time. Then if we go back with news that the siege of Arvad has been broken up, the people will support the Royal Council when it demands that Pygmalion get rid of traitors who would have sold us as slaves to the enemy."

"What about Queen Elissa?"

"She can have her choice of remaining in Tyre—with the rank of a queen. Or of establishing a new colony on the Libyan shore and ruling it herself."

"She will expect you to be beside her."

"Not after the talk we had today. I discharged any obligation I had to Sicharbas as a friend when I saved both her and his treasure. The important thing now is that Tyre may be saved and we can be married as we planned."

"But if I married you and caused you to become an outcast in your own land, I would always feel that I had betrayed you," she said. "I want nothing to mar our life together."

"Nothing will," he assured her. "I promise it."

"Everybody is talking about your plan to attach the leather pipe to the leaden cone over the spring," she said. "When do you expect to do that?"

"Tomorrow—while the weather is still quiet. With luck, we will fill the cisterns of Arvad in the space of a day and a night and build a fire under the leaders of the Assyrian force at the same time."

iv

Considerable preparation was required for tomorrow's attempt to restore the water supply of Arvad. Busy as he was, however, Straton could hardly have missed the sight of a line of porters carrying the chests containing Sicharbas' treasure from his own gaoul to Diomedes' galley, nor feeling a sense of relief that he was no longer responsible for it.

The rents in the leather flange at the lower end of the pipe, made when Assyrian galleys had torn it loose from its attachments to the leaden cone over the spring, had long since been repaired. The method of attaching leather to lead consisted of rawhide lashings at each of the four quarters of the flange, so arranged that they could be quickly pushed through corresponding openings on the top of the leaden cone and tied into place.

Once the column of water started flowing up the pipe—King Aziru had assured Straton from experience gained in the previous attempt, when his divers had been killed—its very force would act almost like a rod, supporting the leather tube and helping to guide it to its target on the ocean bottom. As an added precaution, Straton had ordered four stones of as nearly equal size as possible lashed to the bottom end of the tube, insuring that it could be carried down rapidly, along with the diver—himself—whose task it would be to guide the tube into place and secure the rawhide lashings to the rings on the leaden cone.

Fortunately, the depth of the water had been measured long ago when the tube had first been put in place. And when Straton examined it as it was laid out on the quay the night before, ready to be loaded on the deck of his gaoul, he found that the length of the tube was roughly the same as the depth of the water in Mochus' cove and within his diving range.

In order to catch the enemy as nearly as possible by surprise, Straton had decided to make the crucial dive just after dawn. Much of the night before was spent in getting the great gaoul ready, taking on as many of King Aziru's bowmen, in addition to his own, as could crowd upon the deck without interfering with the activities going on there in connection with lowering the leather tube.

The bulwark of shields was erected on the sides of the gaoul so as to afford a protection to the men who would fight there if it came to an actual battle. And the four stones were attached to the bottom of the tube by separate lashings so as not to interfere with his securing the leather flange to the leaden cone over the spring, but at the same time overcome the upward-buoying effect of the current of water rising from it. This latter effect, Straton surmised, would probably give them their greatest difficulty, since the presence of such a swift stream moving upward from the bottom materially affected the water for some distance around it.

The long spar supporting the upper edge of the great sail also played an important part in Straton's plan. Extending well beyond the side of the ship, it allowed the tube to be lowered into the water by means of lines running across its end. And as an added precaution, he had rigged a second spar or gaff extending down at an angle from the outer end of the main spar to the foot of the mast in order to serve as an additional support.

The task of guarding the entire operation from attack by the enemy had been assigned to six of King Aziru's largest vessels. And a line of shields had been attached to the bulwarks of each to form a floating fortress from which Arvadite bowmen could shoot down upon any galleys the Assyrians might send against them.

It was well past midnight before the preparations were complete and Straton was able to get only a few hours of sleep before it was time for the gaoul to move into place and drop heavy anchors fore and aft to hold it directly beside the column of fresh water gushing up from the ocean floor below. The ships that were to protect the gaoul during the daring maneuver followed, as the small armada was moved out of its anchorage in the northern harbor of Arvad, the decks of each lined with rows of bowmen and an adequate supply of arrows. Behind them came the waterboats, ready to fill their tanks as soon as the pipe was put into place. All sorts of small craft with every large container available had also been pressed into service as water carriers, ready to join the procession of boats as soon as the signal came from Straton's gaoul.

Straton left the gaoul only once, when Ares called him for a conference ashore just before leaving the quay. At the insistence of Diomedes, he signed an acknowledgment of the list of treasure chests which had been transferred from the gaoul to Diomedes' galley and placed in the care of Luli as Queen Elissa's steward. Busy with the task of bringing the gaoul to the spot chosen for an anchorage beside the spring and preparing to lower the great leather tube from the spar as soon as the sun rose, Straton had no time to seek out Hera and ask for her prayers, but he was a little disappointed that she had not interrupted her morning's sleep to come to the gaoul before it left the quay and wish him well.

Hardly had the gaoul moved into place beside the spring when they detected a flurry of activity ashore. Shortly, several galleys put out, obviously with the intention of assaying the situation. But they came no closer when they saw the ships of King Aziru accompanying Straton's huge vessel.

With the leather tube suspended from the end of the long spar and its stone anchors already in place waiting to carry it to the bottom, Straton stripped to a loincloth and stood upon the rail, breathing deeply as he had learned to do long ago in preparation for a deep dive. He was looking out to sea and so did not understand the reason for the sudden murmur of astonishment that ran through the ship—until he turned and saw Hera emerging from the deckhouse.

Her hair was plaited in a tight braid and secured to her head with a ribbon. She was barefooted and wore a robe of heavy linen, girt about the waist with a cord.

"What are you doing here?" he demanded, stepping down from the rail as she came up to it. "We may be attacked by the Assyrians at any moment."

"I am not afraid."

"It was still foolish of you to come."

"You want to get the tube in place, don't you?"

"Of course."

"Ares tells me King Aziru's divers were killed when they tried it once before."

"So he was the one who smuggled you aboard! When did he manage it?"

"While you were talking to Father on the quay—about the treasure chests. Both Ares and I love you enough not to want you to risk your life unnecessarily."

"This is man's work," he protested. "There is liable to be fighting."

"There was fighting in the temple of Melkarth and Astarte at Tyre," she said simply. "I used a bow to help then, and it is even more fitting that I should help now. You know how skilled I am at diving."

"No one else here can equal you," he admitted.

"Then why can't I help you?"

Straton could marshal no real argument, since there was no denying that a second diver would materially aid in the difficult task he had undertaken.

"All right," he told her. "Get ready as quickly as you can!"

"I *am* ready." She loosened the cord binding the robe around her waist and, stepping out of it, handed it to Ares. As when Straton had found her diving in Mochus' cove, her only garment was the single woven loincloth worn by Greek divers, and he heard a sudden murmur of appreciation for her almost unadorned beauty from the men on deck. Then she stepped upon the railing and dived overside, emerging seconds later beside the main column of water surging to the surface from the spring.

Straton knew it was unreasonable of him to be angry because over a hundred men had seen her almost naked, since Minoan court dress on Crete, as well as the costume of Greek women there even now, often left the breasts bare. But he loved her enough, even when exasperated with her as he was now, to be jealous of men who admired her.

Hera had seized a line hanging over the side of the ship and was supporting herself in the water while she gulped in great breaths of air that would enable her to stay down for the longest possible time. Straton, too, dived from the rail and came up beside her, reaching out to take hold of the line that supported her.

"Did you have to strip naked for everybody?" he demanded.

"Don't you want other men to admire me?" Her eyes twinkled mischievously. "Or would you rather I looked like a crone?"

"Of course not. It's just that—"

"You're jealous?"

"Well—yes I am."

Her eyes suddenly softened. "What difference does it make—when I am yours alone?"

"Then you have put aside all that foolishness about my becoming King of Tyre?"

"Unless you want it?"

"I want nothing except to marry you and sail for the Isles of Purple. Now listen closely. If we tried to dive to the bottom by swimming, we would never reach it. You can feel the force of the spring now and it is large enough to cover an area surrounding the main column itself."

She nodded to show her understanding. "Then you're going down with a leather tube and the stones?"

"Yes. The weight of the stones should carry us and the tube to the bottom without effort. Our job is to try and keep the tube centered over the column of water as it goes down and to lash the cuff at the bottom to rings on the leaden cup that covers the spring itself."

"Pray Juno the cone wasn't dragged from over the spring when the Assyrians tore the cuff loose," she said, voicing a fear that had been in his own mind ever since he had proposed the plan.

"King Aziru tells me the father of one of the divers, who was killed by the enemy, remembered his grandfather describing the cuff to him once. He helped to put it into place a long time ago and he said it was very heavy, so it probably wasn't moved when the tube was torn off."

"Suppose it was?"

"We won't worry about that until we find out what is on the bottom of the sea. If anything happens, try to get to the tube and the force of the water will bring you up."

"Are you going to leave the stones attached to the cuff after it is secured?"

"Yes. They will help hold it in place. There are additional lashings for securing the cone to the cuff."

"I understand." Before he realized her intention, she had swung around the line and her body touched his, as she put an arm around him beneath the surface and quickly kissed him upon the lips. "Juno protect you, my darling," she whispered before releasing the line to swim over to where the lower end of the tube was poised just above the bubbling column of the spring.

"We are ready to lower the tube," Amathus called from the deck.

Straton swam to a position directly opposite Hera on the other side of the leather flange, with his arm thrust through a loop in the lashings, as she had already done, in order to maintain his hold when the descent began.

"Give us a few breaths," he told the pilot. "When I signal, let it sink as rapidly as it will."

Straton breathed in deeply a few times, as did Hera. When she nodded, he raised his right hand and brought it down in the agreed-upon signal, and the stones plummeted downward through the water, dragging the tube and the two divers with it.

The descent was more rapid than Straton had expected it to be and the strain upon his left arm and hand from the loop in the leather lashings was considerable. The upward current, too, buffeted his body mercilessly, alternately smashing him against the relatively rigid leather and then swinging his body away. Trying desperately to keep from striking the tube with enough force to deflect it from its course, he had little chance to look at Hera, beyond an occasional glance that told him she was being knocked about fully as much as he was. But it was all over in a matter of seconds when the lower end of the tube slammed home over the funnel-like opening at the top of the black leaden cone that covered the "boil" of the spring on the floor of the sea.

Propelled by the momentum of the force that had carried them to the bottom so rapidly, Straton's body continued to shoot downward, even after the tube had stopped. He would have been smashed against the unyielding surface of the cone itself if the loop of rawhide around his wrist had not caught him up with a jerk that almost dislocated his arm. A quick glance at Hera across the tube from him told him she was at least no worse off than he, but the force of the water against their bodies made it difficult for them to work on the lashings. Even worse, the flange had not come down squarely upon the cone.

Working desperately, Straton set his feet against the leaden surface and strained to shift the flange into a more secure position over the opening. Hera, too, caught the import of what he was trying to do and he saw her straining with him, though the effort, coupled with that of staying down and the pressure to breathe building up in his chest, made him dizzy. For an instant, nothing happened, then suddenly the cuff shifted and he was able to rotate it into a position where the rawhide lashings rested directly over the rings set into the lead. The task of securing the lashings was still far from easy, however, because the force of the water spurting from the sandy bottom outside the main "boil" of the spring tended to thrust them back to the surface.

Straton had rehearsed in his mind a dozen times just how he would lash the rawhide thongs to the rings on the leaden cone. The actual operation, however, had to be carried out largely with his eyes closed, because the pressure of the subterranean stream bursting from the floor of the ocean filled the water with grains of sand that tended to get beneath his eyelids and cause intense discomfort.

It took only a moment to complete the first lashing and move on to the second. But as he finished the last knot, he looked across to Hera and saw that, not having practiced upon the knots as he had, it would be quite impossible for her to secure the second of her two rawhide thongs before she would have to go back to the surface. Seizing the strand from her grasp with his left hand, he gave her a shove upward with his right, and saw her disappear from his range of vision as he worked desperately to secure the final knot.

The pressure upon his chest was so great now that he was barely able to keep from expelling the air which would keep him buoyant and send him shooting to the surface. When the final knot was tied, he released hold of the rawhide and felt the upsurging current of water seize him. Moments later he was at the surface, intensely relieved to see Hera clinging to a line that had been thrown her from the gaoul.

"I was going back after you," she said, as his arm went around her unashamedly, even though the whole crew of the gaoul was watching.

"The cuff is secure," he gasped and, with Hera beside him, swam over to where the upper end of the leather pipe was spouting a stream of water well above the surface. Holding to the tube, they tasted the water gushing down upon their heads but found no tinge of salt.

"You can fill your containers," he called to the waterboats waiting in the protection of the gaoul as eager hands reached down to lift him and Hera to the deck. There Ares wrapped her in the robe she'd dropped before diving from the deck, while King Aziru himself poured wine and gave it to them.

"Our cisterns will soon be filled," he said happily, pointing to a waterboat that was maneuvering into place beside the fountain of fresh water. "You have saved us from capitulation."

"What about the Assyrians?" Straton asked, as Ares rubbed his body dry with a towel. With so many people crowding the deck of the gaoul, it was almost impossible to see the enemy shore.

"You were right about the course they would take," King Aziru said. "Two of their galleys put out from shore, when you moved into place here, but they turned back when they saw other ships join you."

"Your spies are watching them closely, I hope."

"We will know of any change in the Assyrian camp within a few hours of its happening," King Aziru assured him.

"The bait has been cast, then. All we need now is the strength to bring in the catch."

Ten:

AT STRATON'S SUGGESTION, King Aziru had instructed his spies on shore to spread the rumor that the great gaoul was only the advance guard of a large fleet from Tyre, sent to help her sister city to the north. With a plentiful supply of water now flowing from the great spring to hearten the inhabitants of Arvad, the enemy saw nothing to be gained by delay, and much to be lost, if help did arrive from the south. Nobody was surprised, therefore, when watchers posted upon the ramparts of Arvad noted considerable activity on shore, proving that the enemy commander had reasoned exactly as Straton had hoped he would and decided to launch his attack without waiting for the galleys said to be on the way from Tarsus.

Ashore, preparations were going on apace under Straton's direction. Brackets were being fitted to the bulwarks of King Aziru's largest ships, so a row of shields could be erected there, turning them into floating citadels from which the Arvadite bowmen could shoot down upon the decks of the Assyrian galleys. The sails of the Arvadite vessels were removed to lessen the danger of fire, but Straton's plan of battle required keeping the sail upon his own ship. On his orders, however, workers swung down over the already bronze-sheathed prow of the great vessel, applying additional plates of metal as a further protection against the rams of enemy galleys, which would certainly be directed against it in the traditional plan of battle at sea.

The people of Arvad were busy meanwhile, making arrows and spears and preparing fire arrows by wrapping bits of cloth around the ends of the shafts and tying them into place. Dipped in a mixture of boiling pitch and brimstone and set afire, they made torches that were quite difficult to douse. Additional quantities of the pitch and brimstone mixture were also prepared, ready to be heated in great pots on the decks of the fighting ships and poured down upon the slaves chained to the rowers' benches of the enemy galleys.

While inspecting these preparations two days after the pipe had been re-attached to the leaden cone over the great spring, Straton received a message from Queen Elissa demanding that he present himself before her at once. He had been avoiding her ever since the quarrel following his arrival, but he had been half-expecting this summons and did not attempt to evade it.

He found her in the apartment King Aziru had assigned to her, with Luli—as he had expected—in attendance. Today, Elissa chose to be gracious, but he suspected that the warmth of her welcome was designed to influence him to agree with some special wish for which she had summoned him. She had dressed for the role in royal robes lent her by Queen Tabnith of Arvad and wore a small coronet upon her elaborately coiffed hair.

"You have made yourself a hero, Straton," she greeted him warmly. "All Arvad is singing your praise."

"I have dived as deeply many times in the cove off Mochus' garden."

"But never to so important a purpose as saving a whole city from dying of thirst."

"We still have a battle to fight," he reminded her. "And, against superior odds."

"You will lead the fleet to victory. Obviously, the gods look on you with great favor."

"We should know that, too, before long." Straton waited for her to reveal the purpose for which she had sent for him.

"I talked yesterday to Queen Tabnith," Elissa said. "She promised to speak to her husband about sending a fleet to Tyre with us—after you drive back the Assyrians."

As in a game of senit, the divining sticks had been cast from the cup and the first piece moved on the board. Straton knew he was expected to make the next cast, but he, too, was an expert at playing the favored Egyptian game and refused to accept the challenge.

"It would be a mistake to consider the enemy beaten yet," he said. "Both King Aziru and I know that very well."

He saw her teeth press into her lip, holding back an angry retort, but when she spoke, her tone was still controlled. "How soon can we return to Tyre, then?"

"We barely escaped with our lives a few days ago," he reminded her. "Mago is still alive and, with the additional mercenaries Hamil hired for him among the Amorites, he probably still controls the city."

"He could not stand against an Arvadite fleet led by your great ship."

"I imagine King Aziru would hesitate to attack a sister Phoenician city when there has been no provocation."

163

"The King will do whatever you ask of him," she said. "How can he deny you anything, after you save his city from destruction and his people from slavery?"

She had thought the whole thing out carefully, he saw. Nor could he find much to disagree with in her conclusions, if his battle plan resulted in an Assyrian defeat. King Aziru would hardly refuse to place the Arvadite fleet at his disposal. In addition, word could be sent to the Royal Council in Tyre by way of the fishermen in the coastal villages, who formed a very effective network of spies, assuring them that the invading fleet sought only to remove the control of Mago over the city and place Elissa on the throne. And since the merchant members of the council would be only too pleased for that to happen, he doubted that a single ship would be launched against them.

"What about Pygmalion?" he asked. "Would you let him remain as King of Tyre?"

"After he murdered my husband and tried to kill me?" she cried. "Pygmalion forfeited any right to the throne when he did not lift his hand to stop Mago and Hamil."

"What will be his fate, then?"

"The Royal Council can send him wherever they wish," she said with a shrug. "I never want to see him again."

"And the throne?"

"Naturally, I shall continue to be Queen of Tyre." Her voice softened and she extended her hands to him in a gesture of warmth. "But with you as my consort."

"Consort!"

"I don't wonder that you are startled," Elissa told him. "We will not announce it until you return from the Isles of Purple with a shipload of The Dragon's Blood. Then Tyre can deny you nothing and, with you controlling the Fleet and the Army, we have no fear that anyone could unseat us."

"Haven't you forgotten your vow?" he asked.

"Vow?" Her bewilderment appeared to be sincere. "What do you mean?"

"The vow of celibacy you swore while Sicharbas was still alive, in the hope that Astarte would give him back his life in return."

"I swore no such vow." Elissa flushed angrily. "What sort of a trumped-up story is this?"

"Perhaps you should ask Luli."

"What is this?" Elissa wheeled upon the priest, who had been standing back of her. "Did you say I had made any such vow, Luli?"

"The noble Straton is mistaken." Luli's voice did not falter in the lie. "Perhaps he seeks a way to escape his promise to your husband—because of his passion for the Greek girl."

"The daughter of Diomedes?" It was Elissa's turn to be surprised.

"It is common knowledge that the noble Straton gave her the usual ransom in the name of Astarte on the night he arrived in Tyre from the West."

"Is this true?" Elissa wheeled upon Straton, her eyes hot with anger.

"I paid the ransom—yes."

Elissa gained control of herself with an effort. "Where you have satisfied your desires in the past is of no concern to me," she said with lofty disdain. "Naturally, when you are Prince Consort of Tyre you will give up the girl—unless you keep her as a concubine."

"Hera is descended from the Minoan kings of Crete, who ruled there when your family and mine were still caravan drivers," Straton said icily. "She is named for the Queen of the Gods."

"Greek gods cannot be compared to Baal and Astarte," Elissa said with a shrug. "Luli assures me they favor my return to Tyre as Queen."

"Just yesterday I sacrificed a sheep and examined the liver," the priest agreed. "The omens said—"

"Are these the same omens that told you to arrange the ceremony of blessing my ship so Mago and Hamil could kill Sicharbas when he was outside the temple for the first time in months?" Straton demanded hotly. "Or are they the ones that told you to make up the lie that Queen Elissa had made a vow of celibacy."

"Cease!" Elissa commanded. "Luli is High Priest of Baal and Astarte and has my full confidence. Instead of accusing him of lies, Straton, you should be thankful that he has read the omens as they were—letting you become Prince Consort of Tyre."

But Straton had had his fill: of Elissa's condescension in naming him consort; of Luli's lies concerning the vow; and, most important, of Elissa's slurring remark about Hera.

"I swore to Sicharbas that I would guard you," he told her. "If we are not all killed by the Assyrians and if it is still your wish and the wish of the Royal Council of Tyre that you rule as Queen, I shall put you on the throne. But I will be nobody's consort, and what you do about the throne of Tyre is for you and the Royal Council to decide. I want no part of it."

He turned and stormed toward the door, without asking Elissa's leave. But even in his haste, he did not miss the look of gloating triumph in Luli's eyes. Angry as he was, Straton did not think of the reason for the priest's glee, until Ares gave it to him as they were walking from the palace to the waterfront. Giving vent to his anger with words, he had told Ares of the interview with Elissa and her offer to make him consort. When he came to the end of the account, the little servant nodded sagely.

"You could not hope to outthink the High Priest Luli, Master," he said. "After all, a priest's life is all deception. Else how could they keep the people convinced that a statue of bronze is really a god?"

"Give me your thoughts on religion later, if you please."

"Luli's powers of deception are worthy of a Greek," Ares continued, as if he had not spoken. "Just look at what he has accomplished: First, he convinced you that Queen Elissa had sworn the vow of celibacy, so he would not have to worry about your marrying her and becoming king. And now, by talking her into offering to make you Prince Consort —knowing you would refuse—he has made sure that she will never give you another chance." He wagged his head. "I am disappointed in you, Master. You played right into his hands, and now you are not only committed to placing her on the throne of Tyre, but Luli will be High Priest of the richest temple in all of Phoenicia—with the field clear for him to become consort later on."

As much as he hated admitting it, Straton was sure Ares was right, but the certainty did nothing to relieve his own frustration.

"Since you are so clever, what would you have done in my place?" he demanded.

"Become Prince Consort, of course," Ares said with a shrug. "After all, you would not be buying a piece of land you had not inspected already. And even if, after the wedding, the beauteous Dido only admitted you to the royal bedchamber when her will decreed, you would not lack beauties to keep you warm on cold nights. In fact, a few might even be left over from King Pygmalion's seraglio."

"Stop talking foolishness. You know I love another."

"It is always good for a man to remember an old love for a woman he did not possess," Ares said philosophically. "Then in his old age he can dream of what it would have been like. Believe me, Master, such an aphrodisiac is even better than the powdered horn of the unicorn— and much less expensive."

ii

King Aziru was waiting for Straton amidst the feverish activity upon the waterfront. "The Assyrians will launch their invasion tomorrow at dawn," he said. "A spy from the mainland just brought me word."

"Are you certain of your source?"

"As I am of myself," Aziru assured him. "I have been watching the shore from the highest rampart for the past hour and everything I saw bears out the spy's report. They have already started towing the rafts away from the beach to make room for the galleys that will push them, once the real attack begins."

"Then, if you will order the ship commanders to gather here, we will go over their instructions for the last time before the battle."

"You command them," King Aziru told him. "It is time they got accustomed to obeying your orders."

A trumpeter was dispatched at once to the masthead of Straton's gaoul to sound a call for the masters of all the ships that would take part in the defense of Arvad, along with the commanders of the sea-borne troops. When he stood upon the roof of the afterhouse a half hour later and looked down upon them, he saw that they covered almost the whole deck of his ship, a grim-faced group of men, weather-beaten from sea and sun, the kind who inspired confidence in a commander.

"We have lured the enemy into attacking before he is entirely ready," he informed his listeners. "But that must not make us overconfident, and I offer anyone among you whose heart is not in the fight the right to raise sail and set his course for Cyprus or wherever else he wishes. We want no laggers and none who will quail at the sight of what we know is a superior force."

Straton had been much impressed by the Arvadite mariners and was hardly surprised when not one man stepped out of the ranks to accept the offer.

"I have gone over the plan of battle with you once before," he told them. "But we will rehearse it again so everyone will know his task fully. Assyrian forces always attack in the same way on land, and we can expect them to follow similar practices by sea. They put machines of war in the forefront to batter holes in the walls of fortified cities, so their fighting men can push through and seize control. But in the attack on Arvad, the rafts bearing their catapults will have to be pushed near enough to the walls to hurl stones against them. Our whole defense will be based on the awkwardness and the weakness of this maneuver."

He signaled to Ares, who was perched on the back of the afterhouse along with Tarquin and another tall mercenary. Immediately they unrolled a broad sheet of white cloth on which Straton had spent some time marking out with a piece of charcoal the outlines of the island of Arvad, the mainland shore opposite it and the channel between.

"We do not expect the Assyrians to disturb the leather pipe which now brings fresh water to the surface," he said. "Since they are confident of capturing the city, they will want to preserve the water supply, so it will be available for their use. For that reason we will not try to defend the spring, as they no doubt expect us to do. Instead, once the invasion is under way, we will surprise them by attacking at their most vulnerable spot, just behind the rafts containing the engines of war."

Using a spear handle, he pointed out the location of the spring and the open space of the channel between island and mainland.

"Our spies report that the Assyrian battle plan will be to push the rafts they have been building toward Arvad by means of a fleet of smaller galleys which will be lightly armed. These will be followed by other vessels carrying soldiers, who will go ashore upon the city itself, once the walls have been breached and a landing has been accomplished. Our first purpose, therefore, must be to break up the galleys back of the rafts and, if possible, set them afire with our flaming arrows and brands. At the same time, we will try to destroy as many as we can of the soldiers upon the galleys and on the rafts, by shooting down upon them from the superior height of our ships. My gaoul will lead the attack and, by using our superior weight and brazen prow, we hope to crush many of the galleys and drown a large number of the Assyrian soldiers."

"What about the rafts?" one of the captains asked. "Are they to be allowed to go on without being attacked?"

"The rafts are not important, once the galleys pushing them are sunk," Straton explained. "The wind should drive most of them upon the shore where King Aziru's forces can seize some of the catapults. Then, with such engines raining stones down upon an attacker, Arvad should be almost invulnerable in the future."

"Leave the rafts and the catapults to us," King Aziru agreed. "We will catch them when they wash into the harbor, after you destroy the galleys pushing them."

"Does everyone understand his part?" Straton asked.

There were no more questions from among the commanders, so he gave the order to dismiss. Busy with the last-minute details of the preparation, he was occupied until after nightfall. And rather than torture himself and Hera by seeing her again, he purposely remained away from the section of the harbor where the Greek galley was moored. Gerlach, too, was to remain behind with King Aziru, so Straton could hardly help feeling a little lonely, when he sought his couch finally on the gaoul, where the fighting men were already sleeping on practically all of the available deck space.

When sleep did not come at once, Straton occupied his mind with a detailed rehearsal once again of the battle plan for the morrow. Everything that was likely to happen had been foreseen, he decided, except the one imponderable factor that could bring success or failure—the breeze which usually sprang up toward morning with the cooling of the air near the water. Restless and still unable to sleep, he stepped upon the quay to see if he could feel any first promise of the breeze. But the air was still, and he was about to go aboard the gaoul once again, when he saw a shadowy figure moving along the quay. He was on the point of calling for the guard, when the light of a torch burning nearby revealed Hera, in a long cloak over her night robe. She recognized him at the same moment and came running to throw herself into his arms.

"You were going to leave without telling me good-by!" she accused him.

He glanced quickly at the men sleeping on the deck and, when no one moved, took her hand and led her to his quarters on the gaoul, closing the door behind them. The moon was just rising in the east over the Lebanon range back of the Assyrian camp and its rays filled the room with a soft glow.

"I thought it would be less painful for both of us," he explained. "But I was wrong. I'm glad you dared to come."

"I belong to you," she said simply. "So my place is with you."

"After tomorrow I pray we will never be separated again."

They sat close together in the warm darkness, their arms about each other in a period of quiet communion that was closer than anything they had ever experienced together before.

"What about Queen Elissa?" Hera asked finally.

"I told her this morning that I would have no part of what she offered."

"As Prince Consort?"

"How did you know?"

"One of Queen Tabnith's ladies-in-waiting is a friend of mine from Herakleon."

"I would have said the same, if she had offered to make me King of Tyre," he assured her. "As Ares says: one who is loved by a goddess cannot be tempted by a mere queen."

"I wish I were a goddess. Then I could weave a magic spell to protect you tomorrow."

"With a good ship, brave men at my back, and a goddess to come back to—how could I fail?"

"Father says it all depends upon the wind."

"The morning breeze will come. I am sure of it—now that you are here with me."

"Straton, I have something to say to you, but I don't know just how to say it." His arm was around her and he could feel the rapid pulse of her heart beating against it.

"We are betrothed," he reminded her. "You can tell me anything you wish."

"I—I ran away that night in the grove, but I kept the ring you gave me. I am wearing it now around my neck on a chain that a goldsmith in Thebes made for me. It is true that I don't worship Astarte, but if you want me I am prepared to pay the price Astarte demands of those who accept a gift in the sacred grove."

"If I want you!" For a moment Straton's throat was so full that he could not speak. When his arms tightened about her she came willingly into his embrace and her lips beneath his were yielding and soft. He held her thus for a long time, knowing that, if he took her then, she would not resist. Finally, however, he released her.

"The gift of her body is the greatest trust a woman can place in the man she loves," he told her. "But I would betray your trust if I took that gift now."

"Then you don't—want me?"

"I desire you with every fiber of my body. But I also want you to be the mother of my children, the wife I will come home to at night, the strong staff I can lean upon in time of trouble and uncertainty, and the companion of our declining years. Such a union is not built in a night of passion before sailing on a hazardous mission, Hera. It is built in marriage and a gradual understanding of each other through the years."

Her fingers were like the touch of a feather as they moved along his cheek. "I was hoping you would say that, but I wanted you to know just how much I love you." She stirred in his arms. "It is late and you should get some sleep. I must go."

"No, stay," he told her. "Ares has orders to wake me an hour before dawn. He will take you back to your father's ship then."

She made no objection and they settled down upon the cushions. Straton quickly fell asleep, but Hera was still awake when Ares came to awaken him. Together they walked to the quay where the little servant waited to take her to her father's ship.

"You brought me luck," Straton told her jubilantly. "Feel how strong the breeze is? By nightfall the battle will be won. And before the week is out we will be on our way to Crete."

He kissed her quickly and climbed the ladder from the quay to stand upon the massive rail that surrounded the deck of the gaoul. Lifting the curved trumpet he took from the peg upon which it hung against the mast, he sounded a mighty blast arousing the fleet. By the time Ares returned from seeing Hera to her father's galley, the crews of the fighting ships had gulped the ration of thin wine and leavened cakes that made up the morning meal. And as the little Greek seized a line dangling from the spar supporting the great sail and swung himself aboard, the rowers began to push the great gaoul away from the quay.

A cheer went up from the other vessels when the gaoul, with its double banks of oars pulling as one, moved past them on the northward course that would take it to the spot from which Straton planned to launch his attack. On deck, pots of pitch and brimstone were already beginning to bubble. And the bowmen, a select group whose skill had been tested on distant targets, were busy adjusting bowstrings and laying in a supply of arrows behind the shields that topped the bulwark, giving an added band of armor to the defenses of the vessel.

All along the waterfront similar preparations were going on aboard the other ships moored there. But as yet only Straton's gaoul was in motion, spearheading the battle for Arvad according to the plan he had worked out with King Aziru.

Eleven:

*The cables crack; the sailors' fearful
cries
Ascend; and sable night involves the
skies.*

WHEN THE GREAT gaoul cleared the northernmost point of rock on which Arvad stood, Straton climbed to the masthead. The bright disc of the sun was just beginning to show above the green-clad Lebanon ridge to the east. In its light, the vast might of the fleet the Assyrians had gathered for the final assault on Arvad would have been an inspiring sight—but for the threat it represented to them all.

Ares, whose sight was as keen as any aboard the ship, had climbed behind his master. As they stood now, crowded close together upon the small platform at the top of the mast, where a single lookout was ordinarily posted when under way, the little Greek whistled with astonishment.

"Surely, Master," he said, "such a fleet as that has never been assembled before."

"In numbers, probably not." Straton, too, could not help being a little awed by the sight. "But no vessel there is half as large as ours."

The front of the already advancing wave of ships and men was made up of the great rafts of logs, which the Assyrians had spent the past month lashing together into supporting platforms for the catapults. These machines of war now rested upon the logs, their timbered frameworks looming like a group of giant skeletons in the morning sun. In addition, each floating platform carried its own pile of stones, arranged close to the catapults, so they could easily be placed upon the long arm of carefully hewn timbers that would hurl them at Arvad.

Upon the rafts, a wall of boards had been built on each side of the catapults, slanting backward to form a protection for the men who would serve the great machines. Behind the rafts was a fleet of galleys, the rowers straining at the oars to shove the somewhat unwieldy platforms ahead of them. And following these, row on row, were larger galleys, each packed with fighting men.

Seen from the masthead, the plan of the Assyrian general was as clear as had been Straton's own diagram of the battle area the day before, when he had given the individual ship commanders their final instructions. The great rafts, Straton decided, were the most formidable part of the vast armada. For not only would they fend off any ship that might attack them from the front, but they also formed a platform across which—once the walls of Arvad had been breached by stones tossed from the great machines—men debarking from the galleys in the rear could reach the land and carry the attack into the city itself. Fortunately, however, they were also the most vulnerable part of the enemy fleet. For, having no means of propulsion of their own, they were helpless, once they were cut off from the main part of the Assyrian fleet.

Clouds of smoke were already arising from huge pots of pitch and brimstone boiling on the deck below. But the fumes which otherwise might have made it difficult for Straton and Ares to breathe, as they clung to the masthead, were swept away by a fresh breeze from the northeast which had sprung up in the hours before dawn. The sail had not yet been hoisted, since the double banks of rowers were driving the ship almost directly into the wind. But the topmen stood ready on the deck, waiting to raise it when the vessel was brought about according to plan.

"I see none of the Tarsus galleys," Straton observed to Ares. "And those carrying the fighting men do not seem to be armored."

"What Assyrian would be clever enough to foresee an attack such as you plan?" Ares said. "In two hours those ships will be broken into faggots and the men aboard will be at the bottom of the sea, anchored by their armor and weapons."

"I pray Melkarth you are right," Straton said fervently. "But their numbers are large."

"With Juno herself as your patron, how can you lose?" Ares said blithely. "I will descend and make ready the unguents and the bandages. Any moment now, some fool down there is sure to set himself afire with one of his own arrows."

Straton found he could still laugh. And with it, some of the immediate depression he had felt at the sight of so massive an armada—compared to the puny forces he and King Aziru were able to pit against it—was driven away, as the fumes of brimstone had been dissipated by the morning breeze.

The water was already beginning to roughen a little and whitecaps occasionally laced the crests of the wavelets with foam. Straton had hoped for a choppy sea, since it would hardly disturb the hull of the huge gaoul but could seriously hamper the Assyrians in pushing the great rafts across the channel to Arvad, which now lay somewhat to the southwest. And it appeared now as if his wish had been granted.

Making allowance for the freshening breeze, he deliberately let the rowers drive the gaoul a little beyond the point he had selected in his mind for the swing into an opposite course. The Assyrians, he hoped, would assume that the Tyrian ship was running away from an almost certain defeat for the Arvadites, who had been foolish enough to think they could stand against the might of the Land Between the Rivers. Only when the foremost of the huge rafts were halfway from the mainland shore to the island bastion that was their target, did he give the order to bring the gaoul about and raise the sail.

Straton remained at the masthead while the nimble topmen swung along the spar, to which the top edge of the sail was attached. The ends of the spar extended well out over the bulwarks of the ship and some of the men were hanging over the water, as they loosened the sail and unfurled its vast expanse to the wind, while those hauling upon the lines below drew it taut. As the wind filled the billowing sheet of tough black cloth, reinforced with strips of cord sewn vertically into its surface, the ship lifted its prow and suddenly plunged ahead, like a spirited charger at the touch of a spur, eagerly bearing its rider into battle.

Turning his attention briefly to the harbor of Arvad, Straton saw that the gaouls of King Aziru's fleet were beginning to move away from the stone quay right on schedule. Droplets of water splashed up by the blades of the oars shone in the morning sunlight like showers of jewels and, even though the fleet was small, it was an impressive sight.

Satisfied that the second phase in the defense of Arvad was also under way, Straton turned his attention back to the most important task of all at the moment. The gaoul must be skillfully guided in its first smashing impact against the vast armada accumulated by the Assyrians, striking a target just behind the front row of relatively unprotected galleys pushing the rafts. In this way he hoped not only to achieve the greatest possible amount of damage at first impact, but also to create a sudden confusion in the enemy's ranks which the Arvadite ships following him would be able to exploit to the utmost, when they delivered a second attack on the very heels of the first.

Two enemy galleys from the second rank had already swung into a northward course, he saw, undoubtedly for the purpose of intercepting the gaoul. But the prospect of early battle did not lead him to change course, except to point the heavily armored prow a little more to the east so it would pass between the two galleys.

"Draw in the oars," he shouted to Amathus, who was standing between the great steering sweeps, ready to relay his orders to men at the wooden bars that controlled them. "And set the deck rowers to tending the fireboxes."

Amathus gave the order and the galley slaves, following a maneuver rehearsed many times during the past few days, drew inboard the oars with which they had propelled the vessel until the sail had been raised. The long oars of the upper tier were carefully stacked on deck against the bulwarks in racks built there for them, so they would not roll free in the midst of the coming action and disturb the footing and aim of the bowmen who thronged the deck in ordered ranks. The racks of oars against the bulwarks served a double purpose, too. For by using them as footholds, the bowmen could rise quickly into the openings between the shields erected upon the rail surrounding the deck and send their missiles off with twanging bowstrings, then drop back to a position of relative safety behind the shields, while another rank stepped forward with arrows fixed to take their places.

The galley slaves, who handled the shorter oars of the lower tier through ports cut in the planking of the hull a little below deck level, had drawn in their oars, too. But instead of stacking them, as those on deck had done, they let them lie across the benches and remained in their seats. Thus, if a sudden change of plan or failing of the wind demanded propulsion by oars, each man could slide the oaken shaft out, drop it into place against the tholepin, and pick up the rhythm of rowing on no more than the third or fourth beat of the overseer's drum.

The distance between the gaoul and the two Assyrian galleys sent to cut it off was lessening rapidly when Straton slid down to the deck by means of a line from the masthead. He ran back to climb upon the afterhouse, where a protected lookout had been erected for him, so he could remain above the level of the battle and the row of shields surmounting the bulwark. From this elevated point of view he was able to see just what was happening and issue whatever orders were needed to cope with the situation as his own ship headed between the enemy vessels.

Assyrian arrows were already striking the shields along the rail of the gaoul, and dropping into the water. On the foredeck, one of these penetrated an opening to transfix the shoulder of a man working at one of the firepots, but Ares raced to him as soon as he fell. Breaking the shaft of the arrow, the little Greek pulled it through almost before the first cry of pain had burst from the wounded man's throat, and stanched the flow of blood with two pads expertly bandaged into place.

"Make ready to change course," Straton spoke to the steersmen, as the distance between the vessels closed and the shower of arrows grew thicker. So far, not a single arrow had been loosed from his own ship, a maneuver designed to lure the attacking galleys more certainly to their own destruction.

"Over hard!" he shouted suddenly and, as the steersmen threw all their weight against the bars controlling the sweeps, the great gaoul swerved and headed toward the enemy galley on the eastern side.

Too late, the Assyrians saw the meaning of the maneuver and realized, from the sunlight reflected by the bronzed plating upon the prow, what sort of vessel they had had the temerity to attack. A group of specially skilled bowmen stationed along the western rail of Straton's ship had already begun to pick off the steersmen of the galley on that side and the rowers at their benches on the deck. Moments later the gaoul crashed into the galley, crumpling the side of the hull as if with a giant hand.

On Straton's orders, the flaming arrows and brands with which they planned to sow both confusion and destruction among the ranks of the enemy had not yet been used. Nor was there any need to use them now for, while the second galley drifted with half its rowers dead or wounded and the bodies of the steersmen hanging over the sweeps, the first began to list sharply and fill. And though they scrambled frantically for footholds, many of the armed men upon the deck slid off into the water, where they sank—as Ares had predicted—anchored by the weight of armor, which made it quite impossible for them to swim.

Against a single galley Straton would have used a much simpler maneuver more in keeping with the classical pattern of battle between moving ships, striking the enemy a glancing blow and smashing the oars on the side toward his own ship. But he had deliberately sought a test of the bronze-sheathed prow, so he would know in the next encounter just how safe it was to drive at full speed against an enemy vessel.

Calling to the steersmen to resume their previous course, he jumped down to the deck and ran its length to where, by means of a line cast overside, Amathus was already swinging down over the prow to study it carefully. As Straton leaned over the bow of the ship, Amathus came up the side hand over hand, his weather-beaten features split by a broad grin.

"Not even a dent, sir," he cried jubilantly. "You have changed the whole pattern of war at sea this day."

Straton felt a surge of jubilation at the news and embraced the grizzled pilot impulsively before moving back to his own position and calling the good news to his crew. A cheer arose at his words, followed almost like an echo by a second one from the slaves huddled over the lower tier of oars inside the hull.

A quick survey revealed no damage on deck, either, beyond the one man who had been wounded. And a glance backward showed that the galley they had by-passed was now drifting toward the rock of Arvad under the force of the northeast breeze that was steadily freshening, while those aboard fought desperately to get her under control again. The vessel whose hull had been smashed was only a waterlogged hulk, its deck already awash.

Jubilant though he was, Straton did not allow himself to become overconfident. Two enemy galleys had been put out of action, it was true—one of them permanently, and the second probably rendered unfit for any further use that day. But nearly a hundred more vessels of several different types still remained in the great armada and he did not delude himself that anything more than a fraction of their task was complete. Meanwhile, Ares had finished bandaging the wounded man and was helping him into the afterhouse, which Straton had designated as a lazaretto for the duration of the battle.

"The wound is clean," the little Greek reported as his master climbed once again to his protected perch on top of the deckhouse. "He can use a bow again tomorrow, if need be."

"I pray it will all be over before then," Straton said. "Meanwhile you might call on your Greek gods for help. We shall need all we can get."

"They have been fighting on your side since we left the quay," Ares assured him. "Juno herself promised to invoke their help only this morning, when I took her back to her chariot."

The separation of the two enemy galleys from the main force to attack Straton's vessel had left a breach in what had appeared at first to be a solid wall of ships. Deciding to drive directly for this rift, Straton ordered the course changed until the prow was pointed southward toward the black masts of the Assyrian fleet.

"Get the flaming arrows and brands ready," he called down to the deck. "Bowmen, aim high to strike beyond the nearer rank. And throwers, hurl your flaming brands for the nearest target."

They were close enough now for him to see the consternation and fear on the faces of the Assyrians in the front rank of galleys just behind the rafts, as the great ship bore down upon them at full speed. None of the enemy, he was sure, had ever seen a vessel of such size; moreover, the certainty that it would crash directly into their flimsy wooden hulls, crumpling them as it had crumpled the other galley only a few moments before, must be equally terrifying. Arrows were striking the shields upon the rail like rain now, but so far the enemy had not tried to use fire.

"Prepare to ram!" Straton shouted and crouched behind the temporary protecting wall erected for him upon the roof of the afterhouse, seconds before the impact of bronze against wood shook every timber in the great vessel. The sound of impact was more than simply a crash, however. Rather, it was a ripping and shearing, as planking and timbers were snapped, a terrible sickening sound that rose in pitch when the screams of dying men were added. The gaoul hardly hesitated, however. Driven by the vast billowed-out sail, it continued to plow through the ranks of enemy ships like a tornado ripping through the trees of a forest.

"Launch your brands and arrows!" Straton ordered, and from all parts of the gaoul's deck—except the area just fore and aft the sail, where there were no firepots for fear of setting the sail itself aflame—a rain of fiery objects poured down upon the ships of the Assyrian fleet.

The arrows, as Straton had ordered, were purposely arched high in order to fall upon more distant galleys which had not been affected by the first smashing impact of the gaoul. The brands, flaming torches roughly the length of a man's arm, were tossed over the bulwarks to fall upon the decks of the galleys which had been crumpled like scorched parchment by the smashing impact, as well as upon the next rank which might otherwise have come to their aid. Meanwhile, the slaves who ordinarily pulled the deck oars were ladling the boiling mixture of pitch and brimstone over the side, scalding the enemy and creating further confusion.

Straton had counted on the surprise of the Assyrians at his daring to attack such an armada with one ship, plus their consternation at the damage inflicted by the first blow, to play a major part in the success of the venture. One thing had given him serious concern: the question of whether the initial momentum of the gaoul, even with the pulling power of the great sail, would be sufficient to drive them completely through the Assyrian fleet in that first smashing attack. But the freshening of the morning breeze beyond his expectation had encouraged him to believe they would not be stopped. And, as the situation developed, it was not the wind but the utter demoralization of the enemy that was the deciding factor.

The sight of the greatest ship they had ever seen, ripping smaller vessels apart with its brazen prow and spreading fire and destruction in its wake, was too much for some of the galley commanders at the southern edge of the Assyrian armada. Before the gaoul could reach them, they began to pull back frantically, breaking the almost solid front of the fleet as they sought to escape destruction. Just when Straton's ship was beginning to slow markedly, he saw a path open up as enemy galleys sought to get out of the way, not realizing in their excitement and fear that the now barely moving gaoul was more vulnerable at that moment than it had been at any other time during the battle.

Until now, Straton had relied upon the propulsive force of the great sail, which was still pulling like a spirited charger against the slanted mast. But when he saw a lane of water suddenly open ahead as the enemy ships frantically broke ranks and felt the gaoul charge forward, clearing the southern edge of the Assyrian fleet, he shouted for the rowers inside the hull to shift their oars out and begin to pull. At his order, the topmen also climbed swiftly to the long spar supporting the top edge of the sail and began to reef in the fabric as it was lowered by those on deck. A few minutes later, the deck oars were broken out and the gaoul made a sharp turn, swinging into the wind, where it was held by the rowers while Straton climbed the mast to gain a look at the scene behind them.

Smoke from burning ships partially obscured the field of action, but he was able to see that their path through the enemy fleet was littered with sinking or severely damaged galleys. For the time being at least, he was sure, all communication between the main part of the fleet and the advance group that had been pushing the great rafts ahead of them had been cut off. And exactly according to plan, the ships of the Arvadites were now moving into the breach, ignoring for the moment the remainder of the Assyrian armada and concentrating upon sinking the galleys whose task it had been to maneuver the platforms bearing the giant catapults into place before the walls of Arvad.

One of the great rafts, Straton saw, had already drifted ashore and burst the bonds holding the logs together, letting the machine it carried sink, and littering the area with logs. These, in turn, made the task of the other rafts more difficult and decreased the possibility that they ever would be able to get within range of the walls of Arvad. Three galleys which had been pushing another of the rafts had just surrendered to the Arvadite ships, and the floating platform of logs that had been their particular charge was being herded intact into the quiet waters at the outer fringe of the port, where it could be turned around and anchored for later use.

Satisfied that King Aziru's men were following the instructions he had worked out so carefully beforehand, Straton turned his attention to the remainder of the enemy fleet. Here utter confusion reigned, for, besides the ships damaged by direct crushing contact with the immensely heavier gaoul, a number of others were burning fiercely from the fire arrows and flaming brands. On perhaps half the remainder, both crews and fighting men were working desperately to put out the fires started by the flame arrows. But, because of Straton's shrewd use of a mixture of pitch and brimstone in which to soak the arrowheads, the fires were doubly hard to extinguish and they were making poor progress as the freshening breeze fanned the flames.

"Half of the enemy put out of action by a single ship!" Ares, who had scampered up the mast beside his master, exclaimed in awed wonder. "Not even Jason and his Argonauts ever fought such a battle!"

Straton was familiar with the tale, but this was no time for comparison with previous naval history. Roughly half the enemy fleet had indeed been put out of action, much of it permanently, in that first smashing run southward. But behind the broad swathe of confusion and destruction, enough of the Assyrian galleys remained unhurt to still turn defeat into victory.

An opponent, who had patiently spent over a month hauling dry logs down from the hills and lashing them together into great rafts, was not likely to give up at the first backset, he decided. And, besides, only a minor advantage would have been gained, even if the Assyrians withdrew, unless the major part of their fleet was damaged or destroyed beyond their ability to repair the vessels and mount another attack before the coming of winter drove them back into the Hollow of Syria east of the Lebanon range or perhaps homeward to Assyria.

The situation obviously called for a decision, and Straton did not hesitate to make it.

"Set your course northwestward around Arvad," he called down to Amathus. "We must strike them again."

"You are gambling for high stakes, Master," Ares said beside him. "But with the gods of two lands watching over you, how can you lose?"

iii

Two hours had passed before the gaoul, following a course north and west of Arvad so as to clear the rocky island, was able to swing back upon a northeasterly course once again. The morning breeze had freshened by now to a small gale and the task of driving the ship into the wind by oars alone had been more time-consuming than Straton had anticipated. When they finally cleared the rock on which Arvad was located and once more were able to view the battle area, the slaves at the oars were almost exhausted.

Straton had used part of the time to examine the planking of the hull for damage and was pleased to find but little, the extra bronze plates at the bow having done their work well. The seams had opened slightly in a few places and a small amount of water was sloshing around the footing of the mast, but there were no major leaks which could not be repaired in a day or less, once the fighting was over. His only concern, as he climbed once again to the lookout perch atop the mast, was for what had been happening in the channel east of Arvad, where the battle for all of Phoenicia had been going on during the past two hours without his ship. Tarquin joined him at the masthead this time, so they could survey the situation and plan what action should be taken next.

Two of the rafts bearing the huge catapults had been smashed against the rocks, they saw, and only a few hewn timbers cast upon the shore and logs floating here and there remained as evidence of them and the engines of war they had carried. Three more had been captured and towed into the harbor of Arvad where they had been turned around, as Straton had suggested to King Aziru, so the catapults resting upon them were now directed toward the channel between island and mainland, ready to toss stones at the Assyrians. Only two of the rafts appeared to be still in enemy hands, and these were under attack by Arvadite ships.

King Aziru's forces appeared to have complete control of that portion of the conflict which had occurred close to Arvad, so Straton turned his attention to an area nearer to the mainland shore. Here, part of the battle area was still obscured by clouds of smoke rising from galleys set aflame during his passage through the Assyrian fleet and blown southward by the wind. An accurate evaluation was difficult for this reason, plus the fact that, as Straton had often seen happen with the fires that raged in the tree-clad Lebanon slopes during the hot, dry summer season, clouds were beginning to form overhead, tending to hide the sun and deepen the haze that already hung over the whole area.

In the northern section, however, the Assyrian galley commanders had fared better and had managed to collect a number of vessels which had been hurt little—or none at all—in the first engagement.

Even without the catapults, these still posed a serious danger, for their number equaled, perhaps even excelled, the size of the Arvadite fleet, which had also suffered some losses.

"The enemy was hurt badly," Tarquin observed beside him. "But he is far from dead."

"Too much alive to please me," Straton agreed. "But at least the catapults will not be able to batter down the walls of Arvad."

"Do you think the Assyrians will build more rafts and machines?"

Straton shook his head. "The logs they used today were cut months ago so they could dry. Green logs would not support such heavy burdens."

"Then, the enemy must finish the attack now—or give it up until another year."

"He doesn't have much choice," Straton agreed. "Nor do we."

"Then you are still going to attack again?"

"Yes—unless we are to leave the battle half-finished."

"My men will be ready." Tarquin did not even consider the latter alternative, but seized a line and slid down to the deck.

"Hoist the sail!" Straton shouted. "All oars inboard. The course is southeast."

A sudden flurry among the galleys which had been forming into a fleet a little northeast of Arvad revealed that the change of course had been noted, but Straton did not delude himself that their task this time would be anything like as easy as it had been earlier in the day. It was true that he had developed a new method of naval warfare by using a ship larger than anything ever seen in these waters and exploiting to the full the demoralizing effect of the brazen prow, arrows and brands flaming with pitch and brimstone, and bowmen trained to strike down steersmen and other highly trained members of the galley crews. But having come through that attack, someone among the enemy galley commanders would certainly have the intelligence to realize that the tactic of fire, at least, could be used against a vessel whose effectiveness depended largely upon the driving force of the great sail.

"Amathus!" Straton called down to the deck, as the sail billowed out and grew taut. "Send some topmen aloft and have containers of sea water hauled up to soak the sail."

The pilot understood the reason for the stratagem at once. As the topmen ran up the mast, or swung themselves hand over hand up the sheets securing the sail, those on deck tossed lines which were dropped across the spar supporting the upper edge. Meanwhile the deck oarsmen, whose long sweeps once again rested in the racks beneath the rail, were set to hauling up pots of sea water and emptying them into containers attached to the ends of the lines which the topmen had dropped over the spar. As soon as each container was full, others on deck hauled away on the ends of these lines, sending the containers of water swinging upward to be dumped over the sail, soaking it and decreasing the likelihood of its catching fire.

Straton, meanwhile, had slid down to the deck and taken up his usual battle position. As he had hoped, the enemy ranks had begun to open with frantic haste, when some of the galley commanders nearest to his ship realized that they were to be the target of a second smashing attack and sought to get their relatively frail craft out of the way. But before they succeeded, the great Phoenician ship swept down upon them, crunching oars as easily as if they had been the size of arrow shafts.

Screams of pain sounded as rowers on the deck of the Assyrian galleys were swept overboard by the sudden slamming impact against the long sweeps they were wielding, or were transfixed by fragments of split oak, hurtled across the deck by the impact. Tarquin and his fighting men wasted no time assessing the extent of the enemy's wounds but, as methodically as they had done on the first attack, sent flaming arrows arching up to fall on the massed galleys of the enemy fleet. Meanwhile, those of the deck crew not engaged in drawing water to soak the sail were busy tossing flaming brands overside and spilling burning pitch and sulphur down upon the decks of the stricken vessels, where it ran in rivulets of flame, seeking any opening and pouring through it into the hulls to set up additional fires there.

The stiffening breeze carried the entire engagement southward along the channel while the battle was taking place. Soon the gaoul entered an area where smoke from galleys already burning, combined with that from those which had burst into flame upon the second attack, made it seem almost as if night had already fallen. Only a few of the enemy commanders had fought back with the weapons Straton feared most, the fire arrows and brands that could destroy the sail which gave the Phoenician craft such added force and mobility. Fortunately, too, his tactic in placing men along the spar from which the sail was suspended and pouring water over the fabric had worked quite satisfactorily so far. And though arrow after arrow had struck the wet fabric, it was only to splutter and drop to the deck, where they were quickly doused.

The cordage, however, was another matter, for the water that soaked the sail and kept it from catching fire had little effect upon the tightly twisted and heavily tarred rigging. Several brands struck among the lines holding the spar in place, but either the lookout or one of the top-men stationed there was able to disengage them before they could set fire to the cordage. Only when they were smashing through the last row of enemy galleys, with the clear sea visible ahead, did the disaster Straton had been fearing finally strike. And when it did, the sequence of events happened so rapidly that Straton could hardly keep track of it.

A scream of pain from aloft had drawn his eyes to the masthead in time to see the lookout, an enemy arrow transfixing his body, tumble toward the deck. Almost at the same instant a fire arrow struck in the midst of the cordage where the lookout had been standing. If the man had been there, he could easily have kicked the flaming arrow away from the rigging. But the lookout platform was empty and, to Straton's horror, he saw the mainsheet holding the spar in place suddenly burst into flames.

The nearest of the topmen, who had been soaking the sail, started to work his way along the spar toward the fire, which was now burning briskly amidst the cordage. But from his position on the deckhouse at the stern of the gaoul, Straton could see that the man would be too late.

"Slide!" he shouted to the topmen, certain that at any moment both spar and sail would crash to the deck. But before he finished the com-mand, the fire had eaten through the rigging supporting one side of the sail and the now uncontrolled timber plummeted toward the deck, swinging about in the grip of the wind, like a charger suddenly gone mad in the midst of a battle.

Straton shouted to the steersmen to put the bars controlling the steer-ing sweeps over hard, hoping to swing the ship around into the wind so those on deck could grapple with the wildly flapping sail and control it. Amathus, too, realized the danger and ordered the rowers stationed within the hull to extend their oars and bring the gaoul under control. But as the prow began to swing westward, relieving the pressure against the sail, the loose end of the spar was seized by the wind and whipped across the deck like a giant reaping hook, though fortunately at a high enough level to pass over the heads of those crouching there.

In his command post atop the deckhouse, Straton stood directly in the path of the spar. Before he had time even to drop behind the barri-cade erected there to protect him, he suddenly felt himself plucked up by a giant hand, as it were, and flung clear of the deck into the sea. He heard only Ares' cry of "Master!" and saw the small figure of the servant racing across the deck toward the afterrail. Then he struck the water and, as the gaoul plunged on, saw one of the giant cedar logs from which the Assyrians had built the great rafts bearing down upon him. It must have looked, he thought in a flash of insight and cold fear, much the way his own ship had looked to the Assyrians in the galleys that morning as it bore down upon them. Then the log struck him, driving him down into the depths, and he knew nothing more.

Twelve:

*Who knows what hazards thy delay may
bring?
Woman's a various and a changeful
thing.*

IT WAS ALWAYS a losing battle. Each time he sought to escape, strong
hands held him powerless until, exhausted, unconsciousness claimed
him again. But finally there came a day when no hands sought to hold
him down and he recognized the anxious face of Ares bending over
him. That in itself was strange, for Ares had been aboard the gaoul
when the spar had swept him off the deckhouse into the sea.

"Where are the Assyrians?" Straton asked. "The ones who have been
keeping me prisoner here?"

"Those weren't Assyrians—but friends," Ares said. "We had to hold
you to keep you from rushing out in your delirium."

"Delirium? I have my senses."

"You have them now—yes. But for ten days you have been in the grip
of a high fever, babbling all sorts of things."

"I remember being swept off the ship by the spar after the rigging
caught fire. And swimming there when a giant log swept over me."

"The log almost killed you," Ares told him. "But it saved you, too."

"This is no time for riddles," Straton said irritably. He was tired and,
when he moved, every part of his body seemed to be stiff and sore.

Ares grinned and picked up a steaming pot that had been set over a
brazier filled with coals. From it he poured a cupful of fragrant liquid
and, stirring into it a large pinch of brownish powder, lifted Straton's
head and held it to his lips. "Drink this," he said. "I will tell you all
about it afterward."

Straton could feel the hot liquid warm his body as he swallowed it,
but even the small effort of drinking had exhausted him and he could
only lie supine, watching Ares' face grow less distinct.

"When I saw the spar knock you off the afterhouse, I could think of
only one thing—going after you," the little Greek said. "Fortunately, I
landed on the log that struck you. And when I saw you bob to the surface, I was able to seize you by the collar and drag you onto the log
beside me."

186

The warmth of the potion Straton had drunk was spreading even to his fingertips now and the effort of holding his eyelids open proved too much for him. All he wanted to do was to yield himself to it and, when he heard Ares' voice trail off, made no attempt to remain awake any longer.

When he awoke again, he felt strong enough to shout, "Ares!" but, to his astonishment, the only sound that emerged was a whisper. Ares heard it, however, and was by his side in an instant.

"How—how long did I sleep?" Straton demanded.

"Since yesterday. The mulled wine you drank was exactly what you needed."

"But the battle," Straton tried to raise his head, but merely managed to clear the pallet on which he lay and fell back, exhausted by the effort.

"The battle was almost two weeks ago," Ares told him. "You were completely waterlogged by the time the log we were on floated ashore south of the Assyrian camp. And afterward you developed a fever."

"Where am I now?" Straton could see that he lay in a room with whitewashed walls and a roof of thatch.

"I couldn't carry you alone, so I had to leave you on the shore until I could find some fishermen. They are King Aziru's people and were gathering booty that had drifted ashore after the battle. We made a litter and bore you to this house in the hills. Since then I have been too busy keeping you alive to do anything else."

"Then you saved my life twice."

"Fishing you out of the water was no trouble, though it was hard to stay on the log. You can thank Asklepios for healing you—and perhaps Eshmun." Ares grinned. "When it seemed certain that you would die a few days ago, I even prayed to your god, though—as you know—I have a low opinion of foreign deities compared to our Greek ones."

"What about the ship?"

"I lost sight of it in the smoke, but the fishermen say it came through the battle and returned safely to the harbor at Arvad."

"Then the city did not fall?"

"When you smashed their fleet a second time, the Assyrians lost all heart for fighting on the water, Master. Two days ago they started retreating eastward into the Hollow of Syria. Arvad and Phoenicia are safe for another year—thanks to you."

"Did you send word to Arvad that I am alive?"

"Until the day before yesterday, when your fever broke, I wasn't even sure myself you'd live another day. Besides, it was too risky, with part of the Assyrian army still on the shore. But as soon as they are out of the way, we will take you down to the sea and ferry you across to Arvad in one of the fishing boats."

"Tell your friends to hurry. Hera will be worried."

"There is no hurry. The Greek galley sailed from Arvad three days ago."

"They must have given us up for lost—but I can easily follow them in the gaoul."

"It sailed, too, Master—almost a week ago."

For a moment, Straton was stunned by the news. But he needed only a few moments of thought to think of an explanation.

"Father must have gotten word to the Royal Council that Tyre is safe from the Assyrians," he said. "With that information, they probably forced Pygmalion to dismiss Mago and accept a reconciliation with Elissa."

"I hate to have to tell you this, Master," Ares said. "But the gaoul didn't sail for Tyre."

"Are you certain?"

"Some fishermen along the north coast reported that its course seemed to be toward Cyprus. The Greek galley followed by only a day, but a few days later it came limping back to Arvad."

"And no more has been heard from the gaoul?"

"Nothing that we have learned about. But Amathus is a good pilot. He will surely keep the ship safe."

"Why would Diomedes and Hera leave Arvad and then return so quickly?"

Ares shook his head. "I don't know the answer."

Straton could no longer escape the conviction that something was badly wrong. It must involve Hera, too, since Diomedes had apparently pursued the gaoul, but then returned to Arvad.

"How soon can your fishermen friends get me to Arvad?" he asked.

"I sent word this morning for a litter to be brought up from the shore to carry you down. It should be here tonight and we can leave early in the morning. The fishermen have to move carefully, for the Assyrians are great scavengers and roving bands are still plundering the countryside."

The wisdom of the decision by Ares and the fishermen to proceed cautiously, in spite of Straton's impatience to reach Arvad, was proved toward noon the next day, when the tough Zahis, bearing the litter on which Straton lay, paused at a high point in the hills overlooking the valley leading eastward toward the Hollow of Syria. The Assyrian column looked like a giant serpent, as it followed the winding narrow gorge through the Lebanon ridge. It stretched as far as Straton could see, though its western end had only just left the shore before Arvad. The withdrawal was orderly but, as Ares had said, foraging parties intent upon securing food for the army and booty for themselves were roving outward from the main column. And, in fact, Straton and his companions were forced to hide among the rocks almost until nightfall, before they could begin the task of carrying the litter down to the beach.

Straton had not been able to repress a shiver, as he watched the Assyrian army move eastward through the gorge where a stream ran to the sea. The enemy had failed in this year's attempt to engulf Arvad and the other Phoenician cities—largely due to the strategy Straton himself had devised and executed. But he did not doubt that the serpent would return, or that its coils would draw ever tighter about the Phoenician cities, which it must conquer before going on to gobble up the rest of Canaan and Egypt.

More than ever now he was convinced that the new city which Ares had labelled Carthage, since he had trouble pronouncing the Phoenician Karthadasht, should be built on the Libyan headland overlooking the sheltered bay he had discovered on his last voyage. But to do that, he must regain his ship and find once again the woman he loved.

ii

As soon as the last of the Assyrians had left the shore the next day, the fishermen who had carried Straton down from the hills put him into one of their boats and rowed him and Ares across the channel to Arvad. Beyond the rafts of logs which were already being readied for floating southward to the Nile, where they brought high prices in the markets of the Egyptian river ports, the city showed little evidence of the siege through which it had so recently come. Waterboats were clustered around the end of the leather pipe from which fresh water now gushed steadily. And crews of men were hard at work erecting the machines of war taken from the rafts upon stone platforms at either side of the main harbor of Arvad, from which positions they could hurl stones at an invader and render the city much less vulnerable to a future attack.

King Aziru was happy to see Straton alive and on the road to recovery. He embraced him happily and ordered purses given to the fishermen.

"Your father is safe," he said at once. "Shortly after the battle, a Tyrian ship put in here with word that King Pygmalion had given some merchants in Tyre permission to send out a fleet to join Queen Elissa

189

in establishing a new city in the West. Gerlach knew how much you wanted to see such a city rise on the Libyan coast, so he returned to Tyre to help arrange it. I think he felt that what Ares calls Carthage would be a fitting memorial to you."

"The fishermen spoke of seeing my gaoul sail northward—possibly toward Cyprus."

"Your father lent the vessel and crew to Queen Elissa, to take her to Libya. It was he who suggested that she go by way of Cyprus, where she could load supplies, since our reserves have dwindled during the siege."

"What about Diomedes?" Straton asked. "The fishermen reported that his galley sailed northward but returned to Arvad."

"Diomedes is here," King Aziru said. "Perhaps you should hear his story from his own lips."

Certain now from Aziru's manner that something was wrong, Straton allowed himself to be taken to a sunlit room in the east wing of the royal palace. There Diomedes lay, with King Aziru's personal physician in attendance. The Greek shipmaster's face was pale and drawn, but it lit up with pleasure at the sight of his visitor.

"Zeus be praised!" he cried. "You are alive!"

"I give thanks to Melkarth and Astarte that I have been preserved," Straton said. "But where is Hera?"

A spasm of pain passed over Diomedes' face and the physician moved to support his right leg, which was encased in a bulky dressing extending from hip to toe.

"She is gone, Straton," the Greek shipmaster said. "Taken prisoner by Queen Elissa."

Straton groped for a chair, as he reeled under the impact of the news. "H-how could that happen?"

"It's a long story, beginning when your gaoul came back to port on the evening of the battle with news that you had been lost overboard. Hera and I could hardly believe it. But when two days passed with no word that any ship had found you, we were sure you had drowned after the spar swept you overboard."

"Ares saved me," Straton explained. "But the water in my body brought on a fever and I knew nothing for almost ten days."

"Hera was beside herself with grief, as we all were," Diomedes said. "When word came from Tyre that a fleet of ships was preparing to sail from there to Utica to build a new city at the spot you described to me, Gerlach offered the use of your gaoul to Queen Elissa so she could join them in Libya—and she accepted. They sailed for Salamis on Cyprus, while I was readying my galley for the voyage home to Crete. Hera was prostrated with grief for you, so Queen Tabnith was kind enough to let her remain in the palace. Only when I was ready to sail and sent for her, did I discover that Queen Elissa had spirited her away."

"Why would Elissa do that?"

"Isn't it true that she offered to make you Prince Consort if you would lead an Arvadite fleet to Tyre and force Pygmalion to abdicate?"

"Yes—but I refused."

"Because of Hera?"

"I would have refused even if Hera had not been involved," Straton said. "Pygmalion should be removed by the Royal Council, not by a revolution."

"You and I can see that clearly," Diomedes agreed. "But a proud woman might feel that you had scorned her for another—and take her revenge upon the woman she thought had supplanted her. Believe me, Straton, Elissa was only acting as many women would under the circumstances."

Straton did not argue the point. Knowing Elissa's temper, he was sure that Diomedes was correct. "Do you think she would dare to put Hera to death?"

"I feared that at first and followed the gaoul to bring my daughter back. But concern for Hera made me careless, I suppose. We were halfway to Salamis, when I fell over some cordage and broke my leg. In falling, my head struck against the timber and I was unconscious for two days. My pilot was afraid to go on, so he returned to Arvad seeking a physician. By that time my leg was so swollen and inflamed that the physician here says it would mean my life if I tried to follow Hera now."

"You said just now that at first you feared Elissa would put Hera to death," Straton said. "Do you fear it no longer?"

"I've had time to think about the whole situation," Diomedes told him. "Queen Elissa was obeying an impulse to punish one she felt had interfered in her plan to go back to Tyre, but once her anger subsided, I hope she saw her error. It would have been simple for her to put Hera off at Itanos on the way to Libya and, as soon as my leg improves enough, I plan to go there on the way home."

"But can you be sure that Elissa did not—"

"A ship touched here from Salamis only a few days ago," Diomedes said. "Aboard it was a delegation from that city protesting the seizure by a Tyrian ship—which could only have been yours, from the description—of eighty-five young women, presumably to be sold as slaves. I talked to a member of the delegation and he told me a girl answering Hera's description was aboard the vessel under guard."

Straton recalled the report he had given to the Council of Merchants on his arrival in Tyre from the West and remembered that he had spoken then of the eagerness with which the Libyan chiefs sought white-skinned female slaves from the East. He wondered now whether Elissa, too, had not remembered that same report and seized both Hera and the young girls at Salamis in the hope of receiving a warmer welcome from the Libyans. It was a faint hope and, even if true, only increased the necessity that he reach Utica as quickly as possible, before his beloved could be handed over to some Libyan prince.

"How bad is your leg?" he asked.

"Bad enough, I am afraid," Diomedes admitted. "King Aziru's personal physician here says I will lose it, and also my life, unless I stay in bed until it heals."

Straton turned to the Arvadite physician. "My own physician saved my life only a week ago, when I was dying of a fever," he said. "He learned his profession in the service of the Greek god Asklepios. Would you allow him to examine the noble Diomedes?"

The physician bowed. "The wisdom of the priests of Asklepios is known wherever the sick and wounded are treated. I should be honored by consultation with one so skilled."

"Send for the physician Ares, who accompanied me to the palace," Straton directed one of the servants. "Tell him his services are needed here at once."

Diomedes smiled at Ares' new title, but carefully controlled it lest the King's physician realized that Ares was only a servant and be offended.

"Examine the leg of the noble Diomedes, O physician," Straton said formally, when Ares approached a few minutes later. "And tell me what you discover."

The little Greek's eyes glowed at the formal salutation and his quick, appraising glance took in the situation. "Of course, noble sir," he said and turned to the Arvadite physician. "Will you please remove the dressing?"

When Diomedes' wound was exposed, even Straton could see that good judgment had been used in requiring the Greek shipmaster to remain quiet. The bone had snapped near mid-thigh, tearing a great hole in the flesh. And though the fragments appeared to be back in place, for the limb was straight again, there was considerable inflammation and swelling, extending from ankle to groin, and a foul discharge was pouring from the wound. Its edges were already pink with the healing process, however, and the Greek shipmaster was able to move his foot under Ares' direction with very little pain.

"My colleague has shown excellent judgment in treating this limb with dressings moistened in warm sea water," Ares reported. "If the leg remains still, and the dressings are continued until healing is complete, it should be almost as good as it was before."

"Can't I at least be removed to Crete?" Diomedes begged.

"You would be risking your life, noble sir," Ares told him. "And the gods have already favored you."

"Lend me your galley and its crew, Diomedes," Straton suggested. "I will follow Hera, even if it means going all the way to Libya."

"But you have been wounded yourself—and are ill," Diomedes protested. "How can you make such a trip?"

"My physician will be with me, and your pilot no doubt knows the sailing directions for Itanos," Straton said. "By the time we reach that port, I should be strong enough to take command for the rest of the voyage."

"Then, may Juno guide you," Diomedes said fervently. "The galley is yours."

"What of the treasure that was transferred to it before the battle?"

"Queen Elissa took that with her. But you will find some chests aboard my ship with enough silver to pay for anything you need to buy. And if you take on new supplies at Itanos, they should see you safely to Utica." He reached out to grip Straton's arm. "May the gods guide you, for what you seek is my most precious treasure."

"Mine also," Straton reminded him. "Be sure I will bring her back safely."

But as he was being carried to where Diomedes' galley was moored at the waterfront, Straton could not help feeling a sense of despondency. For he remembered well the avidity with which the Libyan chiefs sought light-skinned women for their harems. And one as lovely as Hera would be the greatest prize of all.

Thirteen:

Ere yet the tempest roars,
Stand to your tackle, mates, and
stretch your oars.

FOR THE SEVENTH consecutive day Straton sat disconsolately in Gerlach's warehouse at Itanos on the extreme eastern tip of the island of Crete, staring at the rain and the wind-lashed palms on the quay outside. Battered by the beginning of a storm which had come howling down upon them from the north a day out of Itanos, Diomedes' galley had managed to make its way under oars alone to the safety of the harbor.

Straton had felt little satisfaction in what those on board the galley had considered an almost miraculous feat of seamanship in getting them to Itanos at all, however, even though it had earned him the loyalty of all. For during the time they had been forced to remain immobilized by an unusual summer storm in the harbor of Itanos, he could envision the gaoul bearing Elissa and Hera fleeing westward toward Libya.

For the third or fourth time he questioned the agent who handled the affairs of Gerlach at Itanos, but the answer was always the same.

"As I told you, sir," the man replied patiently, "the ship put into port nearly two weeks ago, and a few days later the fleet from Tyre joined Queen Elissa here. They stopped only long enough to take on food and water, then sailed westward."

"And you are sure you did not notice the lady Hera aboard the gaoul?"

"How would I know her among eighty-odd women?"

"She would be fairer than the others, with hair like gold."

"The women on board the gaoul were from Cyprus," the agent said. "I saw no such one as you described."

Crete was Hera's native island, Straton had reminded himself, so Elissa would hardly have let her go ashore where she might have been recognized by some of the inhabitants. There was a chance, then, that she might still have been aboard the gaoul, but even that thought did nothing to lessen his anger at the storm that had bottled them up in Crete.

"How large a fleet did you say joined the Queen here?" he asked.

"Six large gaouls from Tyre with many people aboard, both nobles and artisans. They were led by the merchant Hadras."

Straton knew Hadras well, both as a member of the Royal Council and as a friend of his family. Ordinarily, he would have rejoiced that Hadras had chosen to be among those who would build a new Tyre in the West. But even that thought brought little surcease from his concern for Hera.

"Did they say what was happening in Tyre?" he asked.

"Only that those aboard the gaouls preferred to follow Queen Elissa into exile."

"Did the Queen speak of the new city on the Libyan coast?"

"She talked of little else after the fleet came from Tyre—and seemed eager to go on."

Straton had developed no plan of future action beyond sailing to Utica or to the harbor of Carthage, if the Tyrian fleet was anchored there, and confronting Elissa with a demand that she release Hera and return his ship. From what King Aziru and Diomedes had told him, the gaoul had only been lent to Elissa for the purpose of bearing her to the Libyan port, so he did not anticipate any trouble in getting it back. Knowing Elissa's temper, he was not nearly so optimistic as Diomedes had been about the Queen's having a change of heart where Hera was concerned. But he was prepared to fight for his betrothed, if need be, and once aboard the great gaoul he would worry no more. Fortunately, everything he needed for the voyage into the Western Sea in search of the Isles of Purple and The Dragon's Blood would be available in the Tartessian port of Gadir. And from Utica, the Greek galley belonging to Diomedes could be sent back to its home port of Herakleon on Crete.

As usual, Ares had spent most of the time prowling the city, in spite of the rain, and had discovered more in the drinking houses and brothels than Straton was able to learn anywhere else.

"They say here in Itanos that there was much rejoicing on board the fleet from Tyre, when the men learned of the women Queen Elissa had seized at Cyprus," he reported. "She promised enough land to build a house on to any who would take one of the women in marriage, and nearly all were spoken for before the fleet left Crete. The rest were quite willing to go on and find husbands among the Libyans."

"Elissa doesn't possess the land yet," Straton said.

"No. But with Sicharbas' treasure, she could buy all of Libya and make it her courtyard. A shipload of Phoenicians from Itanos even joined the fleet before it left here, so the Queen will have enough to populate a small city before she reaches Carthage."

Concerned as he was over Hera, Straton had to admit that Elissa—or the advisers from Tyre who had joined her—had acted wisely and in a way calculated to get the new Phoenician city off to the best possible start. The fact that the women from Cyprus were no longer captives also removed much of the onus from Elissa's rather high-handed action in seizing them but, unfortunately, did nothing to ease his own tortured thoughts.

"You heard no word of my betrothed anywhere?" he asked Ares.

"Nothing definite, but several people did remember noticing that a strict guard was maintained on board one of the gaouls while it was in port."

"That would have had to be done to protect the treasure."

"One man also says he heard a woman calling for help in Greek from the ship and remembers that he thought it odd to hear such a sound from a Phoenician vessel."

It was only a faint ray of hope but, since it was all Straton had, he was forced to comfort himself with it.

Fortunately, the skies began to clear the following day, and by another dawn the promise of fair weather was sufficient for the galley to leave Itanos and head westward along the southern coast of Crete.

Diomedes' pilot was not accustomed to sailing boldly out to sea for any great distance, since Greek galleys still set their courses largely from harbor to harbor and were rarely out of sight of land for any long period. Some of the crew grumbled when, with the western tip of Crete fast dropping behind them, Straton set a course directly for the trading station of Thapsos on the Isle of the Siculi. But the weather held and they reached it safely.

The people at Thapsos had no information concerning a Phoenician gaoul in that area, however, so Straton judged that Elissa and her cohorts had sailed directly to the location of the new settlement, guided by the expert navigation of Amathus, who had been over all this area before. To please his Greek shipmates, Straton was forced to follow around the coast for some distance from Thapsos. But after taking on water and supplies at the Phoenician settlement of Motya, just across the narrow channel from Utica, he set the course for Libya once again and, on the morning of the second day, saw a familiar-looking headland looming on the horizon ahead.

ii

Straton had hoped to find his gaoul and the rest of the Tyrian fleet at anchor in the bay beneath the protection of the promontory. But since they were not there, he surmised that they must have gone to

Utica to negotiate the purchase of the land for the new city from Prince Hyarbas.

He would have preferred to sail on to Utica that same day and search for Hera, but the wind was from the wrong direction and the galley had arrived in the bay so late in the afternoon that under oars the approach to the harbor would have had to be made after nightfall. With the galley's Greek crew already disturbed about what might happen to them in a Phoenician port far west of home, he decided to go ashore and inquire at a group of fishermen's huts lying just back from the beach, hoping to learn whether a fleet of gaouls had recently visited this spot.

With his gift of mimicry and tongues, Ares usually managed to learn a smattering of the language at any port they visited and could speak a few words of the dialect spoken in Libya. When, under Straton's direction, the pilot of the Greek galley had gingerly brought the trim vessel almost to a grounding point in the shallow, the two dropped over the side into the shallows and waded ashore, while the Greek crew immediately moved the galley to what they considered a safe distance and dropped anchor to await his signal that he was ready to return.

From the galley, Straton had seen people moving about in the Libyan fishing village, but it was empty when they reached it. Hoping to gain some clue to the whereabouts of the Phoenician fleet, he decided to climb the headland but had barely started up the slope, when he heard Ares' shout of warning behind him. Turning quickly, he saw a band of mounted men, in the flowing robes and turbaned headdresses favored by the Libyans, emerge from where they had obviously been waiting behind a sand dune.

As they bore down upon him and Ares, two of the riders swept past the little man and, reaching down, caught him by the arms to lift him from his feet and carry him, struggling and protesting, while they went on to surround Straton. Ares tried to interpret, while Straton sought to explain to their captors that they were Phoenician traders like those who visited these tribes from time to time, but made little progress. And after a few moments, Ares gave him the reason.

"We are lost, Master," he wailed. "They can see that we came in a Greek galley, so they think we are here to raid the coast for slaves."

iii

Their hands and feet having been securely tied by their captors, Straton and Ares were each thrown across the back of a horse in front of its rider, like a sack of grain. As they were borne swiftly along, Straton could only hope that his explanation of their presence in Libya—as interpreted by Ares—had exerted some effect upon their captors. He had made a point of speaking the name of Hyarbas frequently, certain that the Libyan prince who ruled in this area would be known to their captors. But whether he had made any real impression upon the men who had seized him he had no way of knowing.

It was about an hour later when the band finally stopped. The men upon whose horses they had been carried dumped them unceremoniously on the ground, but others kicked them until they struggled, hands still bound, to their feet. Having entered Libyan ports before and always found a welcome, Straton was at a loss to understand why they were being treated as culprits—unless, as Ares had said, their captors had taken them for the much-hated Greek slave pirates.

He saw now that they had been brought to one of the camps that native Libyan traders set up as centers from which to conduct barter with people in the small villages scattered over this fertile area. At its center was a large square tent of the type favored by the inhabitants of that land, the fringed purple hangings covering the entrance to the tent indicating the wealth and importance of the owner.

Straton dared to hope it would be one of several Libyan princes and chiefs he had met at Utica when he had stopped there on the way to and from Gadir. But the swarthy man with the hooked nose who sat among the cushions inside the tent, eating from a silver tray held before him by a slave girl, was a stranger. Furthermore, he showed no sign of welcome.

"How much of this language do you understand?" Straton asked Ares in a low voice.

"Only enough to order wine and pay the hire of dancing girls."

"That isn't liable to help us much. Our only hope is to demand that we be taken before Prince Hyarbas."

"I will try," Ares told him dubiously. "But don't beat me if I fail."

The chief had been talking to the leader of the band who had captured them. When the brief colloquy ended, Ares used the few Libyan words at his command to announce that Straton was a Phoenician nobleman and a friend of Prince Hyarbas, and that they had been on the way to Utica when seized on the shore. The Libyan chieftain listened intently, interrupting Ares from time to time with a question. Finally, the servant turned back to his master.

"He insists that we are Greeks," he reported, "and says that, if we were Phoenicians, we would be with the fleet from Tyre that is at Utica now."

The fact that Elissa—and, he hoped, Hera—had arrived safely in

Libya was good news. But Straton knew very well that he and Ares were still in danger of losing their lives unless they were able to convince the Libyan merchant that they were not there to raid the coast for slaves.

"Tell him we seized the Greek galley and followed the others," he instructed Ares. "And promise him a large ransom if we are taken safely to Utica."

"Where will we get the money? You know the Queen wouldn't pay a debenweight of silver for your ransom, after you spurned her for a younger woman."

"Prince Hyarbas will lend it to me. He has traded with the House of Gerlach before."

Ares translated the order and, when he saw a gleam of cupidity appear in the eyes of the Libyan chief, Straton was sure that greed had triumphed over other emotions, for the time being at least. The leader gave an order to the man who had brought them in and they were prodded out of the tent and taken to a smaller one, outside which a guard was posted. But though their bonds were not removed and they were given no food, a copper pot containing water was shoved into the tent. While one held the pot in his bound hands, the other managed to quench his thirst, so they could have fared much worse than they did.

"Something is wrong here, Master," Ares said when they had finished drinking and made themselves as comfortable as they could upon the ground.

"For once, at least, you are speaking the whole truth," Straton agreed.

"I mean, in the way they are treating Phoenicians. When we were last in Utica the native merchants sought us out eagerly. But as these fellows were bringing us here, I heard one of them say Prince Hyarbas would surely reward them for bringing him a Phoenician upon whom he could avenge himself."

"Avenge himself for what? He is rich already from selling us ivory and black slaves."

"I couldn't understand any more of what was said. But I wouldn't depend too much on your friendship with Prince Hyarbas if I were you."

Fourteen:

*Know, gentle youth, in Libyan lands
you are,
A people rude in peace, and rough
in war.*

AFTER AN UNCOMFORTABLE NIGHT, Straton and Ares were put upon horses again the next morning. This time they were allowed to sit upright, though their hands were still bound before them, so the ride was less painful than had been their brief journey from the shore to the camp of the Libyan trader. Straton had spent some sleepless hours during the night puzzling over Ares' observation that the Libyans, who hitherto had always been friendly, seemed to have become antagonistic toward the Phoenicians. But he had found no answer then—nor did he now.

Located on rising ground at the mouth of the principal river in that section of the Libyan coast, Utica was a fairly large settlement and an outlet for the products of a very fertile region in the interior. Phoenician traders had been active there for at least three centuries, but the harbor was not a very good one, compared to Straton's proposed town some two hours' sail to the southeast, and the growth of the port had been slow because of this lack.

The route of their captors took them around the edge of the city away from the harbor, so Straton had no chance to see whether his own gaoul was among the ships of the Phoenician fleet which Ares had heard their captors say was at Utica. Nor was any unusual number of Phoenician faces visible among the people in the streets, as the small party rode through them about midmorning. All of which only increased the sense of foreboding he'd had since their capture, a feeling that all was not well here in Libya as far as the future of Phoenician relationships was concerned.

Prince Hyarbas' palace was familiar to Straton from previous visits and so was the audience chamber to which they were ushered. The Prince's manner, however, was far from friendly, and he studied Straton and Ares dourly for a while without speaking, before finally ordering their bonds removed.

"The Son of Gerlach has chosen a strange way to visit my country," he said bitterly at last. "As a slave trader."

200

"Your Highness has been wrongly informed," Straton said.

"Were you not in a Greek galley? And are not Greeks known to raid our coast for slaves?"

"I did come here in a Greek galley," Straton admitted. "But we seek no slaves. During the battle for Arvad I was swept overboard from my own ship and was thought to be dead. When I finally got back to Arvad my ship had already sailed for Utica, so I followed in a galley belonging to a Greek merchant named Diomedes."

"Is the great gaoul yours, then?" Hyarbas asked.

"Yes, but those on board think me dead. My father let Queen Elissa use the ship to come here. Is she safe?"

"She is safe." There was no missing the bitterness and anger in Hyarbas' tone now. "And free to sail elsewhere."

Ares shot Straton a quick glance of triumph at this verification of his suspicion that all was not well between Phoenicia and Libya since the arrival of Elissa and the fleet. Observing Hyarbas' anger, Straton decided to approach the subject of Elissa and her mission carefully, lest he arouse the Libyan prince even more. Obviously, something had gone badly wrong since he had talked to Hyarbas on the way home from Tartessus only a few months before. For then the other man had been very enthusiastic about Straton's dream that a great western center of Tyrian power might rise upon the headland, where he and Ares had been taken prisoner the day before. Yet now the whole atmosphere seemed to have changed—for the worse.

"The Queen has suffered much recently," Straton said soothingly. "Her husband was brutally murdered and she was forced to flee for her life. Besides, she was relying upon me to seize the throne of Tyre again and, when she thought I was killed, she must have seen most of her hopes of going back fade. Under the circumstances, I am sure you can understand how she might be troubled and uncertain."

"From a woman one expects uncertainty," Hyarbas said. "It is part of their charm. But I rule here, not Tyre."

Straton was beginning to get an inkling now of what must have happened. Not knowing the extent of Hyarbas' realm and the power he wielded, Elissa must have thought him merely another native chieftain. But the princes of Libya were as proud of their heritage as Elissa was, and he could see how, like flint against flint, sparks might have been struck at their first meeting.

"I may be to blame for any difficulty that has arisen," Straton said. "After talking with you when I was here not long ago, I spoke so glowingly of the new city and the opportunities for trade that much interest was created in Tyre. Queen Elissa commands great wealth and can build wherever she will. I was hoping that, since you are my friend, it would be you who would profit by the opportunity for trade, as the King of Tartessus has profited from Gadir."

It was a shrewd argument and, when he saw Hyarbas' manner begin to thaw somewhat, he added: "The merchants of Tyre were particularly interested when I told them of the markets among the people to the south for weapons and other articles of metal, in addition to the trade in ivory and black slaves."

"How can such a city ever be built, much less prosper, when a woman rules who doesn't even know her own mind?" Hyarbas demanded, but most of the truculent note that had characterized his first words was gone now and Straton dared to hope he might be able to repair the damage that had been done before his arrival.

"Women in high places always need advisers and usually lean on one most of all." He paused briefly to let that idea sink in before launching the second prong in his attack upon Hyarbas' hurt pride. "And who would be better qualified to advise Queen Elissa here in an area of which she knows nothing than the greatest prince of that land?"

"Hah!" The Libyan's snort was one of exasperation, Straton was sure now, and no longer of anger. He allowed himself the luxury of drawing a deep breath of relaxation but did not let the iron cool, while it was still upon the anvil and the hammer was in his hand.

"Had I been here, I would have advised Queen Elissa of the help you would be able to give her," he assured Hyarbas. "But without the advice of someone who knows this region and what the city can mean, she was naturally uncertain. I am sure she will gladly pay for the land she needs."

"She offered to pay—through her minister."

"Minister?" It was Straton's turn to be startled.

"The High Priest of Melkarth and Astarte in Tyre who followed your Queen into exile. I forget his name."

"Luli!" Ares spoke automatically, and Hyarbas nodded agreement.

"Did not Queen Elissa visit you herself?" Straton asked.

"She granted me an audience—as she would a conquered chieftain begging for mercy," Hyarbas said bitterly. "And she offered to buy from me the headland you named Carthage, with the surrounding area including the harbor, the bay and all that would be needed for a city and an anchorage."

"And your answer?"

"I told her I would not sell her even so much land as lay beneath her foot," Hyarbas said triumphantly. "But she cannot say that I did not give her a gift, the very peak of that same headland, if she wishes, a piece of land as large as a byrsa—"

Straton frowned. "The word is not familiar to me."

"The hide of a bull. You carry many such in trade."

The momentary elation Straton had experienced, when Hyarbas' mood showed signs of softening, suddenly faded. He knew the proud Libyan would not go back on his refusal to sell. And Elissa—equally proud—would not beg him to reconsider. Between them, he thought grimly, Elissa and Luli had managed with a few words to wreck his whole dream of a new Tyre in the West.

"Where does the situation stand now?" he asked.

"Your Queen's fleet is still moored to the quay here in Utica. But I hear that she plans to negotiate with Prince Barca to buy a section of shoreline east of here in his domain."

Now, at last, Straton understood the main reason for Hyarbas' anger with Elissa. It was bad enough that Luli had apparently treated the Libyan prince as if he were merely a chieftain subject to Tyre, instead of the ruler of a large area in his own right. Elissa, too, had apparently followed Luli's lead and added further to the fire of Hyarbas' anger by dealing with Prince Barca, the only other one among the Libyan rulers who was rich and powerful enough to threaten Hyarbas' ambition one day to be king of the whole area.

If the new Phoenician trading center were built in Barca's territory, Utica would shortly wither on the vine and, with it, much of Hyarbas' source of riches, so Straton could not blame the other man for being bitter. All he could do now was try to repair the damage already done by Luli and Elissa and bargain for Hera's freedom in return for whatever he was able to accomplish in that direction. More than anything else, he wanted to ask about her, but he had no intention of calling the attention of even Prince Hyarbas to so beautiful a captive as Hera.

"Prince Barca has no spot on his whole coastline that can even approach the one I chose for a port," Straton observed.

"So much the better for us here at Utica."

"And he will surely make Queen Elissa pay dearly for what land he sells her."

"Perhaps not," Hyarbas said. "Barca has a passion for light-skinned female slaves who are also virgins. It is said that your queen possesses one of surpassing beauty—a Greek with hair like gold and the body of a goddess. No doubt an exchange can be arranged."

"An exchange!" Straton's control suddenly snapped, breached by the thought of Hera in the harem of Prince Barca. "The girl is betrothed to me and was stolen from Arvad while I was ill. I followed her here in her father's galley."

Hyarbas gave him a startled look. "Is this true?"

"You may have my head if I lie. How far have these negotiations gone?"

"I don't know. So far it is only a rumor."

"Then it can still be stopped—if Queen Elissa gets the land we first considered."

"Which means that I will have to sell it to her," Hyarbas reminded him. "Would you have me go back on my word—and lose the respect of my people?"

"If a sale can still be arranged, wouldn't it solve the problem?"

"No sale will be needed." Hyarbas' voice took on an even more stubborn note. "I have already given your Queen the land, at any spot she chooses, so long as it is not more than can be encompassed by a byrsa." He reached over to a table beside his chair and picked up a small papyrus roll lying there. "I had it all written in your tongue by a scribe. This scroll was to be sent to your Queen today, but you can carry it to her if you wish."

Straton felt a sudden excitement rising within him but was careful to keep his voice under control. "Could I see the scroll, please?"

"Of course," Hyarbas said. "It is only a description of my gift to your Queen."

The scribe, as Straton had hoped, had been sparse concerning details of the gift. The scroll merely stated that Prince Hyarbas thereby conveyed to Queen Elissa so much land as was encompassed by the hide of a bull known as a byrsa, at any spot in his territory that she selected.

"Am I right in assuming it makes no difference how large an area the byrsa encompasses?" Straton asked.

"None whatsoever," the Libyan prince said with a shrug. "After all, how large can a bull's hide be?"

"I will go to Queen Elissa and talk to her about this," Straton promised. "It may be that I can save my betrothed and at the same time keep Carthage in your domain."

"Tell me, Master," Ares said as they left the palace, following their audience, and headed for the harbor. "Just how large can a bull's hide be?"

"No larger than the bull from which it is taken, of course. The question is, how much land can be encompassed by a byrsa?"

"Now who's making riddles?" Ares demanded tartly.

Straton smiled. He was beginning to feel fine for the first time since the spar had swept him overboard during the battle for Arvad. "You will learn the riddle in good time," he promised. "As well as the answer."

ii

Tarquin was the first aboard the gaoul to spy them. The mercenary captain gave a shout of gladness and leaped from the deck to the quay to embrace Straton exuberantly, then lifted Ares from his feet and carried him up the ladder to the deck.

"I begged your father to let me search the shore opposite Arvad for any word of you," Tarquin said. "But none could believe you were alive—just as I could not believe the gods would let you die."

By now the men of Straton's own crew, with Amathus in the lead, were pouring from all parts of the ship to greet them. For a while there was pandemonium and, as word spread to the other Phoenician ships moored in the harbor of Utica that Straton was alive and among them once again, friends among the merchants and nobles who had chosen to follow Queen Elissa into voluntary exile came aboard to greet him. His first thought was of Hera, but when he spoke of her to Amathus, the older man's face became grave.

"I did not know she had been seized until we were at sea," he said. "I could not refuse to obey the Queen and go back, but when the other women were seized at Cyprus, I remembered that you would never allow trading in slaves and refused to carry them in the ship. Queen Elissa was very angry, but she sent the women to another vessel she chartered there."

"Do you know where the lady Hera is now?"

"I saw her with the other women only yesterday," Amathus told him. "I went to inform the Queen that we had fulfilled the conditions under which your father lent her the ship and asked permission to sail to Tartessus for a cargo."

"Did you talk to my betrothed?"

"I had no opportunity. Queen Elissa was not happy with the idea of our going on to Tartessus before the location of the new colony is decided upon."

"What is the real situation there, Amathus?"

The grizzled pilot shrugged. "Prince Hyarbas refused to sell the land. The Queen considered seizing it, but those who came from Tyre have no stomach for fighting the Libyans. Now there is talk of buying another site farther east from Prince Barca, but I told the Queen the coast in that region has few places suitable for a harbor, and none to compare with the one you selected."

"Do you believe both sides might yield a point, if a way of saving face could be found?"

Amathus shot him a quick glance. "You have seen the Prince?"

"Ares and I came from the palace just now."

"The Libyans are much interested in building up trade, as well as the protection a new city would give them from Greek pirates, who have been raiding the coastal villages lately to steal slaves. Besides, there is a strong rivalry between Prince Hyarbas and Prince Barca. If it had been left to me, I would have respected Prince Hyarbas, as you always did. But the priest Luli is the Queen's closest adviser and he insisted that the Libyans should be treated as a subject people." Amathus shrugged. "You know the rest."

"It seems that Luli and I still have much to settle," Straton said grimly. "Where is the lady Hera?"

Amathus nodded toward a large gaoul moored farther down the quay. "Hadras' ship has been turned into quarters for the women who are not yet married. Queen Elissa also moved there to keep them under close watch."

Two armed guards stood at the foot of the gangplank leading to the deck of the gaoul Amathus had indicated. Because the ship was smaller and the bulwarks much lower than those of Straton's own vessel, the deck could be reached by ordinary gangplanks, whereas with the larger vessels, ladders were necessary. When Straton would have set foot on the gangplank, however, one of the guards dropped his spear to bar the way.

"No one enters, noble sir," he said, "except by permission of the Queen or the High Priest."

Tarquin had accompanied Straton. At the guard's words, his hand dropped to the belt of his sword, but Straton shook his head. "Tell the Queen that Straton, Son of Gerlach, requests an audience," he told the guard.

As the man went to take the message, a sudden rush of footsteps sounded on the deck of the gaoul, and Hera flew across it to throw herself into Straton's arms before the other guard could stop her.

"I thought you were dead!" she cried and, for the first time since he'd known her, broke into sobs and buried her face against his breast. The guard stepped forward, as if to seize her. But when Tarquin's sword dropped between him and the two lovers, he took one look at the grim face of the Etruscan and decided not to intervene. Straton held Hera close until her sobs began to subside, then lifted her chin and kissed her. She clung to him like a terrified child still and he could feel her heart racing as he held her in his arms.

"It's all right, my dearest," he soothed her. "We'll never be separated again. I promise you that."

"Noble Straton." It was the guard who had gone to request an audience with Elissa. "The Queen will see you now."

"What about Father?" Hera asked as they crossed the deck. "Is he—"

"Diomedes fell and broke his leg when he tried to follow you. The pilot of the galley took him back to Arvad, but when I saw him there the wound was healing and he should be well soon."

At the door to the deckhouse, Hera drew back. "The Queen is much troubled," she said in a whisper. "I try to stay out of her sight so she will not be reminded of—of us."

Elissa was more subdued than Straton ever remembered seeing her and dark circles showed beneath her eyes. "They told me at Arvad you had drowned," she said in greeting. "Else I would never have left there without you."

"I would be dead, but for my servant's skill with medicines," Straton explained. "We were washed ashore on a log from one of the rafts, and Ares, with some of the fishermen, carried me to a cave in the hills, where he nursed me back to life. By that time the Assyrians had retreated."

"Then Tyre is safe?"

"For another year at least."

"And I need not have fled?" Her tone was bitter.

"I still don't know how much you could trust Pygmalion," he demurred. "In my opinion, you are better off at Carthage."

"As queen of a country no larger than a bull's hide?" She was regaining some of her spirit. "Oh Straton! I have made a mess of everything and betrayed all who trusted and followed me!"

"You acted unwisely at times, perhaps because you were not properly advised," he agreed. "It was certainly a mistake to seize the girls at Cyprus."

"I soon realized that and gave them a chance to return, when we reached Itanos. But they decided to come on and find husbands among the colonists."

"I'm sure Hera had no wish to come."

"For that I alone am to blame," Elissa admitted frankly, with a humility that surprised him. "I am all too human, Straton. To be rejected by you when I had offered to make you Prince Consort wounded my pride. I naturally lashed back at whatever I could find to hurt you, and

Hera was near, but I've had time to think on the voyage from Arvad and I realize now how wrong I was. All I want to do is to make Carthage a great and prosperous city, but I find myself foiled by the pride of a native chieftain."

"Hyarbas is much more than that. Actually, he rules an area considerably larger than our whole Phoenician coast. Besides, he is a very proud man with a royal heritage among his people fully as old as yours and mine."

"Believe me I had no wish to offend Prince Hyarbas," she said. "But Luli said I must exercise my authority and make the native chiefs realize I would be absolute ruler of this new city. Now I cannot yield and beg the Prince's pardon without being in the position of a suppliant."

"It is too late for that," Straton agreed. "If you beg for the land, it will make the Libyans doubt the power and importance of Tyre. You would have trouble ever after in your relations with them."

"Hadras and the other merchants who followed me here say the same thing," Elissa agreed. "But what can I do?"

"I was told that you are considering selling Hera to Prince Barca for a site along the coast east of here."

"That was Luli's idea—as a lever to try and bring Prince Hyarbas to heel."

"Then there is nothing to it?"

Elissa looked away quickly and did not meet his eyes. "So many people have placed their lives in my care, Straton, that I can no longer think—except as a ruler. Hadras and some of the others from Tyre think I should approach Prince Barca with Luli's idea. They cannot see one Greek girl making the difference between success and failure for a whole colony and perhaps costing all of us our lives."

Now that he heard her answer, Straton knew he could not really have expected her to give any other. Were he in her place, he admitted, and Hera only a Greek slave, his own answer might be the same. For, between saving one person and sacrificing hundreds who trusted you, no ruler could make a decision other than the one Elissa obviously felt herself obligated to make. He could only be glad that a way to solve the whole problem had come to him while he was talking to Prince Hyarbas in the palace that morning.

"If I can still get possession of Carthage for you," he said, "will you promise to do exactly as I say and release Hera?"

When he saw her hesitate, he added, "It will require some very delicate negotiations to get around the prickly point that has arisen between you and Prince Hyarbas. Unless I have an absolutely free hand, I cannot guarantee the result."

"Do you really think there is still a chance of building the city?"

"More than a chance," he assured her. "You visited the harbor and the headland before you came to Utica, didn't you?"

"Yes. Carthage is all you said of it—and more. I'm sure my husband would have no greater wish for his treasure than for it to be used in building a new Tyre there." Her eyes suddenly filled with tears. "But there seems to be no way."

"The cause is no longer hopeless, if only you will put everything in my hands."

"I am tired, Straton." Elissa's shoulders drooped. "Tired of running away and tired of standing tall in my queenly robes to impress others. Do what you think is best; I leave it all in your hands. It would have been much better if I had done that long ago. But it is only fair to warn you that, if you fail, I must make the best bargain I can with Prince Barca. And I can hardly let concern for Hera keep me from doing what is best for those who put their lives in my hands by leaving Tyre."

Fifteen:

There bought a space of ground,
which (Byrsa call'd
From the bull's hide) they first
inclos'd and wall'd.

IT WAS STILL BARELY noon of a sunny fall day, when the flotilla of ships which had sailed from Utica that morning anchored in the protected bay of Carthage. Straton had kept secret his plan for solving the difficulties which, at the moment, seemed to make building a city here impossible. Because of this, plus their curiosity to see whether he could perform a seeming miracle, not only the merchants and colonists who had followed Elissa westward, but also Prince Hyarbas and his immediate retinue, had accepted his invitation to be present.

Elissa had remained aboard Hadras' vessel for the brief trip southward, having made it her quarters since their arrival at Utica. Prince Hyarbas and his retinue were passengers aboard Straton's own great gaoul. But at the insistence of the Phoenicians who had followed Elissa, Straton had finally been forced to leave Hera on Hadras' vessel, since everyone knew that, with her aboard and his own gaoul once again under his command, he could outsail anything in this part of the world— if the plan whose details he had not revealed to them should fail and he elected to escape with the woman he loved.

It had been a pleasant morning's sail, with the land always in sight. Here and there streams cut through the shoreline, forming small inlets upon which fishing villages stood. And occasionally a river leaped over a cliff into the sea, sending up streams of spray which were painted instantly, as if by a divine hand, in the bright colors of the rainbow.

The preponderance of rocky limestone cliffs along the shore in the region of the cape had first attracted Straton's attention to that region. For though a good harbor was the first prerequisite for a Phoenician settlement, so that the trade which was its life blood could be carried on, a second and almost equally important factor was a rocky headland upon which a fortified town could be established with protection against attack both by land and by sea.

Carthage, fortunately, possessed these requirements adequately. Besides a bold cape, it also boasted protected bays to the north and to the south. And in addition, the mouths of both these bodies of water were narrow enough to allow the favorite Phoenician stratagem of building a mole, or breakwater, across them to turn each into a cothon or lake. Upon the shores of these, in turn, quays could be built to support warehouses and allow vessels to be unloaded and loaded in all kinds of weather. And, as if these natural advantages were not enough, limestone for building the various structures the city would need could be cheaply quarried, Straton was sure, from the face of an elevation and lowered by means of tough ropes to the decks of barges drawn up beneath the rocky cliff.

"You have chosen well," Prince Hyarbas complimented Straton, as the anchors were dropped overside close to the shore and the gaoul came to a halt floating quietly in an almost waveless sea. "If Utica had been built here, it would already have become a great city." He turned to look toward the gaoul that had brought Queen Elissa to the spot and which was now being anchored not very far away. "Has your Queen admitted publicly that she was wrong?"

"Would the other Libyan princes respect her if she did?" Straton asked.

"No, I suppose not," Hyarbas admitted. "It is a pity that we cannot come to an agreement. Queen Elissa is a beautiful woman. She even insisted upon giving me a golden bowl worth many times the value of a byrsa's expanse of even my most valuable land."

"I wouldn't be too sure of getting the best of the bargain, if I were you," Straton warned him with a smile. "You realize that I intend to have this whole area for a Phoenician settlement, don't you?"

"Why else would I accept your invitation?" Hyarbas said with a shrug. "If you can resolve this matter and still save face for me and your Queen, we will both be in your debt."

"I shall succeed," Straton promised. "And you shall grow rich. From this harbor coastal ships can draw trade from almost the whole of the Libyan shore both east and west. Meanwhile your caravans can penetrate far southward into the heart of Africa, where the black men dwell and the bright, hard stones that can scratch even glass are found. You are fortunate indeed that the new Tyre will be built here in your land."

Hyarbas smiled. "It will certainly be such a structure as the world has never seen—with its base no larger than a byrsa."

"Did you bring one as I asked?"

Hyarbas tapped a bundle from which came the ripe pungent odor of untanned leather. "Here it is. But don't forget the provisions of my gift to Queen Elissa."

"So much land as can be encompassed by a bull's hide," Straton agreed. "But you cannot complain if I manage to stretch it a little."

"I would have been disappointed in you if you didn't try," Hyarbas assured him. "But just how far will a byrsa stretch?"

"You will see that before long." Straton turned to Ares, who was standing nearby. "Are you ready?"

"Everything is in order, Master." Ares tapped a small case he carried under his arm.

"What is in the case?" Prince Hyarbas asked.

"What else but a stretcher for bull's hides, Your Highness." Ares grinned. "After all, you suggested it yourself."

"Here in Libya we have a saying that a man must get up early to escape being outbargained by a Greek," Hyarbas said thoughtfully. "With a Phoenician, I suspect he should never go to bed at all."

A colorful crowd soon gathered on the beach, borne there by small boats which had been carried on the decks of the Phoenician vessels. The handsome, bronze-skinned Prince of Libya and his retinue, in the flowing white robes and headdresses customary in this land, stood to one side; the merchants from Tyre, wearing robes trimmed with purple, and the men-at-arms from the gaouls on the other. Between them was Queen Elissa in a royal robe of purple trimmed with fur at wrist and neck. She wore a sparkling coronet upon her dark hair and looked far more beautiful than she had yesterday, when Straton had found her in Utica, rejected, uncertain and near to tears. To Straton's surprise, Luli was nowhere to be seen and, when he asked Elissa about the priest's absence, she tossed her head.

"I banished him from my presence," she said.

"Why?"

"He kept insisting that you would betray me into the hands of the Libyan princes and urging me not to come here today. Besides, when I thought about it, I became sure you were right in believing he had something to do with my husband's death. Hadras is my chief minister now."

"You have made a wise choice. But what did you do with Luli?"

"I sent him to the temple of Astarte in Utica. It is only a small one and he can hardly do any harm there as High Priest."

A sedan chair had been brought ashore for Queen Elissa. When she was seated, four brawny slaves lifted the carrying handles and bore it up the slope to the crest of the headland, where Straton had announced that the outlines of the new city would be marked out. He could hardly fail to notice Prince Hyarbas' admiration for Elissa's beauty. She, in turn, chose to be very gracious, and the Libyan ruler hardly took his eyes off her for most of the arduous ascent—all of which fitted into Straton's plan.

When they came around a rocky outcrop at the very crest of the promontory, he was not surprised to hear a massed gasp of appreciation from the crowd. He remembered feeling very much the same way on the day he had first dropped anchor in the bay and had climbed to the top of the cape. Spread out before them as far as they could see to the east stretched the cerulean blue of the Great Sea, while southward a peninsula jutted far out into the ocean, forming the southern boundary of a great bay. To one side was a small lake or estuary, with a short natural channel connecting it to the ocean, and on the other, only a narrow isthmus of marshy ground separated the sea from still another placid inlet.

The slaves had put down Elissa's chair almost at the edge of the elevation. She stepped out to stand with the breeze whipping the folds of her robe about her slender body, while she drank in the scene of almost unbelievable natural beauty spread out before her, and Straton could not blame Hyarbas for being entranced.

For a long moment Elissa stood looking eastward. When she turned back from the edge of the elevation, Straton saw that her eyes were filmed over and knew that she had been thinking of far-off Tyre, which she would almost certainly never see again. Nor could he find it in his heart to censure her, in spite of the trouble she had caused him these past several months and the threat she posed for Hera, should the stratagem he planned to carry out here today fail.

"Prince Hyarbas has been generous enough to give us a piece of land upon which to build a new homeland here in the West." Only the barest tremor in Elissa's voice betrayed the fact that she was not far from tears, or that the whole ceremony must have seemed to her hardly more than a farce. "We are met here to take possession of it today."

Straton stepped forward into the open ground before the spot where Elissa was standing. "Queen Elissa has appointed me her agent in all matters pertaining to the land you have so graciously given her," he said, speaking directly to Prince Hyarbas. "I will first read the document describing it, which you have signed and which bears your seal."

Lifting the small papyrus roll so everyone could see the neat alphabetic script of the scribe who had prepared it, he read: "In token of the friendship that exists between the land of the Libyans and those who dwell in Tyre, Prince Hyarbas does hereby convey to Queen

Elissa so much of any not otherwise inhabited land as can be encompassed by the hide of a bull, known in the Libyan tongue as a byrsa."

The words had been written in sarcasm but, as he read them, Straton managed to give the document all the dignity it would have possessed if Prince Hyarbas had actually been conveying a province to Elissa.

"Does Your Highness acknowledge this document as true?" he asked Hyarbas.

"It is true." Hyarbas' cheeks were flushed, even through the brown of his skin, as if he were ashamed now of having been so churlish, when he possessed so much.

Straton turned to the Queen. "And do you accept the gift?"

"I do," she confirmed gravely.

"Then it remains only to measure the land in the presence of these witnesses." He turned back to Prince Hyarbas. "The byrsa, please."

Two men from Hyarbas' retinue opened the bundle which slaves had borne to the top of the elevation. It contained a bull's hide, nothing more, but such a bull for size as Straton had never seen. An "Ahh!" of wonder went up from the watchers when it was revealed.

"Prince Hyarbas has been generous with the unit of measurement," Straton conceded. "Exceedingly generous."

"The prize bull of the royal herd," Hyarbas confirmed. "Slain yesterday and the hide scraped and washed carefully."

"Being so fresh, it is no doubt more capable of being stretched than if it were older," Straton said with a smile.

"You yourself named me generous." The Libyan's eyes were bright with interest and Straton knew he was wondering just what was going to happen next. From the corner of his eye, he saw Elissa's cheeks begin to burn and realized that her anger, never far beneath the surface, was rising at this seemingly foolish bit of mummery. Before she could speak, however, he turned to Ares.

"Did you bring the tools?"

"Yes, Master." Ares knelt and opened the small case he bore. From it he took a razor which had first been honed on a stone and then rubbed upon a leather strap until it looked quite capable of slicing a hair. To the edge of the blade, a narrow piece of ivory, only a few times the thickness of a thumbnail, had been carefully bound with tough, but thin, thread in such a position that the ivory strip projected a little distance in front of the blade.

"In the name of Astarte, what is that?" Prince Hyarbas exclaimed, stepping forward to look at it more clearly.

"A stretcher for a bull's hide, Your Highness," Straton said gravely.

"You have graciously let the largest byrsa in the kingdom be used to measure the land you have given to Queen Elissa and you also suggested that the hide be stretched. That I propose to do now."

Hardly a sound came from the spectators as, followed by Ares, Straton stepped over to the bullhide and lifted one edge of it. The servant took the same edge between his left thumb and forefinger, holding it taut perhaps a hand's space away from where Straton's fingers were. Carefully he applied the sharp edge of the razor against the fresh tough hide and, as the blade sliced into it, began to trim off a running strip that was at no point wider than the thin piece of ivory which had been bound against the blade to keep it from cutting a wider swath.

Hyarbas had exclaimed in wonder when the slicing began. But as it went on and the small pile of continuous rawhide strand cut from the byrsa by the blade grew steadily larger, he began to chuckle and finally to laugh.

Knowing Hyarbas to be a man of honesty and fairness, as well as the possessor of a fine sense of humor, for all his pride, Straton had counted upon just this happening. When he heard the sound, he knew they had won and was thankful, for the strain of trimming the rawhide without cutting through it was beginning to tell on both him and Ares. Finally Hyarbas ceased laughing and wiped his eyes with his sleeve.

"Cut no more, please," he begged and stepped forward to lift Queen Elissa's hand, placing it upon his head and then carrying it to his lips in a gesture of fealty.

"Of a truth," he said. "If they sliced the whole skin as thin as they are doing now, it would encompass my whole kingdom and I would be a pauper."

"We ask only the headland, the bays to the north and south and the land for an hour's walk back of the shore in this area," Straton assured him.

"You shall have it," Hyarbas said. "My scribe will set it all down upon a scroll for me to sign." He turned back to Queen Elissa, who still seemed hardly able to believe the evidence of her own eyes. "And may the Queen of Carthage have long life and a prosperous realm."

ii

Straton's great gaoul was almost ready to sail two days later, when Elissa made her way across the quay. His ship had brought her back to Utica the day after the dramatic stretching of the byrsa to include the entire area selected for the new city.

"I came to say good-by and wish both of you a safe and prosperous voyage to the Western Isles," Elissa said, when he had helped her up the ladder to the deck. "Where is Hera?"

"Inside. Ares will go for her."

"You are very lovely, my dear," Elissa said when Ares ushered Hera out of the deckhouse. "I hope you both have a long and happy life together."

She was turning back to the ladder, when Hera spoke: "Your Highness, Straton and I would count it an honor if you would do a favor for us."

"Whatever you ask—if it is within my power," Elissa said.

"You are still Queen of Tyre and now of Carthage as well," Hera said. "Would you hear our marriage vows and give us your blessing?"

"I will do more," Elissa said warmly. "Not only will I hear them, but I will make a sacrifice to Melkarth and Astarte this day, asking long life, much happiness and many children for both of you."

The vows were simply spoken and afterward Elissa gave them her blessing. "When you return in the spring," she said in parting, "I shall expect part of your cargo of The Dragon's Blood to be sold at Carthage. Hadras brought artisans with him, among them a number of weavers and dyers, so we can put it to good use."

"You shall have half the cargo," Straton promised.

He and Hera stood together while Elissa descended to the quay and crossed it to where an elaborately fashioned sedan chair waited, borne by four black slaves. Nor was he surprised to see that Hyarbas' personal chair had been placed at the Queen's disposal.

"You could have been King of Tyre—with her as Queen," Hera reminded him softly, as the chair disappeared along the quay toward where the rest of the Tyrian fleet that had come to start the new colony was moored.

"I would rather sail to the Isles of Purple with my bride."

"But can you be sure of finding them in so vast a sea?"

"The southing stars will guide us there—as they guided me back to Tyre in time to find you," he assured her. "And as Ares once said, 'Who would choose a queen when he already possesses a goddess of his very own?'"

Hera's eyes were warm as he lifted her in his arms and bore her across the low sill of the deckhouse he had built for them as a marriage bower, kicking the door shut behind them. Even above the noise of getting the great black ship under way, they could hear the strains of a lute and Ares' voice lifted in a song that was a favorite with Greek mariners:

Haste to your banks; your crooked anchors weigh,
And spread your flying sails, and stand to sea.
A god commands, he stood before my sight
And urg'd us once again to speedy flight.
Oh sacred pow'r, what power soe'r thou art,
To thy bless'd orders I resign my heart.

END

Author's Note

THE STORY OF Queen Dido, or Elissa, and the founding of Carthage circa 814 B.C. is one of the great romantic sagas from the ancient world, told by the Roman poet Virgil centuries later in the stately phrasing of *The Aeneid*, from which I have taken the frontispiece, all chapter heading quotations, and the final song of Ares. Like most poetic legends, the story of the founding of Carthage is now recognized to have a strong basis in fact, and the prophet Ezekiel in the Old Testament graphically described the wonders of Tyre and testified to the virtual monopoly of the sea lanes enjoyed by that great city of the Phoenicians during this period.

From the decline of the great Minoan civilization on Crete during the second millennium B.C. to the Greek conquest of the Eastern Mediterranean by Alexander the Great was a period of more than a thousand years. During this time a small group of Phoenician city-states, lying mainly along what is now the coast of Lebanon, largely dominated commerce by ship in the ancient world, as well as its manufacturing—particularly the purple-dyed fabrics for which they became so famous.

Phoenician ships, larger than the caravels of Columbus and guided by celestial navigation—the "southing stars" of *The Aeneid*—circumnavigated the continent of Africa about 600 B.C. Much earlier, Phoenician seamen explored the east coast of Africa in the service of Queen Hatshepsut of Egypt, and later served King David and King Solomon of Israel, perhaps even reaching India. Some students of maritime history believe they also discovered America at least five hundred years before Christ, though here the evidence is somewhat less certain. But Phoenician seafarers did carry the alphabet, probably an Egyptian product, throughout the ancient world and, as early as about 1100 B.C., established a thriving colony in Spain from which they explored England and the North Sea.

A Phoenician philosopher and mathematician named Mochus may well have postulated the atomic theory of matter before Democritus, and perhaps even some elementary geometry before Euclid. Most ingenious of all, the inhabitants of the city of Arvad are reported by the Roman geographer Strabo to have obtained an adequate water supply for their offshore city by lowering a lead cone over a spring on the bottom of the sea and attaching to it a pipe of leather by which water was brought to the surface uncontaminated by salt. And Virgil testifies to the way a byrsa was stretched, exactly as I have described it, to encompass the boundaries of the great city of Carthage.

I first became interested in the Phoenicians some eight years ago while writing *The Mapmaker*. Further years of study intensified my interest, but the idea of retelling the story of Dido as a novel only came to me when I learned that many historians believe the upheaval that led to her flight from Tyre and the building of the great city of Carthage on the African shore was more than just a palace revolution. Much of the rather sparse evidence, in fact, seems to support the thesis that the desire of the artisans of Tyre for more say in their government led to the attempted revolution. But whatever the cause of the Tyrian uprising, Carthage—known first as *Karthadasht*—came near to destroying Rome and thereby changing the whole future course of world history.

Queen Elissa, or Dido, King Pygmalion, the High Priest Sicharbas, and even Prince Hyarbas are historical figures. In addition, wherever possible, I have used authentic names, such as Straton, Hamil, Mago, etc., which appear again and again in the history of Phoenicia. But, as always in my novels of the ancient world, the major problem has been that of making the actual happenings seem as credible to the reader as those I have invented for my story. Which only proves once again the truth of the cliché that history is often stranger than fiction.

Frank G. Slaughter

Jacksonville, Florida
February 14, 1964